Low-hanging bran
of Mallory's face, tangled in her hair and
snagged on her jean jacket.

Rafe came to a sudden stop, and she nearly toppled him over. They both stood still and remained quiet until she heard it. Footsteps coming from behind.

Rafe grabbed her hand and pulled her along as they took off running. They ran over roots and ducked under low-hanging branches that ripped at her clothes. Mallory's heart beat like a war drum as they raced down the mountain.

The sound of their assailant's footsteps got closer. Adrenaline spurred her on. She turned her head to see how close he was, and without warning, she tripped over a rock. Letting go of Rafe's hand, she fell and rolled over on her side. The searing pain seemed to travel from her ankle to the top of her head.

"Come on, Mallory," Rafe whisper-shouted.

"I can't. I think it's broken." She cradled her foot, willing herself not to cry, but the intensity of the pain was almost unbearable. She pressed her lips together, forcing herself not to scream.

Dear Reader,

This is a story about family and second chances set against the backdrop of cybersecurity.

Growing up in a tight-knit family, I've always been fascinated by the bonds that tie relatives together. That sense of unwavering support and camaraderie served as a major inspiration for me in telling Rafe and Mallory's story.

Their chance at love and a fresh start hinges on their ability to uncover the identity of a mysterious threat to Mallory's daughter.

Because cybersecurity is becoming increasingly critical in our daily lives, I felt it had to be a central theme to the story. And when it comes to second chances, I mean, who doesn't love them? We all yearn for redemption, and the opportunity to rewrite our stories, and Rafe and Mallory are no exception.

In *Breaking the Code*, my characters face many challenges, but throughout, there are two things they can rely on, and that's each other and family.

I hope you enjoy Rafe and Mallory's journey. I know I enjoyed writing it.

Happy reading!

Maria

BREAKING THE CODE

MARIA LOKKEN

Harlequin

ROMANTIC SUSPENSE

Harlequin®
ROMANTIC SUSPENSE™

ISBN-13: 978-1-335-50272-8

Breaking the Code

 Harlequin Enterprises ULC
22 Adelaide St. West, 41st Floor
Toronto, Ontario M5H 4E3, Canada
www.Harlequin.com

Printed in Lithuania

Recycling programs
for this product may
not exist in your area.

MIX
Paper | Supporting
responsible forestry
FSC® C021394

A cozy reading chair and a romance novel are all
Maria Lokken needs to have the perfect afternoon.
The perfect evenings are spent with her husband—
her real-life romance hero. Both her husband and
her large family are inspirations for many of her
stories. Besides being an avid reader, she loves
popcorn, movies and walking around museums.
You can find her at marialokken.com or on Instagram,
@maria_writer_lokken.

Books by Maria Lokken

Harlequin Romantic Suspense

Breaking the Code

Visit the Author Profile page at Harlequin.com.

To my amazing family for everything you do.

And to Carly and Magda, who helped shape this story when my hero was a mechanic.

Chapter 1

The death of a husband would devastate most women. But Mallory Stanton wasn't like most wives. When two men from Interpol arrived on her doorstep with news that her husband, Blake, had perished in a plane crash over international waters, she dutifully played the grieving widow and let the tears flow freely. But inwardly, every fiber of her being wanted to celebrate. Finally, she was liberated from a marriage that had almost destroyed her spirit. If not for his continual threat to take away her daughter, she would have left years ago.

For the last month, she'd been slowly claiming her life back. With Blake gone, so was the feeling of having to look over her shoulder or walk on eggshells, trying to anticipate her husband's sudden mood shifts or angry outbursts. At last, the house was peaceful, and she relished her newfound freedom, doing what she wanted, when she wanted—like creating a playlist of her favorite songs from her single days.

The warm, early afternoon sunshine streamed through the window, and Mallory sang out loud and danced through her spacious kitchen. With her hips swaying to the beat, she piled on layers of creamy cheddar cheese over cooked noodles.

While her husband was alive, she never dreamed of serving mac and cheese, even with a gourmet recipe. Blake considered it too ordinary to be served in his house. Well, it was her home now, and making her daughter's favorite meal without fear of retribution from her maniacal husband filled her with euphoria. She laughed and performed another twirl to the music. Strands of shiny coal-black hair from her messy bun came loose, and she blew them off her face. She sashayed over to the speaker and pumped up the volume. Nothing could ruin this perfect late-August day.

When the doorbell rang, she quickly shoved the casserole into the oven. "Coming. Just a minute." Mallory lowered the music, wiped her hands on the dish towel, and hurried to the front door. She'd been expecting the delivery of a new chair for the family room to replace the one she'd thrown out. Day by day, she removed reminders of her husband. Her latest purchase would replace the stuffy, dark leather chair he loved. The thought made her smile.

Mallory opened the front door, but there wasn't anyone there. She raised an eyebrow. *Odd.*

She stepped onto the walkway and glanced right and left but saw no one, not even a car driving away on the wide, tree-lined street with its spacious McMansions. As she stepped back, she noticed a manila envelope inside the threshold that she hadn't noticed when she opened the door.

She picked up the envelope and pressed back the metal clasp, then pulled out several black-and-white photos. Adrenaline coursed through her veins as she studied one image after the next of her daughter at yesterday's playdate. The neatly typed note on unremarkable plain white paper held an ominous threat that had Mallory letting out a shuddering breath.

GIVE US THE INFORMATION ON THE HARD
DRIVE OR WE TAKE HER. DON'T CALL THE
AUTHORITIES. WE'RE WATCHING.

Mallory dropped the photos and flew up the stairs to
Justine's bedroom. A deep breath of relief whooshed out at
the sight of her precious five-year-old still napping. "Oh,
thank goodness," she whispered, slumping against the
doorjamb. Justine's soft brown curls were splayed out on
the pillow. Her tiny fingers curled into relaxed fists, and
the sound of her gentle snore signaled Mallory's world
was still intact.

Closing her eyes, Mallory willed her heart back into
her chest and focused on slowing her breathing. The ringing phone startled her, and she hurried into her bedroom
to pick it up before it woke Justine.

"Hello?" Mallory said into the receiver.

"We want the drive."

The raspy voice on the other end made her skin crawl.

"Your daughter's pretty."

"You leave my daughter alone. I don't know what you
want, but whatever it is, I don't have it."

"Well, you better figure it out," the raspy voice said.
"'Cause Blake was holding it for us, and now we want it
back. You don't have much time. The clock's ticking." The
line went dead.

A cold sensation swept over her. She'd never let them
get close enough to touch her daughter. Not Justine. Not
her baby. She wrapped her arms around herself and began
to rock back and forth, her mind trying to understand
what was happening. Mallory had no clue what drive they
wanted, where to find it, or how much time she had. *Damn
you, Blake.*

The world thought of her dead husband as a financial genius. They'd dubbed him the Wizard of Wall Street. But she knew better. He was a criminal dressed in thousand-dollar suits. Blake kept her out of his business, but she wasn't stupid. She knew he associated with powerful men who didn't play by the rules. And it would seem he had something they wanted.

Mallory spent most of the night frantically searching the house and Blake's home office for anything that resembled a drive. All she recovered was a hidden laptop and some cash taped to the underside of his desk chair. She'd tried desperately to get into the laptop but had no luck with the passwords she tried. A trip to the local computer store hadn't helped her get any closer to discovering if the laptop was what the men were after. There seemed to be no way into the password-protected computer without wiping out all the contents on the internal hard drive.

Dejected, Mallory drove home, wondering how she would find what these men were after. Deep in thought, she hadn't fully realized her front door was slightly ajar as she came up the walkway.

"What in the world?" she whispered and held on tight to her daughter's hand. She motioned for Justine to keep quiet by putting an index finger over her lips. Tentatively, Mallory peeked inside. "Hello?" Her rapid breathing was the only sound. "Hello? Anyone here?" There was no response. If she were smart, she'd step back onto her walkway with her daughter and call the police. Instead, she stepped over the threshold and into the foyer, where she came to an abrupt stop. With her mouth open, her gaze took in the scene.

She couldn't believe what she was seeing. Slashed sofa cushions, drawers dumped onto the floor, closets emptied with their contents strewn about, furniture turned upside down, and holes punched into the walls. Shock slowly crawled through her like an unwelcome visitor.

"Mommy?" Justine began to cry.

Mallory swooped Justine into her arms, rushed out of the house, and phoned the police.

Hours later, when they could find nothing had been stolen, they labeled it vandalism.

To Mallory, it didn't matter what they labeled it. She knew with certainty it was no longer safe for her and her daughter in Westchester County. It was time to flee.

Mallory's hands had finally stopped shaking as she gripped the steering wheel. The knowledge that her daughter's life was in danger made her sick. How could her husband still be controlling her life from the grave?

"Mommy?"

"Yes, Punkie?" Mallory glanced at the rearview mirror. Her eyes met her daughter, who was sitting in the back seat.

"I thought we weren't going to Grandpa's house until next week?"

"Well…change in plans. It'll be fun, you'll see." Mallory tried to keep the tremble out of her voice.

She'd driven over two hundred miles, and exhaustion was beginning to seep into her bones. The night was coming on fast, and Mallory hadn't planned on stopping, but she wasn't sure how much farther she could safely drive through the winding roads of the Catskill Mountains in the dark. Holding the wheel in a death grip, she leaned forward, looking for an exit sign. She needed to find a place to stay for the night. The once familiar area had undoubtedly changed in fifteen years, and in her hurry to put as much distance between her and the people who trashed her house and threatened her daughter's life, she hadn't even thought to check on possible places to stay. The plan had been to get straight to her father's house in Rochester. She shook her head. There was no way she'd make it tonight. But she remembered a small motel she hoped was still in business. The Sunrise. That was the name. Sunrise, how ironic. She hoped she would see one of those again.

She glanced at the large onboard screen mounted into the dashboard—a lot of good it did. The screen was blank. Dead. Nonoperational. It should have come on when she started the car—but nothing. Unable to make it work, she couldn't get directions or the address of a nearby motel. She scoffed. *Some fancy car.* Once she got to the exit, she'd look it up on her phone.

This was her first time behind the wheel of the brand-new, special-order, top-of-the-line Tesla. The dealership phoned, saying it was ready for pickup. Its arrival had been unexpected. Blake never mentioned he'd ordered a new vehicle. But then, Blake rarely told her anything. Now, he was dead, and she needed a car that wouldn't be recognized. The timing was perfect. Almost too good to be true.

The Uber had taken her directly to the dealership. She signed the necessary papers and drove out of Westchester County as fast as possible, hoping no one followed her. There had been no time to get a demonstration of how the car worked or what buttons to push to get the onboard navigator to work.

As she looked for an exit, she rounded a curve and approached an incline. The car slowed. She increased the pressure on the accelerator but failed to pick up speed. Instead, the car stuttered as if she were tapping on the brake. She slammed the pedal to the floor—and nothing. "No.

No. No." She banged her hand against the dashboard. "You brand-new piece of crap. Don't stop! Come on, don't stop!"

"What's the matter, Mommy?"

Mallory closed her eyes for a moment and let out a breath. The last thing she needed was a wide-awake five-year-old. She glanced at her daughter in the rearview mirror. Curly brown strands escaped her baseball cap, and the quiver in her lower lip broke Mallory's heart. "Oh, honey... sorry. Um...it looks like this car has a mind of its own." She worked at keeping an even voice. "But don't worry, everything's going to be fine." Focusing on the road ahead, she willed the Tesla to keep moving, but her intention wasn't enough. She had no choice but to pull onto the shoulder and put the car in Park.

"Mommy, why are we stopping?"

Forcing a smile, Mallory turned to face her daughter. "The car's acting a little funny." She tried not to sound as alarmed as she felt. "I'm going to step outside and see if I can find out what's wrong. I won't be long."

"Mommy?"

"Yes?"

"I'm really hungry."

"I know, Punkie, and as soon as I can get this car started, we'll find somewhere to eat." Mallory reached between the seats and squeezed her daughter's knee. "In the meantime, how 'bout a pretzel?" She pulled out the snack from her oversized leather tote bag and handed it to her daughter. "Okay, I'm going to check on the car."

"Is everything okay, Mommy?"

"It will be," Mallory lied. All day, she'd managed to convince Justine they were on an adventure, but she wasn't sure how much longer that story would hold. "Just wait here, Punkie."

She jammed a baseball cap over her head, walked to the front of the Tesla, and peered down the road. There wasn't another car in sight. In fact, she hadn't seen another vehicle for the last thirty miles. Strange. Very strange.

Her shaking hands managed to raise the hood. In the dwindling light, it was difficult to see. Even if she found something, she wouldn't have a clue what to do. Her extensive knowledge of automobiles began with putting the key in the ignition and ended with pressing down on the gas pedal. And this car had a keyless ignition, so she was already off on the wrong foot.

Exhausted and frazzled, she studied the engine while muttering unintelligible swear words. Hadn't she already been through enough? Five hours ago, she'd left her home in Pelham, New York, first driving into New York City, then maneuvering onto the New York State Thruway, doubling back onto the Taconic Parkway, and finally taking a back road in an effort to lose whoever might be following her, only to be stuck on the side of the road where she was an easy target. She only hoped she'd put enough distance between her and the people who wanted the drive.

Her father would know what to do if she ever got there.

For the next several minutes, her gaze focused on the horizon as the remains of the day turned to twilight. Mallory bit her lower lip, working out what to do. The fear of being stranded outweighed the fear of getting help, and she swiped open her phone and pulled up a travel app. She waited, but no browser appeared. "Perfect. No signal." Holding it above her head, she walked a few feet away from the car, hoping a different position would at least produce one bar. But still, nothing.

Think, damn it! She kicked at the dirt and turned her

attention back to the car. Exhaustion made it difficult for her to concentrate, and she studied the engine as if the answer would magically present itself. "I have no idea what I'm doing," she said under her breath.

A low rumbling sound coming from the road startled her. Oh, God, had they found her?

She wiped her sweaty palms against the front of her jeans and cautiously inched her head around the hood. A single headlight appeared in the distance. *A motorcycle?* Mallory knew only one thing about motorcycles—gangs rode them. This cannot be happening. *Please, keep on riding—nothing to see here.* She tried to push away her panic and hoped she'd get lucky. But luck left Mallory three days ago, and despite her will for whoever it was to keep moving, the motorcycle slowed and pulled off to the side of the road.

The rider hit the kickstand and straddled the bike. He took his time removing his helmet, the fading light giving his silhouette an ominous look. She couldn't make out his face as he headed toward her.

"Hey, what's the trouble?" the mysterious man asked.

Adrenaline coursed through her body, and her pulse hammered hard. *Deep breaths, deep breaths*, she ordered herself as she folded her arms across her chest to keep from shaking. "Justine, stay right there. Don't come out."

"Hello? Are you okay?" the stranger asked as he continued toward her.

Mallory pulled the bill of her cap lower. "I'm, I'm... not sure," she managed to get out. "My car. It...it...just stopped." Sweat began to pool at the base of her neck, and her mind raced. Leather jacket, motorcycle, long hair, dark stubble. With the brief assessment of his appearance complete, she quickly fixed her gaze on the ground. Had she fled one dangerous situation only to find herself in another?

"Do you mind if I have a look?"

Mallory hesitated. She could barely hear him above the roar of blood pulsing in her ears.

"It'll only take a second," he said.

Reluctantly, she stepped back and indicated, with an outstretched trembling hand, that he was free to look under the hood. She hadn't a clue if she was doing the right thing, but she was stranded and officially out of options.

The rider pulled a mini flashlight from inside his leather jacket and leaned under the hood to examine the engine.

While he was preoccupied, Mallory slowly inched herself closer to the road, hoping an SUV carrying a family would come by. She'd feel safer asking them for help.

Several minutes passed, and she held her breath, watching from a relatively safe distance while the stranger poked around, holding his light over different parts of the engine.

"Looks like one of the cooling hoses is loose," he finally said.

Mallory stepped several feet back. Her gaze focused on her daughter. "That doesn't sound good."

"It's not great, but it's not the worst thing. I know about cars—but electric isn't my specialty. You'll need a mechanic for that. Either way, it doesn't look like you'll be going anywhere in this car tonight."

"Damn," she said under her breath. "Can you tell me how far away we are from Hollow Lake?"

"It's the next exit. Five miles down." He slammed the hood shut.

"Mommy, are you okay?" Justine called out.

"Yes, Punkie, I'm fine. Stay where you are."

The rider walked toward the passenger door, peering

into the car. "She's cute. But it looks like you and your kid are stranded."

Except for the rasp in his voice, he almost sounded familiar. But his words made her uneasy, and she didn't dare look him in the eye. Keeping the bill of her cap low, covering her face, she inched her way back toward the car. "Don't worry." Mallory stiffened, ready to reach in, grab her daughter, and run if necessary. "Thanks for your help."

"Listen, if you need a place to stay—"

"N-n-no. We'll be fine." Mallory quickly got into the driver's seat, slammed the door, and hit the locks.

"Mommy, what's happening?"

"We're waiting for another car to come and help." Mallory hoped. But what if the next car held the men who were chasing her?

"Isn't that man gonna help us?"

"I'm not sure. I'm not sure he can." Mallory faced straight ahead and squeezed her eyes shut, trying to work out a solution. When he tapped on the window, she jumped, and for a moment, her heart stopped before it began to race uncontrollably.

The stranger made a rolling motion with his hand, indicating she should lower her window. But Mallory shook her head in vain.

"Listen, I'm not going to hurt you," he said, loud enough for her to hear. "Let me help get your car towed."

Mallory stared at him through the glass between them. Something about him seemed familiar. A sense of warmth in his eyes almost had her at ease. She knew those eyes. She shook her head again, warding off fatigue and possibly her lack of judgment. This man was a complete stranger, and she needed to remind herself that she wasn't a good judge of character. That had been proven the day she'd married Blake.

"Okay. Look, stay put," the man said.

Stay put? Where was she going to go? How had she allowed herself to be so trapped? Keeping an eye on her side mirror, she watched him walk back toward his motorcycle. *Please get on that thing and go.*

But that was too much to hope for. She watched as he leaned against the seat, crossed his legs at the ankles, and pulled out his mobile phone.

Oh, God, what is he doing now? Who's he calling? How does he even have a signal? She leaned closer to the mirror and squinted. *Is that a satellite phone? Who is this guy?* Mallory tapped the steering wheel with the palm of her hand. *Think. Think.*

"Mommy, what's the matter? How come we're not moving?"

Mallory turned to face her daughter. "Something's wrong with the car. It's going to take a few minutes for me to figure this out."

"Are you scared?" Justine's brown eyes were wide.

"Oh, Punkie. No. Everything's fine," Mallory said, trying to keep the muscles in her face relaxed. "I need a minute to think."

"When you're finished thinking, then can we get something to eat? I'm really hungry."

"I know, and I'm sorry it's taking us so long to get to where we're going. But I promise I'll feed you as soon as we get there." Her voice quivered, and she quickly turned. She didn't want to lose it in front of her daughter. Once they were safe, she promised herself a good cry.

Mallory put her attention on her side mirror as she tugged on the heart-shaped pendant hanging on her necklace. Twenty minutes passed, and her daughter finally dozed, but the rider hadn't moved. What was he waiting for?

Sweat dripped down her back, and she rechecked her mobile—still no signal. She tossed the useless device onto the passenger seat.

The next ten minutes were spent with her focus moving from the nonexistent traffic to the unmoving rider resting against his bike. She was beginning to seriously wonder if she'd stepped into another dimension. How could she have found herself on a road with no traffic?

When lights from a few yards away finally filled her rearview mirror, she decided to take her chances, threw open the car door, and jumped out, waving her arms. "Oh, thank God. Finally, another human being."

As the headlights came into focus, she could make out two vehicles. They both pulled up behind the stranger's motorcycle. *Ohgodohgodohgodohno! What's going on?*

The rider called to her, "Ma'am, that's your tow. Let's go ahead and get you hooked up."

"Hold on." Mallory thrust her palm out, facing him in the universal stop-right-there sign. "I don't know you, and I don't know whoever is in that…that…truck. So don't come any closer."

"It's a tow truck," the rider said.

The headlights from the truck and the motorcycle blinded her, and she shaded her eyes with her hand. Someone walked toward her, and Mallory took a step back.

"Hey," a woman's voice called out. "I hear you need some help."

The figure of a petite woman came into focus. "Who are you?" Mallory asked.

"I'm Abbey Ong. I own the B&B in town. Rafael here

called and said you needed some help and a place to stay for the night. He also said you're not too easy with strangers. He thought if I came out with the tow, you might be more apt to let us help you. Sorry it took so long. But there's a bad pileup down at the last exit. State troopers aren't letting anything through. We had to take the back roads."

"But why?"

"Sorry? I don't understand the question," Abbey said.

"Why are you helping?" Mallory's words came out on a sob. She'd become so accustomed to protecting her daughter with no outside help that the offer nearly made her weep.

Abbey pulled her jacket tight across her chest. "You've got car trouble and a little girl. We're not going to leave you out here on this back road. The night's getting colder."

It had been so long since anyone had been kind. Her instinct was to reject the help. But it was dark. She was stranded, and she'd run out of options. Taking a deep breath and a mental leap of faith, Mallory decided to go with it. "Okay. Thanks."

"Do you have any bags?" Abbey asked.

"In the trunk."

"Okay, we'll put them in my car. You get your daughter."

Mallory nodded and opened the back passenger door, helping Justine out. "You okay?"

"I'm okay, Mommy, are you?"

Mallory smiled at the genuineness of the question. "Yes. These people are going to help us."

"Because our car's broke?"

Mallory nodded, put her hand on her daughter's shoulder, and walked toward the trunk as their luggage was removed.

"The short, rangy guy with the tow, that's Mickey. He'll hook up your car. And this guy here is Rafael," Abbey said, nodding in the rider's direction. "He's the one who called me."

At the second mention of his name, Mallory dared for the first time to really look at the rider, whose features were now illuminated by the tow truck's headlights. He was as drop-dead gorgeous as she remembered. "Oh my gosh. Rafe? Is that you?" Her first reaction was shock. The next thought had her wondering why she hadn't recognized him.

Rafe took a step toward her.

Mallory pulled off her cap.

His gaze scanned her face. "Mallory? Mallory Kane?" He pulled her into a hug.

His arms wrapped around her, and she nearly collapsed in the cocoon of his embrace. Old feelings flooded back in a rush. Oh, how she missed that. She had no idea how much she'd missed him. Quickly stepping out of his arms, her gaze scanned the ground as she tried to collect herself. "Wow. This is a surprise. I never expected to see you." She swallowed back the tears pooling at the sides of her eyes and swiped her nose with the back of her hand.

"I could say the same thing. You…um…look so different." Rafe ran a hand through his hair. "I mean, you look great." The words stumbled out of his mouth. "You…you cut your hair?"

Heat crept up her cheeks, and she self-consciously touched the back of her neck. It felt clammy. The hair that was there yesterday, now gone, made her feel exposed.

"Mommy. Who is that?" Justine tugged on Mallory's jeans.

"Oh. Rafe, this is my daughter, Justine." Mallory took her hand. "Punkie, this is…an…old friend. His name is Rafe."

"That's a funny name. How do you know my mommy?" Justine tilted her head, looking up at Rafe.

"We went to school together." He looked around. "But that was a long time ago."

"You went to school with my mommy?"

Rafe chuckled. "Yes, we were in high school—"

"It was a lifetime ago." Mallory pulled Justine toward her. The less said, the better. She couldn't trust what Justine would say if they continued any conversation. Right now, she needed a place to stay and a new plan.

"Hey, Rafe," Mickey, the tow driver, called out. "We're all set. The car's hoisted."

"That was fast," Mallory said. "Thanks. I'm not sure what we would have done if you hadn't come along." Mallory focused on the tips of her sneakers. "I'm sorry. I didn't recognize you. Must be the beard."

Rafe rubbed the side of his face. "I forgot I had this. Just back from a fishing trip in the woods. A couple of weeks with no razor. Kinda heavenly."

"Anyway, I can't be too careful with my daughter," she said apologetically. "But thanks so much. You saved us."

"Yeah, thanks," Justine piped up.

Rafe crouched at eye level with Justine. "You are most welcome."

"You ready?" Abbey asked. She opened her car door. "Do you need help getting your daughter in the back seat?"

Mallory shook her head.

Rafe smiled. "Well then, I'll be taking off. But you're in good hands. I'll check on you tomorrow, and we can catch up."

"Sure." Mallory gave a thin-lipped smile. The hope was that her car would be ready first thing in the morning, and there would be no "catching up."

But her gaze lingered as he rode off. Seeing him again stirred up feelings she forgot she had. She shook her head as if that would help rid her of the memories. This was not a reunion, and involving him in her situation was not an option. Rafe didn't deserve her troubles. She nearly emotionally destroyed him once; she wouldn't do it a second time.

Chapter 2

Rafe switched off the ignition, pushed the kickstand down, and took off his helmet. His mind was spinning. After so many years, seeing Mallory again knocked the wind and the sense out of him. In a half daze, he strode toward his brother's house and rang the doorbell.

"Bro. You're back. How was the fishing?"

"Hey, Zack." Rafe gave his younger brother a weary smile.

"You look rough, man. Everything okay?" Zack opened the door wider.

Rafe didn't respond or wait for an invitation. Instead, he breezed past his brother into the well-appointed two-bedroom cottage with wide white-planked wood floors.

"Sure, come on in," Zack said, his tone laced with sarcasm. "*Mi casa*...and all that."

"Yeah, yeah." Rafe waved a hand and didn't look back. "Came to drop off your keys."

Like his home, Zack was neat, trim, and concise. Eighteen months younger than Rafe, they bore a remarkable resemblance and, in high school, had often been mistaken for twins. Their deep brown hair highlighted their chocolate-colored eyes. Their most striking feature was a dimple in the center of their chins. As the years passed and life happened for both of them, their styles changed. Rafe wore his hair past his neckline and was comfortable in jeans and T-shirts, while Zack preferred suits and ties and wore his hair in a professional cut.

"I've got a bit of a thirst," Rafe said and walked through the large living room, past the breakfast bar separating the kitchen area. He headed straight for the refrigerator and grabbed a beer. "Want one?"

Zack smirked. "Sure. I'll have one of *my* beers. Thanks for asking. Something on your mind? Or did you come back from a two-week fishing trip worse than when you left? 'Cause I thought you took two weeks at my lake house to give your attitude a little vacation. You know, chill from all the hard work over the past year before we start new projects. Me and Max definitely took the two weeks to vacate—body, mind, and spirit. Sandy beaches. Blue oceans." He cocked his head to the side. "I'm gonna take one of my always correct educated guesses and say you decided to skip the chill. So, spill. What happened?"

Rafe shook his head, grabbed the bottle opener from the drawer, opened the beers in silence, and handed one to his brother. "Well…hold that thought." He took an extra-long pull from the bottle.

Zack made a face. "Whoa. What's going on? I sense we got a problem here. *Dimelo.*"

"That's the criminal defense lawyer in you. Always digging."

"Nuh-huh." Zack wagged his index finger while holding onto the beer. "This isn't about me. I'm not the one walking in here looking like someone smacked me, walked away, came back, and smacked me again. I could've been perfectly happy sitting on my couch watching *Amor de mi Vida.*"

Rafe barked out a laugh. "Sorry, I didn't mean to interrupt your very important *telenovela* viewing."

"Go ahead. Make all the fun you want. You'd be surprised what you can learn from these Spanish soap operas. They're helping me develop my next career as a writer."

"For real?" Rafe said, skepticism showing on his arched brow.

"One hundred percent. With all the intrigue, multiple plot twists, villains, and people rising from the dead, you can't beat it. Anyway, it's my thing. It's how I unwind from our work. So don't knock it till you try it."

"I did try it. Remember when *Abuela* Carmen babysat us? That's all we watched. Not a cartoon in sight." Rafe smiled, remembering his maternal grandmother. Even now, he could vividly recall her signature rose-scented perfume and the warmth he felt whenever she hugged him. Thinking about her took the edge off his taut emotions. He exhaled, letting go of the tightness in his chest. "You know the funny thing about plot twists and people coming back from the dead? Sometimes real life is like that."

Zack gave him a pointed look. "Stop talking in riddles."

Rafe let out a long exhale and leaned back against the kitchen counter. "Dang it, bro. I don't even know where to start."

"Like I tell all our clients. Start at the beginning."

If he were going to tell anyone how he was feeling, it would be his younger brother, Zack. Not that he didn't love and respect the eldest of the three, Max. But Zack was slow to rile. Slow to react. He listened first. Digested. He could quickly untangle facts from emotions. It had served him well for the ten years he worked as a criminal defense lawyer for a major Manhattan law firm, handling white-collar crime and getting CEOs off the hook for embezzlement, money laundering, and fraud. He was good at it. Too good. When he realized helping the bad guys win wasn't the reason he went into law, he packed up and joined Rafe in his start-up cybersecurity business. Zack handled the security, Max oversaw the strategy, and Rafe handled the technology. On the side, Zack worked on his first novel.

"So. What gives?" Zack pulled out a stool from underneath the breakfast bar and sat.

Rafe brushed his hair back and placed his beer on the counter. He didn't really know where to start. With so many emotions bubbling up inside, he launched in at the beginning. "Do you remember my senior year in high school?"

Zack placed his elbows on the breakfast bar and leaned forward. "Is there something specific I should be remembering about your senior year?"

Rafe let out a huff. "Do you remember Mallory Kane?"

"Your girlfriend?"

"She was more than just my girlfriend. I was in love with her. But—" Rafe jutted out his lower lip "—she wanted different things. Or maybe I should say her mother wanted her to have different things." Rafe paused. "And… Mallory went along with it." Rafe tried to hide the hurt. When she broke it off, it nearly crushed him. *Leave it*, he told himself. *That was a lifetime ago.*

Zack sat back and crossed his arms over his chest. "Uh-huh. I remember her mother wasn't your biggest fan. Didn't Mallory end up moving to the city after college and marrying…what's his name?"

"Blake Stanton."

Zack snapped his fingers. "That's the guy." He tilted his head and looked up to the corner of the room. "Didn't they call him the Wizard of Wall Street or something like that?"

"Yup. That's the one. Imagine, of all the people in the

world, I ran into her tonight. Car trouble. Stuck out on Route 23 with her little girl. Thing is, we didn't recognize each other, and…well…her behavior was…strange, like she was afraid of something." Rafe scratched the side of his face. "Yeah. Something was off."

"This just happened?" Zack asked.

Rafe nodded.

"So, let me get this straight. A woman who you were in love with, what? Fifteen years ago? Right? Is stranded on the side of the road, and it's getting dark. Here you come riding on your motorcycle, looking like that—" Zack pointed a finger at him "—I mean, I'd be scared of you, too."

He put his head in his hands when he realized what the problem was. "Oh, man. She was afraid of *me*." Rafe scrubbed his face with his hands. "Oh, man." He looked up. "You think she knew?"

Zack grabbed Rafe's forearm and gave it a gentle squeeze. "Nah, man. You were exonerated. She probably doesn't even know what happened to you."

"I'm not so sure about that. Once she knew who I was… I can't explain it. There was a sense of… It… She was uneasy. Nervous."

"And this is important, *por qué* why? I think you're overreacting. What did you expect on a dark road after all these years?"

"Yeah, I get all that. But what I don't understand is why she's on a road outside Hollow Lake. Think about it. Her father doesn't live here anymore. Where's she going?"

"Now look who's talking like a criminal defense lawyer." Zack took a swig of his beer. "Sounds like running into your lost love got you all in a state."

"I wouldn't say I'm in a state. But I won't deny it stirred up feelings. My gut tells me something's off."

"And my gut tells me it's time to eat." Zack stood, walked to the refrigerator, and pulled out a plastic Tupperware container. "I've got leftover *empanadas* and more beer. I can't talk about important matters on an empty stomach."

Rafe gave a wry smile. "Okay. Let's eat. Then you can tell me what to do about Mallory."

"Sure thing. But listen to me. I bet Mallory doesn't know about your past. It's been forever since you've seen her. She got married and had a kid. I'm not being mean, but it looks like she moved on. And as far as your problem is concerned—I keep telling you, there are a lot of people in this town and in our family who know you could never have committed a crime. That's all I'm going to say."

"Yup. I feel you. A lot of people, except for Pop. For whatever reason, our father doesn't believe I'm innocent. Mom tried to tell him, but he wouldn't listen. She was the great equalizer." Rafe paused. "I miss her."

"Me, too. Every day." Zack shook his head. "Man, cancer sucks."

"It really does." Rafe swallowed hard. "Listen, I wish it were different between me and Pop. But it's not."

Mallory checked the time on the dashboard. Barely nine o'clock and the streets were already tucked in for the night. She was certainly back in Hollow Lake. Grainy snapshots flashed through her mind—images of her time with Rafe. Friday night football, eating burgers at the diner, district math competitions, their magical night at the prom, and the summer they spent before she went to college. So many memories.

She swallowed hard remembering how she broke it off.

Why had her desire to live up to her mother's expectations been greater than her love for Rafe?

From the day they began dating, Sharon Kane had been relentless in her objections. *You're too young to be serious. You have your whole life ahead of you. Rafe's a nice boy, but he's got no ambition outside of Hollow Lake. Don't make the same mistakes I did. I married too young and got stuck. Get out of this nowhere place while you can.* For the longest time, Mallory didn't listen, but when she came home for winter recess and discovered Rafe had quit community college to figure out his life, doubts began to creep in. She wasn't sure they were after the same thing anymore. Maybe her mother was right. Maybe she was too young to know if this was a forever thing with Rafe. And the idea of ending up like her parents scared her.

Even though she loved him, she pulled back. *Who are you kidding? You didn't just pull back. You were harsh.* For the remainder of the semester, she answered only a few of his calls, rarely responded to his texts and found reasons for him not to visit campus. When she finally told him it was over, it was the worst night of her life. She'd seen in his eyes how she'd hurt him. At the time, she honestly thought she was doing the right thing for both of them.

Mallory let out a wry laugh.

"Everything okay?" Abbey asked.

"Yeah." Mallory nodded and thought about how her mother once ruled Mallory's life. But after her parents divorced, Sharon Kane couldn't get away from small-town life fast enough. She traveled throughout Europe for a while before marrying a rich Italian who owned a villa in Sardinia. If not for the yearly Christmas cards, Mallory would never hear from her.

She lowered the car window and inhaled deeply. The

woodsy scent brought her back to her senior year and those
precious summer days she and Rafe spent together before
she listened to her mother. Before she went against her
own heart.

She closed her eyes against the night breeze and tried
to forget everything that brought her here. Even if only for
a moment. But her mind wouldn't still. There was a time
when Rafe was her entire world. He'd sweep her into an
embrace, look into her eyes, and kiss her. She was lost to
him. To his kindness and humanity and his dreams. But all
that ended when he chose a different path. A simpler path.

She wanted to put all the blame on her mother, but the
truth was she'd been weak. She always had a choice, even
if her mother had made it harder for her to choose. She'd
allowed herself to be convinced Rafe wasn't enough.

Years later, when Mallory brought Blake home, her father cautioned her to take it slow. Her mother, however,
had been thrilled. And, like always, she'd been swept up
in her mother's enthusiasm. Blake was everything Sharon
Kane had wanted for her. Even then, Blake was an important person in investment and political circles. The day
her wedding announcement was featured in the *New York
Times*, Sharon Kane purchased dozens of copies, distrib-
uting them to all her friends.

The photo in the announcement featured two people
with large smiles who seemed happy. And at the time of the
photo, they were. Once they were married, Blake changed.
He went from harsh to cruel, and Mallory wanted out.
When she soon realized she was pregnant, she decided to
stay, believing things would change. They never did. They
only got worse. And then it got to the point where he would
only allow her to leave if she left Justine behind. And she
would never do that.

The car pulled up to a three-story red brick building. "This is it," Abbey announced.

Mallory dragged herself out of her past and looked at the familiar building. "This used to be Dr. Roberts's house. Right?"

"Yeah. He retired about five years ago. So I bought it and turned it into a bed-and-breakfast."

Mallory stepped out of the car and reached into the back seat to wake her daughter. "Hey, my little Punkie, you ready to continue our adventure?"

"Uh-huh." Justine sat up, rubbing the sleep from her eyes. "Mommy, I'm hungry."

"I know." She lifted her daughter out of the car. "We're going to take care of that very soon."

"This way," Abbey said, ushering them toward the front door.

Mallory's eyes adjusted to the warm glow of the foyer. Watercolor landscapes dotted the pale yellow walls. With Justine in her arms, she followed Abbey down a wide corridor that opened onto a parlor with a butterscotch-colored sofa and several strategically placed chairs. The elegant yet inviting room made Mallory want to curl up and sleep, but that was not an option. Instead, she gently laid her sleepy daughter on the couch, headed straight for the wide French doors overlooking a patio, and jiggled the handle. The doors were locked, and she leaned her forehead against the glass in relief.

"I can open those doors if you want to go outside," Abbey said. "It's the next thing on my handyman's list. I've been keeping them locked because the springs are broken, and the darn things won't stay closed. The last thing I need is field mice getting in."

"No, it's fine. I was only looking." Mallory leaned

against the door. Her body felt like lead, and fear was the only thing keeping her upright.

"I bet you're exhausted. My husband will take your bags up while you and I take care of the registration. He's in the kitchen—" she took her phone out of her pocket "—I'll just text him."

Mallory crossed the room toward the small mahogany counter that served as the reception desk.

"Unfortunately, I can only offer you this one night. I've only got five rooms, and I'm booked up for the rest of the week through the weekend with a family from Connecticut. They'll be in town to celebrate their grandparents' sixtieth wedding anniversary." Abbey blew out a breath. "Can you imagine? Sixty years together. Amazing."

The last thing Mallory could imagine was a happy marriage, let alone one that lasted six decades. All the hype about growing old together was for greeting cards. As far as she was concerned, she'd grow old by herself. She didn't need a man for company. "Uh, yeah. Well, that shouldn't be a problem. I'm expected at my dad's, and Rafe said it was some sort of hose connection. I don't know anything about cars, but it didn't sound like a big deal."

Abbey shrugged. "Seems simple enough. So, how do you know Rafe? That was a bit of a surprise."

Heat crept up her cheeks, and Mallory bit her lower lip. "Yes. I didn't recognize him right away. You know…it was dark…and that beard. Anyway, it was fifteen years ago. We went to high school together."

"What a coincidence running into him after all these years."

"Hmm," Mallory murmured.

"So where you headed?"

Under normal circumstances, Mallory would have found

the question harmless—simply idle conversation. *How are you? Where are you from? Where are you going?* All perfectly innocent. But not tonight. She was aware any seemingly innocuous revelation on her part might mean her daughter's life.

Whatever answer she gave, it was safer to stick as close to the truth as possible without giving away too much. "We're on our way to see my father," Mallory offered without looking Abbey in the eyes.

Abbey took a registration card from the drawer under the computer and handed it to Mallory. "Sign here, please." She handed her a pen. "Going farther north, then?"

"Yes."

"Where about?"

"Uh… Rochester. He was transferred there some years ago."

"Oh, I've been there once, on my way to Toronto. My husband's family lives there."

Mallory grinned, hoping her smile was friendly but not encouraging—she had things to do, and more small talk wasn't on her agenda. Concentrating on the registration card, she wrote Mallory S and stopped short, quickly changing the *S* of her married name to *K* and signing her maiden name, Kane. She left the address line blank and pushed the registration card back toward Abbey. "How much do I owe you?" She reached into her purse.

"Two-hundred-twenty-five dollars for the night, plus tax. Comes to two-hundred-fifty-six dollars and fifty cents."

Her hand tightened around her wallet. The amount was more than she'd expected for a small town. Using her credit card was out of the question. Without a doubt, the person or people who ransacked her home were the same people who sent the threatening notes. And she was certain they were professionals who were now trying to find her. She wouldn't help them by leaving a financial trail. Blowing out a breath, she loosened her grip and opened her wallet, counting tens and twenties from the stash she found hidden under the chair in her husband's home office.

Abbey's eyes widened at the crisp bills on the counter.

Mallory kept a neutral expression. *Nothing to see here. I'm not a fugitive or a criminal.*

The moment passed, and Abbey tucked the money in a drawer.

Mallory let out a slow, shaky breath. "Can you tell me where we can get something to eat? I'm afraid getting stuck on the road interrupted our dinner plans."

Abbey shook her head. "I'm sorry. At this hour, nothing's open in town. Most folks go to Ravena, the next town over, for a late-night supper."

"I was afraid of that." Just her luck, streets rolled up and she was stuck in a B&B. Not even a vending machine in sight.

"Mommy, I'm awake!" Justine sat up on the couch. "Can we eat now?"

Mallory pursed her lips and tightened her fists.

Abbey must have recognized the frantic look of a mother with a hungry child.

"Hey there, Justine," Abbey said. "How 'bout a grilled-cheese sandwich? Would you like that?"

Overwhelmed at the offer, tears welled in Mallory's eyes. She was nothing but a bag of raw nerve endings, and the gesture nearly put her over the edge. But she needed to keep it together for her daughter's sake. "Thank you." Swallowing the tearful lump in her throat, Mallory picked up Justine, brushed her curls from her forehead, and kissed her. "Grilled cheese sounds good, doesn't it, Punkie?"

Justine nodded enthusiastically.

"Okay, let's follow Abbey."

After they'd eaten, they said goodnight to Abbey and headed to their room. Mallory was bleary-eyed and unsteady on her feet as she trudged up the stairs to the second floor. On the other hand, Justine, now satiated and apparently wide awake, skipped up the stairs, ready for the rest of this adventure.

The elegant furnishings in the room matched the foyer, giving Mallory a measure of comfort that they weren't staying in a dive. If it had been otherwise, it might have broken her. The room featured a queen-size canopy bed with an array of colorful pillows and, mercifully, a private bath.

Mallory locked the door behind her, hauled the suitcase onto a luggage rack, and began rummaging through her things for their toiletries. "Come on, let's get your toothbrush and get you cleaned up and ready for bed." Mallory thought if she tried to maintain some normalcy, then this nightmare she was living wouldn't take over.

"Aha! I knew it was hiding somewhere." She handed Justine the toothbrush and toothpaste. "You know the drill." Mallory forced a smile and pointed her toward the bathroom. When she was sure Justine was fully occupied, she double-checked the window locks and dragged a chair across the room, pushing it under the door handle. Wiping the sweat off her brow, she took a deep breath. "You need any help?" she called out.

Justine came into the room with a smile, "Nope. All done. I brushed all my teeth. Even the back ones."

"That's my Punkie. Come on, let's get your pj's on." Mallory got Justine changed and into bed. "You, button nose, are going to sleep. It's way past your bedtime." She tucked her under the covers. "I'm going to sleep right beside you."

"But where's Teddy? I can't sleep without him." Justine pouted.

Mallory recognized that tone and didn't want to end the day with a full-out crying jag from an overtired five-year-old. If Justine cried now, without a doubt, Mallory would lose it. She leaped off the bed and dug through everything in the duffel bag until she retrieved Teddy.

Holding the bear triumphantly, she smiled. "See, here he is, and I expect both of you to be asleep in two minutes." She tucked him under the covers next to Justine and kissed her daughter on the forehead.

"Give Teddy a kiss goodnight, too." Justine shoved the bear toward her mother.

Mallory hesitated. She never liked kissing that smelly, bedraggled excuse for a stuffed animal. Justine's attachment to Teddy went beyond what Mallory could understand. In recent months, she'd worked on getting Justine to grow out of the Teddy phase but was unsuccessful. After today's events, she knew she needed to drop the subject until things returned to normal. If they ever returned to normal. She kissed her daughter again, blew Teddy a kiss, and turned off the bedside light.

Tempting as it was to crawl under the covers and lie beside her daughter, she had work to do. Men were after her, and she needed to find out what they wanted. Now was not the time to get comfortable.

Mallory grabbed her oversized shoulder bag and pulled out a small silver laptop. Silently edging toward the window, her gaze swept the empty street. Satisfied no one was watching, she slipped into the bathroom, closed the door, and flicked on the light.

She leaned against the white tiled wall and slid down to

the floor. Once the laptop was powered up, she began typing letters and numbers. She'd already tried several possible combinations with no luck. What confusing password had her husband created? Whatever it was, she needed it. She was convinced information in this laptop would tell her who was threatening Justine's life and why. If only she could hack her way in.

Rubbing her forehead with the palm of her hand, she took another deep breath. *What password would a devious mind create?* She placed her fingers on the keyboard and typed in passwords she'd already tried, with the illogical hope they'd miraculously work this time. Putting in her husband's birthday backward, she hit Return, and nothing. Next, her wedding anniversary backward, a date she wished never happened. Again, she hit Return, and... nothing. "Shoot!" She tilted her head toward the ceiling and closed her eyes. "Think, think, think!"

All these years, she managed to hang on. Managed to tell herself she'd find a way out. And here she was, literally free from her abusive husband. He was dead, and you couldn't get much freer than that. She groaned, realizing there was no getting away from Blake Stanton. Until she could get into the laptop, she'd be connected to him. It was as if he were reaching her from the grave. The thought made her whole body go cold.

Mallory stared into space, trying to come up with a solution, but she was exhausted and getting nowhere. She needed a few hours of sleep. She turned off the light and stepped into the bedroom. Smiling at Justine's sprawled-out sleeping figure, Mallory stretched her arms over her head and yawned. She turned to the window and pulled back the curtain. Across the street, in the shadows, she thought she saw someone looking up at her window. Quickly, she dropped the curtain and pressed herself against the wall. Her mind raced. *Don't be afraid. Breathe.* Clenching her jaw with a determination she didn't feel, she inched her way back to the window and peeked out, but the street was empty. Mallory shook her head, trying to clear her thoughts, wondering if what she saw was real or if her exhausted mind was playing tricks.

Chapter 3

Rafe punched in the code to the front entrance of the offices of RMZ Digital Fortress. On any given day, he'd be the first to arrive, but when he crossed the threshold this morning, the rich scent of freshly brewed coffee told him Max had beaten him to it. His older brother couldn't kick-start his workday without his hands wrapped around a cup of black gold.

The large antique railway clock on the wall read 6:30 a.m., and Rafe chuckled. Max must have been as anxious as he was to handle what was probably a mountain of work after a two-week vacation. He passed the all-glass reception desk and headed straight back toward the rec room.

The company offices were housed on the top floor of the old post office building on Main Street. The whitewashed brick walls, exposed-beam ceilings, and massive windows allowed natural light to pour into the large space. The concrete floors and open architecture gave it a modern look.

The redesign had been Rafe's doing. In today's world, most clients never came to the office, preferring video chats. So, he made the space comfortable for the people who worked for his firm. In addition to the low sofas and plush chairs, there were cutting-edge tech stations with high-resolution monitors, ergonomic keyboards, and noise-canceling headphones. The rec room at the far end of the floor resembled a combination coffee bar slash adult play-room.

When the analysts, techies, and office personnel weren't staring at their computer monitors, they could grab a snack or relax with a game of ping-pong, foosball, or air hockey.

Rafe slid a puck across the hockey table, walked past the pool table, and toward the barista counter where Max was making his morning cappuccino. The hiss of the milk steamer and the smell of the chocolatey espresso dripping from the porta-filter filled the air.

"Hey, bro. Let me have one of those."

Max turned and smiled. "Make your own."

Rafe ignored the tease and held out his hand, wriggling his fingers. "Come on."

Max gave a half eye roll, handed him the steaming cap-puccino, and proceeded to make another.

"Thanks. So, how was your trip?"

Max closed his eyes and smiled. "What's not to love? White sandy beaches by day, candlelight by night."

Rafe thought he detected a blush creep up his brother's neck. "So, you and Gloria had fun?"

The quizzical expression on Max's face told Rafe every-thing he needed to know. "So—not Gloria?"

"Nope."

"Who then?"

"No one you know."

Rafe laughed. His brother had been a quantitative ana-lyst on Wall Street, and he'd brought all that brain power to RMZ Digital Fortress. At work, he was a genius and all business. But when it came to relationships, being smart wasn't his forte.

"Oh, man." Rafe shook his head. "At some point, all

that messing around with a different woman every week is going to catch up to you."

Max raised an eyebrow. "Do I look worried?" He poured the steaming milk into the espresso. "But there is something that has my concern antenna tuned in real fine. I spoke to Zack this morning. He told me you ran into Mallory Kane... or should I say Stanton."

"You spoke with Zack this morning? When it's not even seven o'clock."

"Good morning." Their receptionist, Brittany, walked toward them, stopping their conversation. "Welcome back. Hope you all had a good vacation."

"Thanks." Rafe checked his watch. "But what are you doing here so early?"

"Zack has a video conference with a new client in London, and I wanted to get the conference room all set up."

"Oh, shoot. I forgot we arranged that before we left. I wanted to be on that call." Max turned to Rafe. "I need to get a sense of what IT systems they have in place before the meeting. Let's talk later." Max grabbed his coffee and headed toward his office.

Rafe nodded. It seemed he wasn't the only one with Mallory on his mind. Last night, he'd dreamed about her, and when he woke, he had the same uneasy feeling that Mallory was hiding something. Whatever it was, he was going to find out. But first, he needed to start his workday and put out any potential fires that were likely brewing after he'd been completely off the grid for two weeks.

The private offices at RMZ Digital Fortress lined one long wall. Tall windows on one side and all glass on the other allowed light to filter across the bullpen area where the analysts and techies worked.

The number of emails and voicemail messages waiting

for Rafe almost made him wish he'd never taken his fishing trip. After ten years in business, the brothers had developed a solid reputation among Fortune 100 companies and several government agencies. They were in high demand. In fact, none of the brothers had taken more than a day off in over eighteen months. And now he knew why it had taken so long to go on a vacation. Rafe loved his work and the company he created, but re-entry sucked.

An hour passed, and he wasn't halfway through his emails. Rafe sat back, stretched his arms over his head, and put his feet on the desk.

Zack stuck his head into Rafe's office. "The meeting went well—London's on board. And, hey, *Tía* Ellie called. She needs you to go over and fix that leaky faucet in the upstairs bathroom."

Rafe rolled his eyes. "I love her, but why doesn't she call a plumber?"

"With three strong nephews living in the same town? Pfft. Never gonna happen, man." Zack rapped his knuckles against the doorframe. "Get to it. It's your turn. I got rid of the squirrel in the attic last month."

"Ha! You called animal protection services. Not the same thing."

Zack stepped back into the hallway. "*Adiós*, bro," he called over his shoulder.

Rafe sighed and looked out the window. He sat straighter and squinted when he saw Mallory and her daughter crossing the street toward the diner. He checked his watch. "Maybe I'll have a little breakfast first."

Hollow Lake's picturesque Main Street featured one- and two-story shops and office buildings set back from a tree-lined boulevard. Except for the addition of several specialty artisan shops, the town hadn't changed much.

The slight breeze and the crystal blue, cloudless sky reminded Mallory of the late August mornings of her childhood, when she played from dawn to dusk, squeezing every last drop of freedom before school started.

The memory was bittersweet. Her life had been so simple then. Full of promise. Why hadn't she listened to her father all those years ago? How often had he warned her about Blake against her mother's insistence? One more issue her divorced parents hadn't agreed on.

"I should've listened," she muttered.

"What did you say, Mommy?"

"Nothing, Punkie. Talking to myself."

"What did you say to yourself?"

"Nothing important. Are you hungry?"

Justine nodded. "I'm so hungry I could eat twelve whole donuts."

For the first time in days, Mallory let out a laugh. "I know just the place." Taking Justine's hand, they crossed the street and headed for Fritz & Dean's diner. She hadn't been inside since she was seventeen. She'd loved its 1950s vibe, complete with a picture window and a red-and-white-striped awning. It was the kind of place where a person could drown their problems in a bottle of maple syrup drizzled over a stack of pancakes.

Before heading in, Mallory scanned the block. Nothing looked out of the ordinary, but then, she didn't know what she was looking for. Trusting her gut, she held onto Justine's hand and walked in.

As they entered, the bell above the front door rang. The unexpected sound caused Mallory's stomach to drop, and her throat went dry. *It's a bell, Mallory. Get a grip.* She took a deep breath, and her eyes adjusted to the light. The place hadn't changed.

The morning rush buzzed all around her, with the chatter of diners, the ring of the cash register, and the waitstaff taking orders and pouring coffee. The red leather stools at the counter were taken, and the tables in the middle of the room were equally occupied. Scanning the far wall, Mallory noticed a couple leaving a booth and headed straight for it.

She slid into the booth and tucked her shoulder bag between herself and the wall. "You good over there, Punkie?"

Justine grinned. "Yup!"

A server arrived, cleared the dirty dishes, and wiped down the table. Her name tag read Penny, and every inch of her youthful face was covered in freckles. "Would you like coffee while you look over the menu?"

Mallory nodded.

"And how about a booster seat for your little one?" Penny asked.

"I don't need another seat," Justine answered.

Penny smiled and looked Justine in the eyes. "Got it. No booster. How about a phone book?"

Justine tilted her head to the side. "Huh?"

"They still have those?" Mallory asked.

"Yeah, welcome to Fritz's, where nothing gets thrown out. You need a 1956 mixer?" Penny laughed and turned back to Justine. "Before computers, before the internet, if you needed to find someone's phone number, you looked it up in a big book. Anyway, we don't use those anymore, but they're pretty thick. Thick enough for you to sit on. It'll make it easier for you to reach the table. You wanna try it?"

Justine closed her eyes for a moment. "Okay, thanks."

Penny winked. "Coming right up."

Once Justine was settled and they'd ordered, Mallory took another look around for anything that might be out of the ordinary.

The low hum of conversations competed with the Muzak pumping out of the speaker above the register. The seats were filled with several men and women in business casual and others who looked like retired regulars. A family of four sat at a center table, backpacks hanging over their seats. Tourists, she thought, and felt a prick of envy, wishing she could be that carefree.

Her gaze rested on the counter area, and Mallory recognized the wiry man behind the register with the graying temples as Fritz, the owner. With a ready smile, he seemed to know everyone by name and greeted them with an effusiveness that had small town written all over it. A sense of nostalgia overcame her like a wave. The familiarity of the diners' voices merged with the clinking of plates and glasses. Memories flooded her mind—all the Sunday nights she spent here with Rafe sipping an ice cream soda. She smiled.

Stop it. Don't get comfortable, came the silent warning in her head. Too much needed to be done. First, she'd make sure her daughter had a good breakfast. Then, she'd locate the garage that had her car. Once all that was sorted, she'd search for a computer store. Getting into her dead husband's laptop was a priority.

The bell above the front door rang, and Mallory glanced toward the entrance. Rafe stepped through the door. Their eyes met before she could look away, and Mallory had no choice but to acknowledge she'd seen him and gave a small wave.

"Who you waving at, Mommy?"

"Rafe. My friend who helped us with our car last night."

"I wanna wave at him, too." Standing on the booth's bench, Justine turned and put both hands in the air like a cheerleader at a varsity game. "Hey, Rafe. Come sit with us."

Several diners turned to stare.

"Sit down," Mallory urged.

"Come over," Justine said, ignoring her mother. "We're having breakfast."

Rafe nodded, and diners stared as he strode toward their booth. He cut an imposing figure dressed in a black shirt and black jeans that accentuated his tall, athletic body. He was difficult to ignore, and his effect on Mallory was almost instantaneous. An electrifying surge shot through her—and a longing she hadn't experienced in years. Her cheeks grew hot, and she turned to gaze at the pictures on the wall. She didn't want him to know that his appearance flustered her.

"Hi," Rafe said.

"Sit down. Mom says it's not polite to stand at the dinner table."

"Justine!" Mallory raised an eyebrow.

Customers continued to stare. Mallory couldn't afford to be noticed. "Please, Rafe, eat with us." Mallory slid several inches to the left, making room on the bench, hoping the other diners would get back to their own business.

"Mornin', Rafe." With quick, practiced movements, a cup and saucer were placed in front of him, and Penny poured him coffee. "What can I get you?" She took a pad from her apron pocket.

Rafe smiled and ordered.

"Be right back with your food," Penny said.

"So." Rafe cleared his throat. "I'm glad I ran into you. We didn't get much chance to talk last night, I—"

"One more thing." Penny placed a coloring book and crayons in front of Justine. "Enjoy."

Justine clapped her hands.

"That was nice," Mallory said.

"That's Hollow Lake for you. Welcome back." Rafe smiled. "So, we didn't get much of a chance to talk last night. Did we?"

"Yeah, I know." Mallory chewed on the inside of her cheek, looking past him, watching the front door.

"I didn't expect to see you...again." Rafe took a swallow of coffee. "What's it been? Sixteen years?"

"Fifteen." She shifted her focus and really looked at him for the first time. The snake tattoo on his inner left wrist was new, as was the small crescent-shaped scar above his right eyebrow. Apart from that, he was the same but older. Lines marked the edges of his deep brown eyes. The soft, ready smile on his full lips was as she remembered. Despite her circumstances, he could still make her stomach behave like a circus performer executing multiple somersaults. She cleared her throat. "You shaved." Of all the things she could've said, it was the only one she could think of that would keep the conversation neutral.

"Yeah." Rafe rubbed his chin. "Mountain man wasn't exactly a good look for the office."

Just as she thought, he worked here and never left town.

They smiled at each other, and the conversation, such as it was, lulled into nothing. Mallory didn't know what to say or ask. Her situation was so untenable she remained cautious and closemouthed. The silence was punctuated by an incessant rhythmic beat, which Mallory soon realized was coming from her foot tapping against the floor. *Nerves.* She put a hand on her thigh to stop the motion. *It's Rafe. Keep it light. Act casual. And get through breakfast.* "So you work around here?"

"Yeah." Rafe pointed straight ahead. "The building across the street."

"You work at the old post office?"

Rafe let out a laugh. "Well, yes and no. I bought the building a few years ago. I have a company with my brothers. You remember Max and Zack?"

Mallory nodded.

"You have brothers?" Justine put her crayon down.

"Yes. Two brothers."

"And you went to school with my mommy?"

"Yes, I did." Rafe chuckled. "Your mom was a math genius," he said in a conspiratorial whisper.

While Justine peppered Rafe with questions, Mallory wondered what her life would have been like if she'd never left Hollow Lake and stayed with Rafe.

Justine's laugh pulled her out of her reverie. She hadn't seen Justine this animated in a very long time. Her daughter's nonstop curiosity had driven her husband crazy, but Rafe seemed to be totally engaged.

Mallory pursed her lips and mentally juggled whether she should confide in Rafe. Maybe too much time had passed. Too much unsaid. Too much to undo. There was no denying that she'd dreamed of Rafe over the years, especially when everything turned sour in her marriage, but never imagined she'd see him again. *Was it fair to involve him?* No. The right thing to do was get her car fixed and get to her father's house. Leave the past in the past.

"Here you go." Penny placed a stack of pancakes in front

of Justine with a glass of milk. A bacon, egg, and cheese sandwich for Rafe and a single English muffin for Mallory. "More coffee?"

Mallory nodded, pushing her cup toward Penny with one hand and grabbing the syrup bottle from Justine with the other.

"Mommy, I'm not finished," Justine protested.

"I think your pancakes may just float away. Why not eat what's on your plate and see if it's enough before you pour anymore?"

"Oh-kaaay." Justine sighed. She picked up her fork, dug into the pancakes, and took a bite. "Mmm, these are good. Like yours, Mommy."

"I'm glad. Now, don't talk with your mouth full." Mallory gave a quick smile, then went back to surveying the people in the restaurant from the corner of her eye.

"So, what have you been up to? What brings you back?" Rafe asked.

"Uh…" She shrugged. "I'm on my way to see my dad." Unable to look Rafe in the eye for fear he'd see that nothing was as it seemed, she began cutting Justine's pancakes.

"Mommy, I don't need any help. I can cut my own pancakes."

"Oh, sorry, Punkie."

Justine took a long gulp of her milk. "Hey, Rafe, you know what?"

"What?"

"I don't have any brothers. But I have Teddy."

"Who's Teddy?"

"He's my best friend. We sleep together." Justine put a bite of pancake in her mouth.

Mallory leaned in and whispered to Rafe. "It's her stuffed animal."

"Oh." Rafe's smile widened. "He must be very special."

"He is. And you know what? We slept all night. We were cozy, and we didn't wake up once." A note of pride rang through her voice, "Right, Mommy?"

"Well, yes. That's right." For the first time in a year, Mallory realized her daughter hadn't woken up once with a bad dream. A tightening sensation pushed against her chest with the knowledge that Justine felt more comfortable in a strange place than she had in her own home. Her heart ached for what she'd put her daughter through. Her husband had been an abusive bully, and she should have figured out a way to leave long before he died.

"Do you want to, Mommy?" Justine said, tapping Mallory's hand.

"What? Oh, sorry, I was thinking about…something else."

"I was suggesting when you're finished here, I could give you a lift to the garage, and we could find out when your car will be ready."

The bell over the door chimed again, and Mallory's heart raced as she lowered her head and raised her eyes to see what looked like a nonthreatening teenager enter. Would she ever feel safe again?

"Hey, so how about that ride?" Rafe asked.

"Uh, yeah, that—that would be great. Thank you."

Rafe waved Penny down for the check, and Mallory pulled out her wallet, but he put his hand over hers. "I got this."

His touch sent a shiver through her, and she closed her eyes for a moment to get focused. "You don't have to do that."

"It's just a friendly gesture."

"All right. Well…thank you." Relieved not to shell out

any more cash, Mallory put her wallet away. She had no idea when or if she'd be able to access her bank account or use her credit cards. In the meantime, she needed to be cautious with the money she had and be ready to run at a moment's notice.

Chapter 4

Rafe helped Justine into the back seat of his truck. "Can you buckle your seat belt?" he asked.

"Yes." Justine smiled.

"Here. Let me." Mallory reached in front of him to help.

Rafe was momentarily unable to move. The subtle fragrance of her familiar citrus scent called to mind warm summer nights by the lake when he held her in his arms, and it was only the two of them with an endless future.

"Excuse me, Rafe. I need to get in so I can reach the buckle."

"Sorry." In a daze, he stepped to the side. He hadn't expected to have such a reaction.

"Punkie, lift your arm. I'll snap in the belt," Mallory said.

Rafe stepped further back and observed Mallory as she helped her daughter. It was the only time she seemed halfway relaxed. Otherwise, her entire demeanor indicated something was off. He'd listen if she wanted to talk, but he wouldn't pry.

After his release from prison, Rafe made it a firm policy not to get involved in other people's business or their lives. It was better for everyone if he kept to himself. But this was Mallory. She'd once been the love of his life, and after fifteen years of no contact, it surprised him how much he cared. Even more startling was the realization that his desire for her hadn't lessened. He took a deep breath as he walked to the driver's side and tried to tamp down old feelings threatening to push to the surface. "All secured?" he asked.

"I'm good," Justine said.

"Yes," Mallory said.

"Okay, then." Rafe put the key in the ignition and waited for Mallory to get in.

"How far is the garage?" Mallory asked as she buckled her seat belt.

"Not far. A few miles away. Right before you hit the county road." Rafe double-checked Justine was buckled up in the back seat, then put on his turn signal and pulled his truck onto the main road.

They drove several blocks before he glanced at Mallory, who was staring out the passenger window. Last night, she'd been so skittish he'd barely seen her face. In the light of day, at the diner, he'd gotten a better look. Physically, not much had changed. She was as beautiful as she'd been when they first met. At five foot seven, her lean, statuesque frame gave her the stance of a runway model. Her once long, coal-black hair was now a pixie cut, and he thought it was hot. The most significant change was the fear in her sea-green eyes. He spotted it last night, and it had only intensified this morning.

While serving time, Rafe developed an antenna for sensing trouble that was 99 percent accurate. His breakfast with Mallory had set off all kinds of alarm bells. For one thing, her husband's death had been all over the news, and she'd never even mentioned it. He'd also observed how her gaze darted toward the front of the diner each time the ringing bell signaled a new customer. Her anxiety only seemed to intensify as they drove. In the short time they'd been in the car, she'd turned her head more than once to check behind them. He noticed the constant bouncing of her leg and her continual glances at the side mirror—all of it indicated something wasn't right. Whatever the reason, there was no mistaking she was afraid.

It was a palpable fear, and he wanted to wrap her in his arms and make her feel safe. But Rafe tried to push the thought from his mind. He couldn't make anyone feel safe until he cleared his name of his wrongful imprisonment and found the person who framed him.

Once more, he glanced at her. She seemed so vulnerable. After everything they'd once meant to each other, could he leave her on her own?

Several minutes later, they pulled up to a single-story building. "This is it," Rafe said.

Chip's Garage and Auto Body sat at the edge of town, just before Main Street turned onto County Road 385. There were several cars and trucks of various makes and models parked along the left side. The front of the building featured three wide openings, and inside the last two bays were a car and a pickup hoisted on lifts.

"Hey, Mickey, how's it going?" Rafe asked as he walked inside the first bay.

Mickey came around from underneath the hood of a truck, wiping his hands on a rag. His five-foot-five frame carried an extra twenty pounds right at his midsection.

"You remember Mallory and Justine from last night?" Rafe asked.

Mickey nodded. "Hi there, how ya doing today?"

"Hi." Justine waved.

"I'd be a lot better if you told me my car was ready."
Mallory bit her lower lip.

"Well, about that." Mickey took off his cap. "It looks
like there is something wrong with the coolant hose to the
battery."

"Can it be fixed fast?"

Mickey shrugged. "Not sure. Depends."

"On what?"

"On how fast they can ship the part. But honestly, you
should call the dealer and let them handle it." He looked over
at the car parked in the last bay. "That's a new car. There's
barely five hundred miles on it." Mickey shook his head.
"I'd call and give them hell. For sure."

"If I..." Mallory cleared her throat. "If I don't go to the
dealer, how long for the part?"

Mickey shrugged again. "If that's the way you wanna go,
but I took the liberty of checking the glove compartment, and
the paperwork's all there. The car's from Leonard Devane's
and from what I hear, he's one of the biggest luxury dealers
on the East Coast." He scratched the back of his neck. "I'm
sure they'd help you out. So, you wouldn't have to pay us."

"Let's not call them. Can't you just call the manufacturer and have them overnight the part?" Mallory wiped
her upper lip with the back of her hand. "I mean, that's
probably what Leonard would do anyway."

The perspiration on her face made Rafe wonder what she
was so nervous about. Why wouldn't she call the dealer? It
would save her from shelling out any money.

"I'd need to make some calls," Mickey said. "But with
the current supply chain issues, I'd guess at least two
weeks."

"Two weeks!" The sound of the whirring air compressor from one of the bays ceased, and her voice reverberated around the garage.

"Wait a minute." Mickey put up a hand. "That's purely a guesstimate. I won't know exactly until I make some calls."

"I can't believe this." Mallory paced in a circle, clenching her fists. "I can't be stuck here. Isn't there anything you can do to get it faster?"

"Mommy, why are you mad?" Justine took a step back.

Mallory stopped pacing. "Oh, Punkie, I'm not mad. I'm… I'm…just surprised." Mallory took in a breath and looked around.

"I'm sure Mickey will do everything he can to get the part and get you on your way." Rafe gave a sympathetic smile and put his hand on Mallory's forearm for reassurance. The feel of her made his pulse race, but she jerked her arm away, and her reaction hurt. Maybe the fear he saw in her eyes did have something to do with him. He clamped down on his emotions and forced himself to shrug it off. It wasn't the first time someone steered clear of him, but he didn't expect it from Mallory. It seemed his past would always be a present-time problem until he cleared his name. The more he thought about it, the more it made sense to help Mallory get her car fixed and out of town. "Maybe calling the dealer is the best plan. Maybe they can get the part faster," Rafe said.

"Nah, man," Mickey said. "The dealer doesn't have the part laying around. They'll go directly to the manufacturer. I suggested the dealer because it's their problem and wouldn't cost Mallory a dime. Maybe even give her a replacement car for her troubles."

"Mickey, I want you to go ahead and make the call to the manufacturer for the part," Mallory said. "I'll just have to wait."

Her response surprised Rafe. Not less than two minutes ago, she needed to leave Hollow Lake as fast as possible. Now, she had time to wait. It didn't make sense.

"I'll get you a card with the number for the garage. I'll be right back." Mickey headed for his workstation when a tall man with black-framed glasses perched on the tip of his nose opened the office door. "Hey, Mickey."

"Yeah, boss?"

"Oh, hi, Rafe, I didn't know you were here."

"Hi, Chip." Rafe lifted his chin, acknowledging the garage owner.

"Mickey, you finished with the Explorer SUV already?" Chip asked.

"Yeah. In fact, as soon as I'm done here, I'm gonna head over to the Bailie's place and drop it off."

Chip slid the glasses on top of his shining bald head. "That was fast."

"Yeah, well, it's their first family vacation in five years," Mickey said. "They're heading out to New Mexico to see his sister. I wanted to help them out."

"You sure did. Let me know when you get back, and we can schedule the rest of the week."

Mickey gave a thumbs-up and turned back to Mallory. "Okay. Let me get you that card."

"Thanks." Mallory's cell phone buzzed, and she retrieved it from her pocket, swiping it open. "Hey, hold on a sec," Mallory said into the phone, then turned to Rafe. "Do you mind if I take this outside? And…uh…could you watch Justine? It'll only be for a sec."

The flick of her eyes toward her daughter and then toward her phone told him she didn't want Justine to overhear.

"Please? Really, it won't take long. I have to take it."

Rafe hadn't a clue what was going on. In the span of

five minutes, she'd seem to run the emotional gamut from jumpy to angry to fearful to—he didn't even know how to describe this current manifestation. All he knew was that someone was on the phone, and when she answered it, she looked desperate.

Of course he would watch her daughter, but he was determined to unravel some truths when she finished the call. "Okay. Sure," Rafe said. "Hey, Justine, you like LEGOs? 'Cause the owner keeps a box of them in the waiting room."

Rafe's soft-spoken kindness toward Justine made Mallory smile. At least that part of him hadn't changed. But the tattoos and motorcycles—that was different, and something she never could have imagined. Not the Rafe she knew. But for some reason made him all the more attractive. She shook her head. Now wasn't the time to focus on him. She put her head down and walked quickly out of the garage.

The moment she stepped into the open air, Mallory carefully scanned her surroundings and headed toward the bushes on the side of the building. When she was fully out of sight, she spoke into the phone. "Dad, hi! I was just going to call you."

"Oh, thank God, you answered."

"What's the matter?"

"Two men came to my office this morning, and they were asking a lot of questions about you. They wouldn't tell me who they were and why they were asking, but I can tell you they weren't friendly. I know this has something to do with that dead husband of yours. Am I right?"

Mallory didn't respond. Couldn't. She was too busy trying to breathe. Her world was crashing in all around her.

"Mallory? Mallory? You still there? Because something's very wrong, and I'm about to call the police."

"No! You can't do that," Mallory shouted before she could stop herself. "Sorry, Dad." She let out a breath. "Just, please, tell me what they said." This was so much worse than she could have imagined. She paced back and forth, unconsciously picking tiny leaves off the hedges along the side of the garage.

"They wanted to know where you were and when I'd last seen you."

Damn it! The one person she'd tried to shield from her troubles, and now she'd brought them right to his doorstep. She hadn't planned on telling him about the threats or the vandalism of her home until they were face-to-face. "What did you tell them?"

"I told them it was none of their business, and I told them to leave. I had security escort them out. But since then, there's been a black sedan parked outside our offices all morning."

She kicked at the dirt beneath the bushes. "Listen carefully, Dad. Me and Justine will be fine as long as no police get involved."

"Don't go to the police? That's crazy. I can't agree to that."

"Dad, I can't get into it right now," Mallory said, gripping her mobile, "but I'm begging you. The only way for us to be safe is if you don't get the authorities involved."

There was a brief silence. "Mallory, what is going on? You're scaring me."

"It does have something to do with Blake, but I honestly don't know what. Some people—I don't even know who—think Blake left me something that belonged to them. And they've made threats about Justine if I go to the police." Mallory lowered her voice and scanned the area again. "Listen, Dad, I promise to explain everything. For the time being, it's best if I don't come straight to your house. Especially if men are watching. I think I'm safe for now. But I need some time to think this through."

Mallory quickly considered her limited options. In all this madness, she was certain that keeping her father in the dark was for the best. The less he knew, the safer he was. Maybe her best option was staying in Hollow Lake and finding a way into that computer.

"I can't believe this is happening. That husband of yours...well, that's not going to help the situation."

Mallory turned her face toward the cloudless sky. Her father had never been one for I-told-you-so's, but he was right. He'd warned her and tried to get her to see Blake for what he was. If only she'd listened before it was too late. "Dad, you're right. You were always right where Blake was concerned."

"I'm not trying to be right. I only want you safe."

"Well, the best thing for all of us is if I stay where they'll least expect to find me. At least until that black sedan is gone and we're sure those men aren't coming back. I need some time to find out what they're after. If I can figure that out, maybe this nightmare will disappear."

"Are you sure you know what you're doing?"

The truth was, she didn't have a clue what she was doing. All she knew was she needed to keep her father as far away from this as possible. And considering she no longer had wheels and couldn't use her credit card, staying put was looking better and better. "Dad, I'll be in touch. But...not by phone. You know what I mean?"

There was another long silence.

"Hello, Dad? Did I lose you?"

"No, I'm here. I understand."

Mallory heard the tremble in his voice and tried not to react.

"This is all so hard for me to take. You're still my little girl, and it's killing me to know you're in trouble, and there's nothing I can do."

"Try not to worry. I love you. I'll see you soon. I have to go." Mallory swiped off the call, leaned her forehead against the cool brick of the building, and stifled a sob. The situation couldn't be bleaker. She was stranded, broke, and scared.

It had been two years since she'd seen her father—a separation not of her choosing. There'd always been a reason she couldn't see him or he couldn't come for a visit. Blake had seen to that.

Too soon after her marriage, she'd become a simpering, subservient doormat. Love, ha! For whatever reason, maybe it was pride, she wanted to believe she hadn't been a total fool. There must have been some love at the very beginning.

When they met, he'd been the perfect gentleman, romancing her with his charm and seducing her with his larger-than-life way of taking on the world. With a snap of his fingers, he could get the hottest tickets on Broadway, the best table at any restaurant, or seats in the owner's box at a Yankees game. Anyone who mattered in New York was part of his circle of friends and business associates. Blake wasn't the most handsome man in any room, but his six-foot, trimmed frame struck an imposing figure in his expensive suits and slicked-back dark hair. Theirs was a whirlwind fairy tale that got ugly fast.

They'd gotten married five months after their first date. Ten months later, Justine was born. Soon after that, everything changed. Blake changed. What began as small criticisms and urgent requests turned into cruel remarks and total control. From hiring a stylist to dress her to a personal trainer to get her body back in shape after giving birth to cooking lessons so she could throw lavish dinner parties for his clients. She went along with these decisions to keep the peace—anything to keep Blake from becoming upset.

After the second year of their marriage, her husband was rarely home. When he deigned to make an appearance, he was either verbally abusive or spent the evening locked in his study.

At one point, Mallory suggested they get counseling. But that conversation hadn't gone well. "You have to realize things have changed since Justine was born," she said one night when he came home early. "Maybe if we talk to someone, a neutral party, we could get back to where we were."

Blake scoffed. "You have everything you could possibly want. All you need to do is smile and look pretty. And when I tell you to show up at a fundraiser or a dinner, be there and play the part of a loving wife."

His words were like a knife piercing her heart. That night, she decided her only course of action was to leave.

"You want to leave—there's the door," Blake sneered— the smell of whiskey on his breath. "But you go the way you came. With nothing." That night had been a barrage of threats. He promised to take everything away from her, including her daughter. While she didn't care about his money or possessions, losing Justine wasn't an option. In his twisted mind, he wanted the world to see a picture-perfect family.

The verbal violence turned physical, and she tried leaving many times, but he was always one step ahead of her.

A shiver shot through her as she stared at her phone. *How stupid.* The people chasing her were probably like her ex, powerful enough to track her. And what better way than through her mobile phone? Her panicked mind hadn't thought of getting rid of it when she fled from home two days ago. The only objective had been to put as much distance between her, Justine, and whoever the hell was after them.

"I hate you, Blake," she shouted.

Overwhelmed with emotion, she squeezed her eyes shut, forcing herself not to break down. Not here. Not yet. But she was unable to hold in her anger and ran toward the back of the building, where there was nothing but an empty field and a railroad track. Taking a deep breath, she screamed into the air, the sound instantly muffled by a passing freight train. She screamed until her throat was hoarse and her head hurt.

Breathing hard, she leaned against the wall, pondering her next move. If they were tracking her now, she needed to send them in the wrong direction.

The wrong direction. Think. Her mind buzzed, and an idea formed. Hadn't the garage mechanic, Mickey, said he'd fixed an Explorer and was taking it to a family headed out West?

Mallory hurried from the back of the garage toward the only Ford Explorer parked out front. Looking around, she cautiously opened the back door of the SUV and jammed the phone underneath the back seat. "Have a good trip," she murmured, her heart beating like a jackhammer as she walked toward the open bay at the front of the garage.

"Hey, Mom, look what we made." Justine skipped toward her, holding a motorcycle made of LEGOs.

Mallory gave a tight smile. With her heart racing, she used every ounce of energy to appear normal.

"And Rafe says I can keep it."

"Oh, Punkie, those aren't yours—"

"She made it all by herself, and I know the owner. He's got boxes of those things. He'd be happy if she kept it."

"Thanks. Thanks for everything," Mallory said, her tone weary.

Rafe smiled. "I'll drive you back."

"Appreciate it," Mallory said without looking at him.

What she really wanted to do was wake her husband from the dead and then kill him herself. Enough was enough. She had to stop running and think.

Chapter 5

Rafe pulled the car keys from his back pocket. "All right. You ready to take off?"

Justine raised her hand and hopped up and down. "I am, I am."

In contrast, Mallory remained silent, never taking her gaze from the road in front of the garage. She seemed frozen in place and hadn't heard him.

This wasn't the confident person he remembered. He couldn't quite figure her out, which was unusual because Rafe could read most people in the time it took to shake their hand—his year in prison taught him a lot about secrets and hiding.

While Mallory hadn't given him any idea what was going on, something happened between the time she took that phone call and now.

His gut was telling him he couldn't afford to get involved. He could think of a dozen reasons to let her go, her secrets intact, and act like this little interlude was simply an old friend passing through town. To put his company and brothers in the middle of whatever this was would be reckless.

Despite the warning signs, his heart told him otherwise. Damn. Mallory could always get to him. They were once inseparable. The feelings he'd had for her were singular, and he hadn't felt that for another woman since. He could not let her go without trying to help. Somehow, they'd have an honest conversation between now and when her car was ready. Maybe he could do something. He'd take her back to the B&B and invite them to dinner this week.

"Ready?" He gently touched Mallory on the shoulder.

"Mmm." Mallory stepped away.

"Mallory? Mallory? You ready?"

She turned to face him and blinked as if she were waking up. "Sorry. Was thinking."

"You seemed a million miles away."

"More than that," she said.

The comment was strange, but he chose to ignore it. "Okay, let's get in. I'll take you back to Abbey's."

Rafe chose the back roads to town, hoping Mallory might chill and enjoy, or at least notice, the perfectly cloudless late-August day. The scenic route did nothing to ease the tension in the car. While Justine played with her LEGO motorcycle in the back seat, Mallory played percussion on the armrest, her nervous fingers tapping out a consistent beat, her gaze never straying from the side mirror.

When they got to town, Rafe turned down Avery Place and stopped at the red light. At the corner, a tall woman with a gray bob, wearing jeans and a light blue sweater, waved and walked to the car.

Rafe pushed a button, and the window slid down.

With a wide smile and eyes that seemed to sparkle, she leaned in and kissed him on the cheek. "*Hola*, Rafael. You just passed my house. Aren't you coming in?" She paused and looked inside the car. "Oh, I see you have company."

Rafe smiled. "*Tía*, what are you doing out here?"

She held up a small brown paper bag. "I was at Judy's hardware store. I got a washer because you'll need it to fix the leak in the upstairs bathroom. I didn't want you to have to go out and buy one."

Rafe chuckled. "You think of everything." He turned toward Mallory. "Do you remember my aunt Ellie?"

Mallory smiled. "Hi—"

"Wait," Justine said from the back. "I wanna meet your aunt."

"Who do we have here?" Ellie leaned in further.

"I'm Justine. What's your name?"

"Ellie. It's nice to meet you."

Rafe turned to see Justine give a shy nod. "So, *Tía*, I'll drop them off and be right back."

Ellie placed her hand on his forearm. "Absolutely not. You'll come over and fix my faucet, and we'll all have lunch together. Besides, I haven't seen you since you came back from your vacation."

"Yay! I'm hungry," Justine piped up from the back seat.

"Punkie, you can't possibly be hungry. You just ate breakfast," Mallory said.

Rafe checked the clock on the dashboard. It was nearly noon. They'd been at the garage longer than he thought. As much as he felt a pull toward Mallory and wanted to try to help, he did not want to bring whatever troubles she had to his aunt's home. But before he knew it, the back passenger door flung open, and Ellie was making herself comfortable in the seat next to Justine.

"I'll ride with you." Ellie buckled her seat belt and smiled at Rafe. "Drive around the block and then park in front of the house."

"Mallory," Ellie said. "It's been ages. How are you doing?"

"Just fine, Mrs. Chavez."

"Call me Ellie," she said, laughing. "We're both adults now."

Rafe parked in front of a yellow Victorian with a wide wraparound porch, sitting atop a small incline.

"Well, here we are." Ellie got out of the car.

Instinctively, Rafe knew this was a bad idea. He turned to Mallory. "If you don't want to come in, I'll tell my aunt you need to get back to Abbey's Bed and Breakfast." Rafe cleared his throat. "You know, she lost my uncle last year—"

"Oh, I'm so sorry." Mallory looked away.

"Yeah, it was rough. But we're all getting through it. Anyway, my cousins live in the city, so she's on her own now. My brothers and I have lunch with her at least once a week. But we haven't seen her since we were all on vacation."

"It's fine. It would be rude to refuse," Mallory said.

That wasn't the response he was expecting or hoping for. Figuring this woman out was proving to be a challenge.

At the sound of the back passenger door slamming, Mallory turned. "Justine, wait for me."

"Oh, it's okay. I've got her," Ellie called from the porch as Justine climbed the stairs.

In a flash, Mallory was out of the car after her daughter.

Knowing there was no way to stop this little get-together, Rafe decided to go with it.

Once inside, Mallory could feel her shoulders drop. It had been a while since she'd been here, but nothing had changed. The bright, open foyer featured a center staircase with a mahogany railing. She breathed in the familiar scent of furniture polish and Pine-Sol. It reminded her of Saturday mornings when she helped her parents with the weekly cleaning. She'd put old rags on her sneakers and glide around the wood floors, polishing them until they shone. The memory soothed her, and she unclenched her hands.

The dining room was to the right of the foyer, and on the left was a parlor with turn-of-the-century pocket doors and a baby grand piano. The rooms were flooded with natural light streaming through the oversized windows at the front and sides of the house.

"Why don't we all head back to the kitchen?" Ellie said. "I've got some lemonade. And today, I've got tuna sandwiches."

"I don't want to put you out." Mallory held onto Justine's shoulders.

"It's no trouble," Ellie said, ushering them on. "Rafe and I have a standing lunch date on Mondays. There's plenty of food. Really."

Mallory followed Justine, whose mood was suddenly buoyant at the sound of a cold glass of anything, her ponytail swinging from side to side as she skipped toward the back of the house.

Glasses, fresh lemon slices, and a tall pitcher filled with ice and lemonade were placed on the table. Mallory remained quiet as Ellie poured the drinks. "So, what brings you back to Hollow Lake after all these years? It's been a long time." She opened the refrigerator, pulling out a large bowl covered in plastic wrap.

"*Tía*, let me help you with that." Rafe rose from his seat.

"*Siéntate.* I'm not too old to make sandwiches for company." She waved him away. "Justine, how many pickles would you like?" Ellie twisted open the cap on the jar.

"These many." Justine held up two fingers.

The smile on Justine's face eased Mallory's rising anxiety.

"Go on, Mallory. I'm listening." Ellie smiled, spreading tuna on slices of bread.

"Well…we were on our way to see my father. And… um…" Mallory slid the heart pendant up and down on her necklace. "You see, my husband recently died."

Ellie turned to face her, knife in hand, the corners of her mouth dipped. "I am so sorry for your loss."

"Yes. I'd heard," Rafe said. "My condolences."

Their sympathy took her by surprise. Rafe probably wondered what took her so long to mention it. They had no way of knowing she was lying through her teeth or that she was relieved her husband was dead or that she was running for her life. Mallory felt her face grow hot and she lowered her head. She was already so deep into the deceit she reasoned she had no choice but to continue. She looked up, hoping her face held the appropriate amount of sadness for a recent widow. "That's why we needed a change. An adventure." She plastered on a reassuring smile in Justine's direction.

Justine nodded. "An adventure to Grandpa's house."

"That's right. Part of this trip was to visit with my father and show Justine upstate New York. It's been forever since I've been here, and…well, you know… I thought it might be fun to show her the different sights. Like…like…the…um… the Hampstead farm with the horses, cows, and chickens."

"We're going to see chickens?" Justine asked. "Will we be able to see them lay their eggs?"

"Oh, sorry. I don't think you'll be seeing any egg laying," Ellie said. "That place has been abandoned for years. Although, when I was at church last week, I heard they're planning on making it a Piggly Wiggly."

Mallory saw the disappointment in Justine's eyes. Her daughter didn't know she'd never had any intentions of visiting farm animals. She was simply trying to fudge her way through what she hoped would come off as a believable story. "Justine, we can probably find another farm before we reach Grandpa's house."

"Can I pet the horses?" Justine smiled.

"Sure you can," she said, knowing she needed to stop talking before she dug herself deeper into this complicated lie she was weaving.

"So when are you taking off?" Ellie asked.

"Well, our car is in the shop and needs a part. And the funny thing is…even if we could get another car…well…I…I spoke with my father this morning, and on top of everything else, he was remodeling his basement when they found asbestos. So he's moving into a hotel, and we need to postpone our trip." She nearly ran out of breath, trying to keep up with the story she was telling on the spot.

"That's awful. Why didn't you say something?" Rafe leaned forward.

"What's ass-bess…ass-bess-toes?" Justine asked.

Ellie laughed, "Oh honey, sorry, none of this is funny. Asbestos is a material they used to put in walls to keep your house warm. That is until they found out it was very bad for you."

Mallory nodded, keeping her focus on Ellie. The kindness in her eyes reminded her of her father. How could she lie to this woman? *You're keeping Justine safe. That's all that matters.* Mallory sat straight and cleared her throat. "So it looks like we'll be here for at least a couple of weeks."

"Really?" Rafe put his glass of lemonade down.

Mallory kept her gaze on her lap as she spoke. She couldn't dare look Rafe in the eye and lie. "Yeah. Looks like it."

"So, will you be staying in town?" Ellie asked.

The question gave Mallory a jolt. Where would she be staying? She remembered Abbey's B&B wasn't available.

"Actually, Abbey's place is all booked up with a sixtieth wedding anniversary. I guess I'll have to find something else in town or at least close by. I don't have a car."

Ellie placed the sandwiches on the table. "Unfortunately, Abbey's B&B is the only game in town."

"Ooh, potato chips!" Justine reached for the bowl and then stopped short. "Can I, Mommy? Can I? Mommy!"

"Oh…sorry, Punkie. Wasn't paying attention."

"I know. I said, can I have potato chips? Pleeeeeease."

"Oh, sure. But only a few. And only after you take a few bites of your sandwich." Mallory felt sick to her stomach. Using her credit card to rent a car so she could find a place to stay was not an option.

"Well, I have plenty of room," Ellie said.

Surprised at the offer, Mallory's eyes widened. "Really? But…but…but this is so random. You haven't seen me in years. Goodness, opening your home? Isn't it an inconvenience?"

"Mallory, you're hardly a stranger. As I recall, you and Rafe were once quite close." Ellie smiled at Rafe. "And that's good enough for me. Besides, I'm alone in this four-bedroom house. It could use a little more life."

Mallory noticed Rafe lean toward his aunt, eyebrow raised.

"I couldn't impose. Really." Mallory kept her gaze on her hands neatly folded on her lap, not daring to look at Rafe. She'd seen the look of incredulity in his eyes. He wasn't wrong. She shouldn't be staying here.

"*Tía*, let's finish lunch. Then Mallory and I can have a chat. After that, we'll figure out where she'll be staying."

Rafe's words sliced through her.

Ellie gave a soft laugh. "*Mira*. Just because you own a cybersecurity firm doesn't mean you have to be suspicious of everything and everyone." She tsked. "This is Mallory and her daughter—no need to run a security check, for goodness' sake. They are perfectly welcome here. And that's that."

Mallory looked up. *Cybersecurity?* "Rafe, I thought you were…well, honestly, I didn't know. I do remember how much you loved science and computers."

"It's true. My handsome, genius nephew was a nerd. He still is." Ellie smiled. "When his brothers and my boys got together, they played touch football in my backyard." She waved a hand toward the back door in the kitchen. "It didn't matter if it was raining or a hundred degrees. But not Rafael. Sure, he'd tag along, but he'd be studying at this table or at the computer in the den."

Rafe coughed.

"Sorry, don't mean to talk about you like you aren't here. But, *sobrino*, I'm proud of you. Your company's a big deal. Mallory, did you know they have some of the largest government contracts?" She squeezed his forearm.

"So, you're involved in cybersecurity?" Mallory cocked her head. This couldn't have been more perfect if she'd planned it. She had the urge to spill her guts and tell Rafe everything. "You know—"

"What's saber secure?" Justine asked, popping another potato chip in her mouth.

Again, Ellie laughed.

"What's funny?" Justine reached for another potato chip.

Mallory moved the bowl. "Punkie. Please eat your sandwich."

"It's cy-ber-se-cur-ity." Rafe pronounced it slowly. "You know how in your favorite superhero stories, there are good guys who protect everyone from the bad guys? And you know how we have locks on our doors at home to keep us safe from strangers?"

Justine nodded, her mouth now full of tuna.

"Well, when we use computers, phones, or tablets, there can also be bad guys who try to sneak into them to steal or mess with our stuff."

"What kind of stuff?" Justine asked.

Rafe gave a one-shoulder shrug. "Oh, you know, like our pictures, games, or even important information about us. So, cybersecurity is like the superheroes or the locks on our doors but for all our gadgets. It's all the things we do to keep bad guys out of our computers and keep our digital stuff safe. We use passwords, just like keys for our doors, and sometimes we use special programs like superheroes to guard our computers."

"Cool," Justine said.

Passwords. If there were a soundtrack that went along with her thoughts, the chorus would be singing "Oh Happy Days." There was a strong possibility that he could help her get into Blake's laptop.

Rafe stretched and pushed away from the table. "Uh, *tía.* I...uh, need to talk to you for a second."

The glances exchanged between Rafe and his aunt were unmistakable. He wasn't keen on her staying with Ellie. Mallory stood. "Go ahead," she encouraged them. "I'll clean these up. Can I put them in the dishwasher?"

Ellie rose and took off her apron. "You don't have to do that. You're a guest."

"That's exactly why I want to. Punkie, come on. Help me clear the table."

"I'll hang up my apron and be right there," Ellie said.

Rafe stepped onto the back porch and leaned against the railing, looking out at the expansive backyard. Two ancient oak trees with flat green leaves flanked his right. Several tall maples stood on his left, marking the plot of land belonging to his aunt and deceased uncle. A thin smile crossed his face as he remembered the many happy family barbeques and Sunday dinners they'd had before all the harsh words were traded between him and his father. Oh, how he wished he could turn back time and take back everything he said.

He heard the screen door slam shut, and Ellie was beside him. *"¿Qué te pasa?"*

Rafe turned to face his aunt. He loved her for her endless supply of kindness. He saw the love in her silver eyes now. It didn't surprise him that she'd offered Mallory a place to stay. Ellie opened her arms and her heart to anything that was hurt. His cousins would bring home all sorts—from injured birds, lost puppies, and baby squirrels to neighborhood kids looking for some of her famous *flan* and a glass of milk. It was common knowledge that Eloise Chavez would take care of them. She never asked questions and only believed the good in people, and Rafe loved her for it. But this time, regardless of the feelings Mallory stirred in him, he was worried.

"¿Qué te pasa?" Rafe raised an eyebrow. "You're asking *me* what's the matter? You haven't seen her in fifteen years. She's practically a stranger to you. We have no idea what she's been up to."

"We know her husband is dead. And you and I can see something's not right—*¿verdad?*"

Rafe huffed. "Exactly why you should be cautious before opening your home."

"Sobrino, you are so protective, a quality I don't particularly like, but in you, I forgive." Ellie smirked and crossed her arms over her chest. "You know, this old house is so big, I only ever use three rooms on a good day. Your friend looks like she could use some taking care of—looks a little

lost. She's got a little girl and no place else to go. I can't *not* help."

At that, Rafe smiled. "You're as stubborn as ever."

Ellie stepped back. "*Exactamente.* Now we're on the same page." She winked and gave a little head nod.

Rafe raised a hand. "Hold on a sec. Max and Zack would have my head if I didn't investigate her before she settles in here."

Ellie's mouth went slack, and an expression of shock crossed her face.

"Don't look at me like that."

"*¿Pero me qué estás diciendo?* Investigate? That's ridiculous—"

"Let me explain." Rafe gently placed a hand on her shoulder. "It wouldn't be prudent to let her stay here without at least asking some questions."

"Well, then ask." Ellie poked him in the chest. "Go in there and tell her you want the truth. If you're satisfied, we'll leave it at that."

His aunt was probably right. He should have a conversation with Mallory. The idea made him nervous, and he wiped his brow. She'd once been his everything. Now, she was a stranger with a situation. "I can't just ask her what's going on with her kid sitting right there." The words came out more defensively than he intended. "Sorry. I'm a bit rattled."

"*¡Ay mijo!*" She stomped her foot. "You and your brothers run a company with big government contracts facing down crime every day. This is one woman. A woman, I might add, who you used to love. And from what I can see, it looks like you still have some feelings."

Rafe flinched.

"So, she's got an issue. So, help her, for god's sake."

Ellie put her hands on her hips. "Now, I'll go in there and tell her about the room. Once her daughter is settled, tell Mallory you want to talk. Take her for a walk by Sullivan Park. Or better yet, go to your apartment where there are no prying eyes. I'll watch Justine. We'll bake cookies." She turned. "Let's go."

Rafe held the screen door open and followed his aunt back into the kitchen.

"So—" Ellie clapped her hands together "—why don't I give you a tour?"

"Do we have our own room?" Justine asked.

"Yes, you do, and it's on the second floor. Follow me." Ellie walked out of the kitchen and toward the center hall staircase. "It faces the back of the house and has wonderful early sunlight. So, I hope you're a morning person."

"What's a morning person?" Justine asked as she held onto the banister and hopped up one step at a time, following Ellie.

"Well, it means you like to get up early. You know, greet the day."

"Oh." Justine stopped hopping, sticking her tongue into the side of her mouth, and looked up. "I'm not a morning person."

Ellie chuckled, glancing at Mallory. "That's okay. I think you'll like the room anyway."

At the top of the stairs was a wide hallway with five doors. Ellie led them to a large room overlooking a vegetable garden at the back of the house. The queen-size bed featured a quilted headboard, and the duvet cover was sage green with a leaf pattern along the edging. A tall dresser flanked one side of the window, and a writing table sat opposite. There were two comfortable chairs against the far wall.

"I'm assuming you'd like to be in the same room as your daughter?"

"Yes."

"Okay, good. The room has its own bathroom," Ellie said. "I hope you'll be comfortable here."

"It's perfect," Mallory said.

Ellie crossed over to the one closet in the room and pulled out a blanket. "The nights get cold," she said, placing the blanket on the bed. "If this isn't enough, there are more in the linen closet at the end of the hall. Just help yourself."

"Thanks. I think we'll be fine."

Justine sat on the edge of the bed and began bouncing up and down.

"Justine…" Mallory gave a raised eyebrow in her daughter's direction.

"Look at the time," Ellie said, glancing at the watch on her wrist. "I was hoping you wouldn't mind if Justine helped me bake some cookies?"

"Yes! I wanna. I wanna." Justine leaped off the bed and raced toward the door.

"Hold on, Punkie." Mallory caught her by the waist. "Ellie, staying here is one thing. But I really don't want you to, you know, take care of us."

Ellie waved her hand. "I'm baking them anyway. Might as well have a helper." She headed out the door, and Justine followed her, silencing any further argument.

No sooner had Justine left than Rafe turned to Mallory, a solemn look on his face. "Mallory, we need to talk."

Chapter 6

The drive to Rafe's apartment on the east side of town was silent, except for Mallory's continuous finger drumming on the middle console. The converted paper mill housed seven luxury condos on an embankment fifty feet from the Hudson River. Rafe had moved into the penthouse a year ago.

The apartment was large and airy. Oversized, multicolored abstract paintings decorated the ten-foot Sheetrocked walls. Moveable dividers separated the kitchen and dining area from the living space. Beyond that, a long hallway led to several bedrooms. The entire east wall of ten-foot windows overlooked the broad, sparkling Hudson.

Rafe tossed his keys into a bowl on a table near the entryway. "Want something to drink?"

Mallory looked around. "Uh…water?" She made it sound like a question.

"Sure thing." Rafe opened the refrigerator and pulled out two bottled waters. "Come on. Let's go upstairs."

Mallory gave him a quizzical look.

"Roof garden." Rafe glanced upward. "Follow me."

He led her toward a spiral staircase that opened onto a landscaped terrace. Complete with flower gardens, gravel paths, benches, and patio furniture.

"This is all yours?"

He let out a one-syllable laugh. "Yes. The apartment. The roof. All mine."

"You hired someone to do these gardens?" Mallory's eyes widened. "They're amazing."

"I wish." Rafe shook his head and put the bottle of water on the wrought-iron table. "Did all the work with these." He held out his hands. "Some tools, and of course, my brothers chipped in with hours of manual labor." Rafe scanned his work admiringly.

When he was released from prison, he wanted a place with lots of open space. He chose the apartment because the barren roof had so much potential. He created this garden terrace, which had been a labor of love. "It took some doing, but I'm happy I did it. I get to enjoy this space so many months out of the year. Sometimes, even in the winter, I grill if it's not snowing or raining. Nothing like steak on the grill—" Rafe cut himself off and put his hands in his pockets. "Look, we didn't say more than two words on the ride over here, and now we're talking about my terrace. You and I both know that's not what we're here for."

Mallory stared for several seconds. The expression on her face told him all he needed to know.

"You sure Justine is going to be okay?" Mallory looked down. "Your aunt—I mean, I know she's very nice—"

Rafe nodded. "Please don't worry." He patted the phone in his pocket. "If anything's wrong, Ellie will call."

Mallory let out a long breath. "Okay."

He wanted her to feel comfortable, so he casually lowered himself into one of the chairs, put his legs out in front, and crossed his feet at the ankle. Keeping his expression neutral, he waited. Whatever was going on, it was clear she needed to tell someone. She'd been acting like a powder keg about to burst since the night he found her on the side of the road. Somewhere in the depths of his soul, he'd already decided to help her take refuge or just be there for her. He knew that trapped look because he'd been there. He didn't want that to be Mallory's situation, no matter what she was about to say. "All right then." Rafe held out the flat of his hand toward the table and chairs. "Why don't you have a seat."

Rafe was giving her the chance to spill her guts. Instead, she froze. Her back felt stiff from days of bottled-up fear and tension. She studied the flowers, tresses, and lanterns strewn overhead. She was stalling. Was she crazy for thinking she could trust Rafe?

Nervously, she twisted the water bottle cap back and forth until she finally removed it and gulped greedily, not realizing how thirsty she'd been. She took a deep breath and slumped into the chair opposite Rafe. "I guess there's no point in pretending I'm not hiding from someone."

"Nope." Rafe's voice was clipped.

She pressed her lips together, and for a minute or so, she looked anywhere but at Rafe.

"Hey, you've already established something is going on." He leaned forward. "Just spill it."

Easier said than done. Where to begin? Closing her eyes, she tilted her head toward the sky. And then, she began to laugh. Not the ha-ha funny kind of laugh, but the uncontrollable, on-the-verge-of-hysteria laugh.

Rafe laughed lightly in response. "What's so funny?"

"You...wouldn't...believe me..." Mallory couldn't speak through the laughter. The release felt better than a good, long cry.

"Try me."

Tears rolled down her face, and the uncontrollable laughter made her sides hurt.

"Mallory, you okay?"

She nodded, but just barely. *He must think I'm mad. Maybe I am.*

"What could possibly be so funny?"

It took several minutes, but Mallory finally got a grip on her emotions. She took a deep breath, stood, wiped her cheeks with the back of her hand, and walked toward the roof's edge. Looking out over the railing, she tried to compose herself and focused on an embankment on the far side of the river. The leaves on the trees glistened in the sunlight. She couldn't hold it in any longer. She didn't want to. Rafe was asking her to tell him. It was now or never.

She kept her back to him. Telling him her story was one thing. Facing him was another. "Nothing's funny," she said. "In fact, what I'm about to tell you is probably the most unbelievable story you've heard in a while."

Rafe rose and stepped beside her.

"Please don't ask any questions until I'm finished." She paused, hoping she was doing the right thing. "I don't even know where to start." Mallory stared at the view, her knuckles white from gripping the railing, afraid she'd lose her nerve.

"How about at the beginning." He placed his hand gently on her forearm, and Mallory had to steel herself from the overwhelming feeling of desire from his touch.

Squaring her shoulders and without any preamble, she began at the beginning.

"All right. Here goes. I worked at a top-ten accounting firm in New York City. I'd just made Vice President of the Forensic Accounting department. The company bought a table at a charity event, and I was invited to attend. That's where I met Blake Stanton. Some people might say it was love at first sight. Looking back, I'm not sure what it was." Mallory hung her head. "Let's just say I was consumed with everything about him. So was the rest of New York. I mean, he wasn't simply a popular hedge fund manager. He was trending in all the right circles. There wasn't a celebrity, banker, or even a government official he couldn't reach with the touch of his phone. Everyone wanted his opinion, and he was envied for his charmed life."

"That wasn't the case?" Rafe asked.

She swallowed hard, preparing to say words she'd never spoken to anyone. "Hardly," Mallory scoffed. "Our life together was not the Camelot he portrayed. Blake was a master at manipulation and had everyone fooled. Before I knew what was happening, I quit my job, a career I'd worked hard for, and I found myself isolated from all my friends and family." Mallory banged her fist against the railing. The words poured out. She couldn't stop if she wanted to. "Rafe—" she turned her head, still holding the railing "—you have to believe me. I tried to leave him when Justine was just two years old." She let out a tired laugh. "I got as far as the airport when he found me. In the steely voice he reserved for business negotiations, he assured me he would always find me and that he'd take Justine. I believed him. Blake's connections included all the power brokers in New York and DC. He had the best lawyers in the city on retainers. I wouldn't have stood a chance."

"That's awful." Rafe took a step closer.

"I'm not done." But Mallory stopped. A war still raged in her mind, battling whether to tell Rafe or let him live a life that didn't involve her and her problems.

Rafe leaned against the railing. "Like I said, I'm listening."

She could feel his expectant gaze, and she cleared her throat. "When Interpol came to my door to tell me that my husband's plane crashed in international waters and no bodies were recovered, I thought I'd been given a second chance at life."

Mallory smiled at the memory. Moments after the Interpol officials left, she slumped against the door and wiped the tears of joy from her face. Then, she blasted the stereo and danced around the living room. When Justine came home from school, she delayed telling her the news. Instead, they ate hot dogs and French fries off paper plates while they sat on the floor watching *Frozen*.

"That look on your face," she said, pointing at his raised eyebrow. "You're surprised because I'm smiling. Right?"

"Yeah. A little."

"Well—" she shrugged "—that was my liberation day. I knew I would never have to be perfect or do things the way Blake demanded ever again." She shook her head. "But, damn it, I was foolish to believe I was ever really…free." The last word came out as a sob.

Rafe placed his hand on her back. It felt good. The warmth of his hand made her want to wrap her arms around him. Instead, she stopped herself and stiffened. Getting help was one thing. Leaning into the comfort he offered would only be the first step in a downhill slope of relying on a man again. She wasn't sure she could let that happen. Her daughter needed her to stand on her own two feet and stay strong. Ultimately, the only person Mallory felt she could ever really trust was herself.

"Mallory? What's going on?"

She hadn't realized she was crying until the teardrop landed on her hand.

"Hey there. Let's sit." Rafe took a few steps to the table. "Here." He handed her the water. "Take a sip."

Mallory took the offered water. "You don't need to hover."

The look on Rafe's face registered hurt. She hadn't intended to make him feel bad—she simply needed some room to breathe. "Thanks. Really. I'm fine," she said, softening her tone.

He sat across from her, leaning forward with his elbows on his knees, chin cupped in his hands. The kindness in his eyes made her relax. "You okay to keep going?"

Mallory nodded and let out a breath. "A month after his death, I received a note and a threatening phone call. In both instances, they claimed Blake was holding a hard drive they wanted. They warned me not to go to the authorities or they'd hurt Justine." A chill ran down Mallory's spine, remembering that afternoon.

Rafe raked a hand through his hair. "My god. Why didn't you call the police?"

"The note included photos of Justine at school, in the playground. Clearly, they were watching us, and...and... I believed they would hurt her."

"This is unbelievable." He reached for her hand.

The panic that consumed her when she read the note hadn't left because her mouth went dry, and her heart stuttered with the memory. It was his nearness and the warmth of his hand that kept her steady. "I had no idea what they were talking about, but I searched the entire house, including Blake's home office."

"Did you even know what you were looking for?"

"No. But I was certain if I could find something, anything that looked like a disc, I'd give it to the company attorney and let them handle it."

"I'm confused. Did you find the disc or not?"

"No. At least, I don't know." She scrubbed her face with the palms of her hands. "I found a laptop and ten thousand dollars in cash strapped to the underside of his chair."

Rafe let out a low whistle. "Do you think it's the laptop they're after?"

"It's all I have to go on." She blew a breath out through her nose. "The note said 'hard drive.' I searched every inch of Blake's home office and couldn't find anything else. The laptop has a built-in hard drive. If I had to guess, that's what they're after. Otherwise, why would Blake go through the trouble of hiding it?"

"Sounds about right."

"I tried to get into the laptop, tried every possible password combination. I was never locked out of the computer, but I didn't have any luck getting in. Before I left, I took the laptop to the computer store in town. The techie said the only reason I'd been able to attempt so many passwords was because Blake never changed the factory setting on the computer. He also said that without the password, the only way in was to wipe the hard drive."

"Yeah, that sounds about right."

"Well, I couldn't let that happen. I need the password because I think whatever is on there is going to save my daughter's life. But I don't trust whoever's after us to leave us alone once they get what they want."

"Your ex was a powerful man indeed, but what makes you think they wouldn't leave you alone?"

Mallory shivered and ran her hands up and down her arms. "When I came back from the computer store, my house had been ransacked—furniture turned over, pillows slashed, closets emptied onto the floor. Even though they warned me not to go to the authorities, I finally succumbed and called the police." Mallory pulled on the pendant around her neck. "A lot of good that did me. They found no fingerprints and no evidence anything had been taken. The police labeled it vandalism and left."

"Maybe it was?" Rafe shrugged.

"No. It couldn't be. I live…" Mallory shook her head. "I *lived*, past tense, in a gated community. There's nothing but miles of expensive homes and everyone has CCTV. And these so-called vandals left not a single fingerprint, and not one camera captured an image?" She raised both eyebrows. "How is that possible?"

"Sounds like professionals."

"That's exactly what I thought." She sat back in the chair. "Not to be melodramatic, but I sense those types of people would want to make sure that whatever was on the laptop was for their eyes only. If they even suspected I knew what was on it, I think they'd for sure want to get rid of me. I couldn't take a chance. I knew I had to get out. I had to protect my daughter."

"How in the world did you end up here, back in Hollow Lake?"

"Well, it was on the way to my dad's new place in Rochester. I thought I'd be safe with him. I'd get into the computer and then figure out my next step."

Rafe pursed his lips. "Okay, so far, I'm tracking with you."

"Well, the day before they vandalized my home, the Tesla dealer phoned. Evidently, some new car Blake purchased had arrived. I didn't know anything about it. Apparently, he'd ordered a custom model, and it was already paid for. That's when the lightbulb went off. I could get out of town in a car I wasn't associated with. Which meant maybe I wouldn't be followed. I hoped by the time they realized

I wasn't home, I'd be long gone and far away." As she recounted the details, her adrenaline levels began to surge.

"I was scared to death, but I had to act fast. I cut my hair and threw on jeans and a baseball cap. I packed what I could, took the laptop and the ten thousand in cash, and called a cab. I knew whoever photographed Justine was watching, so I had the cab meet me in town. I snuck out the back door and somehow managed to walk along the back roads with Justine and the luggage about a half mile into town. I took the cab to the dealership, got the car, and drove. Several hours later, that's when I met you, stalled out on County Road 385."

Rafe was silent.

"I know. I know." Mallory shook her head, eyes downcast. "It almost sounds like a reenactment of a true crime series." Mallory let out a bitter laugh and slumped back in her chair. The weight of what she was carrying, finally out in the open, afforded her some relief. But at the same time, she felt ashamed that she'd lived for so many years with a monster, unable to escape. She covered her face with her hands. "I'm so god-awful tired...of everything." Mallory got up and started pacing along the gravel paths. "I'm scared."

Rafe didn't move.

"Ironically, when Blake went on this last trip, I'd already had an appointment with a divorce attorney. I was going to leave him. Somehow, I was going to figure out how to escape with my baby." She wanted Rafe to know she did have some spine left.

"I'm not sure what to say."

"I know." She stopped pacing and saw the disbelief in his eyes. "Imagine me, a trained forensic accountant, and I couldn't trace the lies Blake fed me from the very start of our marriage. I thought the nightmare was over when he died. How foolish of me. It was only beginning." She stood in front of Rafe. "I need your help. I have to get into that computer because until I do, that bastard will still torment me and my daughter even from the grave."

Rafe took her hands in his. "Mallory, he isn't here. He can't hurt you."

"Oh no? Haven't you heard what I've been saying? That's exactly what's happening."

"When was the last time you were contacted by those men?" Rafe asked.

"Not me."

Rafe frowned. "What do you mean, not me? Is that some kind of non sequitur?"

"I mean, I haven't been contacted again. But this morning, two men showed up at my father's office asking questions. That's what this morning's phone call was all about. He said they wanted to know when I'd last visited and when I would be returning. They're trying to intimidate me by stalking my father. They're waiting for me to show up. I know it." Mallory sucked in a breath. "My poor dad. He doesn't deserve this."

"Is your father all right?"

"For now. No doubt he's out of his mind with worry. But he's strong and trusts I know what I'm doing."

"What are you doing?"

Mallory hesitated. The more she thought about her situation, the more she knew what her next move needed to be. She'd already taken pains to disguise herself by cutting her hair. And now that she'd stuffed her phone in the back of a car going to New Mexico, her instincts told her she had a week, maybe two, to hide in plain sight. "I need to get into that computer. Something in there must be why my daughter's life is being threatened."

Mallory stepped to the side of the round wrought-iron table, picked up her large leather shoulder bag, and reached in. She pulled out the small silver laptop and handed it to Rafe. "Help me. Please."

Chapter 7

Rafe pulled up to Ellie's house and waited until Mallory was safely inside. He put the car in Park and kept the engine running while he stared at the empty porch. He needed a moment. So many emotions were bubbling to the surface it was difficult to know exactly what he felt—anger, hurt, worry, maybe even desire. *Damn.* What had he gotten himself into? He banged his hand against the steering wheel and looked at the laptop resting on the passenger seat.

Yesterday, he'd been happy to see Mallory. Today, he was afraid. There wasn't a doubt in his mind she was in serious trouble. The kind of trouble that could get a person killed. Rafe closed his eyes, realizing he'd brought danger to his family. He should have sent her packing the moment she told him the truth. That's what he *should* have done, but that wasn't what he was going to do. After all, they had a shared history that couldn't be denied. Against his better judgment, he'd already opened himself up to feeling things for her that he thought were buried. Leaving her to fend for herself didn't seem like an option.

Once more, Rafe banged the steering wheel with the palm of his hand. It felt good momentarily releasing some of his frustration. He checked the clock on the dashboard.

It was late, and he hadn't been back in the office since early morning. His brothers would be wondering what happened.

He pulled the phone from his pocket. The battery was dead. How had he let that happen? Hopefully, Ellie hadn't tried to reach them. He plugged it into the console. As it came to life, it dinged several times, alerting him of the five missed calls, two voicemails, and ten text messages from Max, the perpetual worrier, and Zack, the other worrier. None from his aunt. He didn't bother to read any of the messages. He quickly sent a group text to his brothers, letting them know he would be there in ten minutes. He threw the gear shift into Drive and took off down the street.

The elevator doors opened, and Brittany greeted Rafe. "There you are." Her toothy smile faded. "Max is looking for you. He has been for the last hour. Why'd you turn off your phone?"

He smiled and ignored the question. "Is he in his office?"

"No. He said to meet him in the large conference room."

"Thanks." Rafe stopped by his office and popped the laptop into the bottom drawer of his desk. He locked the drawer and his office door and went to the conference room.

Max sat at the head of the long glass table with a sour expression. The oldest of the brothers, Maximo Jesus Ramirez, resembled their father in looks and attitude. He was the consummate rule follower. His chiseled features were set with tight lips and an arched brow.

Rafe slid the door closed, and Max hit a button on the built-in console, darkening the all-glass wall and shutting out prying eyes.

"So. You want to tell us what's going on?" Max pushed his light brown hair from his forehead.

"We got a little worried," Zack said. "I mean, it doesn't

take hours to fix a leaky bathroom sink, so we called *Tía* Ellie, and she gave us a little bit of the tea. You know, the 411."

"But we'd love for you to fill us in," Max added.

Rafe was at a loss. *Where to start?* He strode to the far end of the room, opened a small refrigerator, and pulled out a bottle of water. "Anyone want?"

"Nah. Well hydrated at the moment," Max said.

"Yeah, I'm good." Zack waved him off.

"Bro. You're stalling." Max's tone turned serious. "Having trouble remembering who you spent your morning with?" He pushed closer to the table. "You know who I'm talking about? Right? Woman, slender, pixie cut, car needs repair, curly-haired little girl? Oh, and you—" he pointed at Rafe "—you were in a serious relationship with her back in high school. Am I right?"

"Yeah. Want to fill us in on what you talked about?" Zack joined in. "*Tía* Ellie says it looks like she's in some kind of trouble. And if I'm correctly recalling our conversation from last night, I believe you suspected something, too. In fact, I thought we discussed you were going to let her go her own way."

Rafe made a motion with his hands as if he were patting something down. *"Cálmate."*

"Oh, I'm calm," Max said, sliding his seat further from the table and crossing one leg over the other. "What about you, Zack? You calm?"

Zack put his feet up on the table. "Feeling real relaxed."

Despite their sarcasm, their eyes held an intensity that said they were not joking around. It only reinforced how much danger he'd brought to the family.

"Have a seat, bro." Max pointed to the chair next to him and opposite Zack. Rafe sat, forming the familiar triangle at the head of the long conference table where they held staff meetings.

Max spoke first. "Seems your long-lost love is on the run."

Rafe opened his mouth to answer.

Max held up a hand. "*No me hables.* Don't say a word." He pointed to himself and Zack. "Neither of us are recent graduates in the investigation game. It took us less than the time it takes to make a *jamón y queso* sandwich to find out that your girl, Mallory, is running from something. Her house was ransacked, and she left yesterday in a brand-new Tesla purchased by her husband before his death."

"Yeah," Zack said, sitting forward and rolling his chair closer to the table. "So the husband, who happens to be... wait for it—" Zack pointed to Max.

"Blake Stanton," Max said in a deadpan voice.

Zack snapped his fingers. "That's the one. Anyway, he dies mid-Atlantic. All mysterious like. You know? His plane bursts into flames in the middle of the ocean, and guess what? No bodies are recovered. Fascinating, don't you think?"

Rafe shook his head, not sure what to say. Clearly, his brothers had done some digging. And while it annoyed him, he understood because they did it to protect him. "Well, I appreciate—"

"*¿Pero qué te pasa? ¿Acaso no piensas?*" Max tapped his temple.

"Yeah, what *were* you thinking? Did you somehow leave your brains back in the cabin when you went fishing? Why'd you take her to our aunt's house? *Tía* Ellie doesn't need this." Zack raised an eyebrow.

Max scoffed. "Believe it or not, we worry about you."

"Yeah, I know," Rafe said. "*Pero no te preocupes.*"

"Hold up," Zack said. "We've earned the right to be worried. You were framed once before. Remember? We don't want you getting hurt, and this guy, Blake Stanton, may be dead, but he's got a past I don't like."

His brothers were right. Whoever was after Mallory was on the wrong side of the law. And going back to prison wasn't an option. He needed to be careful. More importantly, he needed to protect his family.

"I see the wheels turning in that head of yours," Max said. "You're thinking you can do this all by yourself." He slapped a palm on the conference table. "No!"

"I second that." Zack raised his hand. "We're brothers. We're in this together."

"Hold up. I'm not totally on board with whatever this is yet. I need more information," Max said.

His older brother was always the skeptic. Anally analytical. Most times, Rafe loved him for it. Today, not so much. For once, he wished Max would just go with it. Rafe sighed. He supposed Max was right. Get all the facts. Then make a decision. Helping Mallory would require his brothers' help.

"Míralo." Zack pointed at him. "I know that look. You're going do what you want to do because that's what you always do."

"Nah." Rafe shook his head. "When it comes to family it's a democracy. This involves all of us, and I won't make the decision on how we move forward unless we all agree."

"Qué milagro." Zack smiled. "A zebra can change his stripes."

Rafe grinned.

"So start. Tell us everything she told you," Max said.

Rafe ran a hand through his hair. "Mallory and her daughter are being hunted."

"Hunted?" Zack sat forward. "You got my attention."

Rafe told Max and Zack everything he knew, including the need to hack into Blake Stanton's computer and the fact that Mallory's daughter would be in danger if she went to the police. And that, as of this morning, at least two suspicious men were asking questions at her father's office.

When he finished, a silence descended. Rafe looked from one brother to the next. "Well, aren't you going to say something?"

Max pursed his lips.

"Ah, man. Don't give me that look," Rafe said.

"What look?" Max asked.

Rafe pointed his finger. "The one that's taking over your face right now. The one that screams Rafe's stepped in it again."

Max stood abruptly and strode to the far end of the conference room. He stared out the window for a few moments and then whirled around. "Honestly? I'm trying to remain calm."

Rafe didn't understand. "I get that you're upset—"

"Nah, man. Not upset. Nope. Scared." Max dug one hand into his pocket. "Let me break it down for you. This is *the* Blake Stanton you're talking about. And if his ex is being chased and her daughter's life is in danger, there's a reason." Max sat. "I need to think." He put his head in his hands.

Zack took out his phone and began to scroll.

Rafe didn't know what to say. When he was arrested for crypto-jacking, his brothers had been there for him. Through their efforts alone, the dark net hacking crew behind the illegal mining of cryptocurrency was discovered. RMZ's reputation had taken a hit, but together, they'd tirelessly worked to restore it. He would go along with whatever they decided. He owed them that much.

"Hate to break into your private thoughts. But we got a problem." Zack stared at his phone screen.

"What now?" Max moved around the table, looking over Zack's shoulder. "Oh, man." Max slapped the table with a palm.

"What?" Rafe stood.

Zack looked up at him. "News alert." He turned his phone's screen to face Rafe.

"I can't read that from here."

"Looks like the black box on Blake Stanton's plane has gone all Bermuda Triangle. It's gone. Vanished." Zack put his phone down.

"If we were analyzing this as a case, with all the information we have now, let's be real, we'd probably pass. Particularly since the main event, one Blake Stanton, was devious at best and an out-and-out criminal at worst." Max paced.

"Hell, that guy had back channels up into the White House. He was well protected," Zack offered.

"Even in death?" Rafe asked.

"Well, you tell me. How does a black box disappear?" Zack asked.

"But we're not protecting the dead husband," Rafe countered. "We need to protect Mallory and her five-year-old daughter. When did we stop caring about individuals? We've all been so busy stalking cyber criminals and the harm they do to big corporations and government agencies. But this is real. This is a person. Not some nameless government agency. Not a bunch of zeros and ones hiding in the dark web. Dammit. She needs our help. Let's not over-think this. The clock is ticking."

Max crossed his arms over his chest. "'Cause Zack and I know this guy's reputation from working on Wall Street.

And Blake Stanton, alive or dead, isn't someone I would choose to mess with. Word was, he knew the kind of people you don't want to meet in a dark alley on a moonless night, if you get where I'm going with this."

A shiver crawled up Rafe's spine. He hadn't experienced that sensation since prison, where watching your back was part of daily life. He tried to shake it off by getting up and walking to the windows. His gaze traveled up and down Main Street just as a black sedan pulled up in front of Fritz & Dean's diner.

Chapter 8

"Mommy's back. Mommy's back!"

"Don't open the door, Justine," Mallory heard Ellie admonish. "Let's see who's there first."

From the corner of her eye, she caught the flutter of the living room curtains and turned to see Ellie looking out and waving and Justine right beside her, smiling.

"We'll be right there," Ellie called through the closed window.

Justine barely gave Mallory a chance to get through the door with her packages before giving her the details of her afternoon. "Mommy, you won't believe what we made. I only got to eat one 'cause Ellie said I had to wait till after dinner or I'll spoil my appe…appe…"

"Appetite," Mallory finished for her.

"Yeah. Appetite," Justine said proudly.

"I'm happy to hear that," Mallory said.

"What happened to Rafe?" Ellie asked.

"Thanks for taking care of Justine." Mallory flashed a grateful smile and continued down the hall toward the kitchen. "Rafe said he had to get back to the office. He'll be by later with our luggage." She placed the bags on the counter and checked the clock above the sink. She'd been gone for more than three hours.

"What's all this?" Ellie said, pointing to the grocery bags.

"Rafe took me to the supermarket. I did a little shopping for dinner." It had taken a herculean effort on her part to convince Rafe to let her go to the local market. At first, he refused. They'd already stopped at Abbey's B&B so Mallory could pack. He'd been in a hurry to get back to his office and talk to his brothers. And he didn't want her walking around by herself. But Mallory was just as stubborn, insisting she had to do something special for Justine, who'd been shuttled around and disoriented. And she didn't want to take advantage of Ellie. He'd finally acquiesced on the condition he went into the market with her.

"It's spaghetti and meatballs as a thank you for the room and lunch and for watching Justine."

"Yay! I love spaghetti and meatballs." Justine clapped.

"I know you do. Hopefully, it's something Ellie likes, too." Mallory looked up expectantly.

"First of all, no thanks necessary. Justine and I had a wonderful time making cookies. Reminds me of when my grandchildren visit. And as lovely as dinner with the two of you sounds, I can't tonight. Tonight is book club night with the girls. It's Grace's turn to make the appetizers, and they're a meal in themselves." Ellie took off her apron and hung it up behind the door. "I'm going to go up and change."

"Oh, okay." Mallory was somewhat relieved Ellie would be out. Now, she wouldn't have to spend all evening pretending her life was normal instead of feeling like a mouse caught in a cat's playpen. She began unpacking the groceries and looking around the large kitchen for things she needed to prepare dinner. "Well, Punkie, it's just you and me tonight. How 'bout helping me make dinner."

"Sure. But when do we get to eat dessert?" Justine asked.

"The sooner we get dinner on the table, the sooner you can have one cookie." Mallory held up her index finger, emphasizing the number one. Her motherly instincts told her that in addition to the cookie already eaten, there'd been a healthy sampling of cookie dough and licking of spoons. Any more sugar and bedtime promised to be a struggle. She bent, put both hands on Justine's face, and kissed her nose. Her daughter's face made her heart ache with joy and trepidation.

"Owww. Mommy, you're squeezing too hard."

"Oh, sorry." Mallory kissed the top of her head.

A dozen times this afternoon, Mallory had vacillated about flying to her father's house and handing over the damn computer to the men who were after her, hoping to end this nightmare. But then the rational portion of her mind would kick in, cautioning her that these men were like her husband. They weren't honorable, and there'd be no guarantee she and Justine would ever escape danger.

No. Her only recourse was to get into that damn computer. Instincts told her if she could get the information these men were after, she'd have some leverage.

For now, she needed to stay put and hope that placing her trust in Rafe had been the right thing to do. Glancing up at the clock again, she wondered what he was doing now. Had he told his brothers? Would they help? When would she ever stop worrying? She blew out an exaggerated breath—time to make dinner.

Before long, Mallory had all the burners on the stove working, and the aroma of freshly made tomato sauce filled the room.

"That smells delicious. Tempting enough to make me miss my club meeting," Ellie said from the kitchen doorway. "But then I'd miss out on all the gossip, and it would take weeks to catch up." Ellie laughed. "I wrote my cell phone number on the pad next to the phone if you need me. But you should be fine. And I'm usually home by nine thirty or ten. Do you need anything before I go?" Ellie asked.

Mallory smiled and shook her head. "No, we're good."

"Yup, we're good," Justine echoed.

Ellie chuckled. "Well, all right, see you in a few hours." She headed out the kitchen door toward the garage.

Mallory checked to make sure the door was locked, then she lifted the lace curtain hanging over the door's window and scanned the backyard. Satisfied no one was lurking about, she went back to the stove. She lifted the lid on the pot and took in the rich aroma of tomato and spices. Her shoulders dropped a little. The kitchen was homey, and she was cooking a meal for Justine. She could almost believe her life was normal. She put up the water for the pasta and gave the sauce another stir. She began to hum the tune to one of her favorite songs and danced over to the refrigerator before she mentally slapped herself back to reality. This wasn't the time to feel as if she'd found *Good Housekeeping* nirvana. Blending in was one thing. Being relaxed, losing her edge, was altogether reckless. She had to stay alert. Period. She squared her shoulders and stood a little straighter.

"Punkie, it's almost time for dinner. You'll have to put that coloring book away and help me set the table."

Mallory put out the plates and grabbed some forks, handing them to Justine along with napkins. "Set those next to the plates."

"I remember, Mommy." Justine sounded a little exasperated, and it tugged at Mallory that she'd put her daughter through so much.

The meal was nearly ready when the doorbell rang. *Who could that be?* Mallory's heart went into overdrive.

"I'll get it," Justine said, dropping the forks on the table. She took off toward the front door.

"Don't open it until I see who's there." Mallory was right behind Justine.

"Yeah, I know. Ellie already told me." Justine's voice came in a singsong.

With shaking hands, Mallory parted the living room curtains and saw Rafe standing on the porch with their luggage. She dropped her shoulders. "It's okay. It's Rafe with our stuff."

Mallory opened the door and stepped aside to let him in. "Hi. Thanks for bringing over our bags."

"Mommy, did you remember to pack Teddy?"

"Of course I did, silly." That stuffed animal was more than security to Justine, and Mallory thought she needed it now more than ever.

"Is my aunt here?"

Mallory shook her head.

Rafe snapped his fingers, "That's right, it's Monday. Tonight's *Tía* Ellie's book club."

"She only left a few minutes ago." Mallory couldn't understand why he was being so casual. She knew he'd spoken to his brothers, and she was anxious to find out what they said. But Rafe acted like everything was normal.

"Where would you like these?" Rafe pointed to the luggage. "I can bring them upstairs if you like."

"Please, don't bother. I can do that after dinner."

"I thought I smelled some deliciousness coming from back there," Rafe said, giving a nod toward the kitchen.

"It's sghetti night," Justine said.

"Spa-ghetti," Mallory corrected.

"Well then, I'll take these upstairs. Spaghetti is one of my favorites, and I rarely say no to a favorite. That okay with you?" He gave Mallory a pointed look.

She felt a flow of intensity radiating from Rafe. He wasn't purposefully being casual; he was being guarded to avoid saying anything in front of Justine.

"After dinner, we can discuss the plan." Rafe turned to head up the stairs with the bags.

"After sghetti we get to have cookies. And I helped make them."

"Can't wait," Rafe called over his shoulder.

A plan. It seemed that Rafe and his brothers would be able to help.

"So it's just the three of us. My aunt doesn't know what she's missing," Rafe said as he entered the kitchen. "How can I help?"

"Oh…well, maybe you could pour Justine a glass of milk and then, I guess, have a seat because dinner is about to be served." She placed the bread on the table, followed by a big bowl of pasta and a green leafy salad.

"Is that bottle of wine for the meal?" Rafe's gaze turned toward the counter. "Would you like me to open it? I know where the corkscrew is."

Mallory gave a half nod, uncertain if opening it was a good idea. Being around Rafe made her feel things she'd buried long ago, and she needed to stay sharp. There was no sense in prolonging dinner. She wanted the meal to be over as soon as possible. She'd give Justine a bath and put her to bed. Then she'd be able to find out from Rafe if he and his brothers found a way into Blake's laptop. From there, she'd figure out what to do next.

He moved through the kitchen effortlessly like he belonged there. As if the three of them having dinner was an everyday occurrence, like a normal family. The picture-perfect family scene, false as it was, almost overwhelmed her. She lowered her eyes and felt a physical sensation that could only be described as a deep ache in her soul for something she'd lost a long time ago.

Rafe took two wine glasses from the cupboard, glanced up at her, and smiled as he easily pulled out the cork. His dark brown eyes and barely-there stubble added to his attraction. She noticed the tattoo on his wrist again. Who had she ever known in her life who had a tattoo? Blake would have called it "common."

For that reason alone, she decided she liked it.

At six foot three, Rafe was taller than Blake. His frame was muscular but maintained a sleek athleticism. His dark brown hair was longer than she was used to seeing in a man. Blake had been conservative in his looks, and while his attire screamed money and power, it was all very understated. His appearance belied the maniacal bully underneath the expensive clothes. With Rafe, all you really noticed was his kind face.

"To old friends," he said, giving Mallory a lingering look and then clinking his goblet against Justine's milk glass.

"Okay, let's eat." Mallory placed the paper napkin on her lap.

After the initial spaghetti slurping, Justine looked up. "Delicious."

"Thanks, Punkie. I'm glad you like it." Mallory smiled.

"I second the declaration. Delicious." Rafe broke a piece of bread in half. "I can't remember the last time I had spaghetti."

"Me either," Justine added. "I wish we could have it

every day." Her wide tomato sauce grin nearly covered her entire face.

Mallory relaxed her grip on the fork. She hadn't seen her daughter this carefree in a long time.

Rafe's easy conversation with Justine reminded her of his unending kindness. In high school, his care and compassion drew her in. If she'd stayed in Hollow Lake and married Rafe, her life would have been different. But she wouldn't have Justine. As much as she despised Blake and every single day of their marriage, her precious baby was the only worthwhile thing to come out of that union.

"So, Justine, tell me about Teddy," Rafe asked. "How long have you two known each other?"

Justine giggled. "He's one of my best friends. Do you have a best friend?"

"Yup, I have two."

"Two?" Justine tilted her head. "Can you have two best friends?"

Rafe shrugged. "I don't know that there's any rule that says you can't. Anyway, I have two. My brothers Max and Zack."

"Are they clean?"

"Clean?" Rafe furrowed his brow.

"Mommy says Teddy smells, but I can't give him a bath, or he'll fall apart."

Rafe threw his head back and let out a belly laugh. Justine joined in.

"I'm pretty sure my brothers take a bath every night." He winked.

"I don't have brothers," Justine said. "I'm an only child."

He pointed his fork at Mallory. "Ask your mother. I come from a very, very, very big family. We're all really close.

And most of the time, I love it." He smirked. "Most of the time."

Mallory remembered Rafe's relatives as a tight-knit Puerto Rican clan. At school, no one started trouble with any of the Ramirez brothers or their Chavez cousins. It was unspoken—if you messed with one, you essentially messed with all of them.

And with scores of aunts, uncles, cousins, and grandchildren. The Ramirez family's annual July Fourth BBQ was the talk of Hollow Lake.

Rafe's mother, Maria, had two sisters, Ellie and Claudia. Each one moved to the area from the Bronx and married. When Mallory and Rafe were dating, she met and socialized with at least fifty members of the combined families living in and around the Hudson Valley. Now, fifteen years later, she could only imagine how many were in the family after even more marriages and births.

"Rafe's right, Punkie. He does come from a big family. By the way, how are your parents?"

Rafe looked down at his plate. "Uh, my mother passed." His voice was barely above a whisper.

Mallory leaned forward. "Oh. I'm so sorry."

"Me too," Justine said.

Rafe cleared his throat. "Thanks. As for my father, well, let's just say we're having a rough patch." Rafe straightened. "For now, I'm just enjoying this delicious meal and exceptional company." He smiled at Justine. "You'll have to introduce me to Teddy later."

Justine giggled.

Despite the sad news, sitting here with Rafe and her daughter, having a conversation and a meal, felt more intimate than anything she and Blake had shared outside of giving birth to Justine.

Mallory smiled, the kind of smile that came from within, and her body relaxed. Not for a minute did she believe this was at all normal. But she decided this one moment, this small window of time, she would enjoy.

And then, in an instant, her small bubble of happiness seemed to deflate when Justine reached for a piece of bread and knocked over her milk. Simultaneously, they heard a loud bang outside.

Rafe sprung from his seat and flew out of the kitchen.

"I'm sorry, Mommy. I'm sorry. It was an accident," Justine said, as tears welled in her eyes. Her hand trembled over her mouth, and she began to cry.

Mallory's stomach churned. "Stay right there, Justine."

"Mommy, I'm sorry." Justine continued to cry.

Mallory stood and eased her way to the kitchen window, her pulse racing. "Please, Justine. Stop crying." Standing on the tips of her toes, she peered out the window and into the backyard. There was nothing there. She jumped when a man came around the side of the house.

Rafe looked up and waved.

She gave a weak smile and tried to put her heart back in her chest.

He jogged up the back porch steps. "It's nothing," he said, closing the door.

"Nothing? What in the heck was that loud bang?"

Taking Mallory's hands, he gave a gentle squeeze and looked her in the eyes. "I guess we're all on edge. Must have been a raccoon. The lid of the garbage can fell to the ground. I'm sure it was loose, and raccoons are scavengers. It was probably looking for food. It's fine. I swear." He held up a hand and crossed his chest like a Boy Scout. He turned toward Justine. "Hey now, what are all the tears for?"

Justine sobbed and pointed to the spilled milk on the table. "I'm sorry. I didn't mean it."

"That's nothing. This is an easy fix."

"I won't do it again. I'll be careful," Justine cried.

Rafe grabbed a dish towel from the counter and patted the table dry. "It's fine. Really. I'm going to pour you another glass of milk, and then we'll start all over. No harm done."

Hiccupping between sobs, Justine asked, "Am I in trouble?"

"Trouble? Not in this house. Really, you don't have to worry about it. See—" Rafe poured her a fresh glass of milk "—problem solved."

Grateful for Rafe's ability to diffuse the situation, Mallory breathed again. "Yeah, don't worry, everything is fine, Punkie," she managed to get out, a slight tremble in her voice. She gave Rafe a sideways glance and could clearly see from the expression on his face that he understood what she'd endured in the Stanton household over the last six years. It was obvious this little milk drama spoke volumes.

"Now, where were we?" Rafe said.

While she appreciated Rafe's attempt at keeping the atmosphere light, Mallory put her fork down. She'd lost her appetite. The rest of the meal was fairly silent, and when Rafe finished, she announced bath time for Justine.

"I don't want to go upstairs and take a bath." Justine's pout was so big it practically devoured her face.

"Justine." Mallory gave a raised eyebrow.

"But I don't wanna. I wanna stay here and talk to Rafe."

"Well, it's kinda close to my bedtime, too," Rafe said, giving an exaggerated yawn. "While you're getting ready for bed, I'll clean up down here."

"Oh, please don't do that. I can take care of it later."

"Not gonna happen. In my family, whoever cooks doesn't clean. And really, there isn't much here." Rafe turned to face her, his demeanor suddenly not so carefree, as he gave her a pointed look. "Go. I'll be here waiting. I have news, and we need to talk."

Chapter 9

Twenty minutes later, Rafe put a mug of coffee on the table in front of Mallory. "It's decaf."

"Mmm…smells good."

"I know where Ellie keeps the primo stuff." Rafe smiled and pushed the milk and sugar over to her side of the table. "Take a load off."

"Thanks." Mallory nearly slumped back in her chair. "So you spoke with your brothers. You want to tell me what they said? Were you able to get into the laptop?"

Rafe stared into his cup. "Let's face it. Your ex knew a lot of people in very high places. The kind of people who could make anything or anybody disappear."

"I already know this, and you're stalling."

"Okay. Whatever you have, or whatever it is they think you have, is important enough for them to threaten you. And to me, that means you need the kind of help that doesn't simply begin and end with a hacker. I say that because my brothers worked on getting into the laptop. They're thinking you need the kind of help we can't give."

"You mean like the police?"

Rafe shrugged. "Maybe."

"I'm afraid of taking the wrong step."

Rafe stood "Come here." He came around the table and

pulled Mallory out of her chair and into his arms. The top of her head reached just under his chin, and he caught a whiff of citrus. He closed his eyes and drank her in. Her body felt small and soft, and on instinct, he wanted to protect her.

Mallory relaxed into him. Her arms slowly wrapped around his waist. He held her and knew he was hugging her as much for himself as for her. Moments passed before she lifted her head and looked at him. She was beautiful. He brought his face close to hers, and when she didn't move away, he lowered his lips onto hers and heard her sigh.

The kitchen door burst open. Ellie swept in with Zack and Max trailing behind.

Mallory stepped out of Rafe's embrace. Her eyes were wide.

"Hello, Mallory. Long time," Max said, then looked at Rafe. "Coffee fresh?"

Rafe nodded. He knew why they were here.

"Get me a cup too, bro," Zack said, pulling a chair up to the table. "Hi, Mallory."

"I'll get some pie," Ellie said. "Just made an apple this morning." She got the pie stand from the pantry. "Rafe, please get the plates from the cupboard."

Mallory clutched at her throat, unable to understand what was happening. She tried to remain calm as Rafe's family filled the room but found it increasingly difficult. They were all acting normal, as if they'd been invited for social hour at a neighborhood gathering. But it didn't take a genius to know something was terribly off. Her heart beat like she was on a treadmill with the speed turned up to nine. "Why do I get the sense you're all here because of me?"

Max turned around, coffee mug in hand, and leaned against the counter. "Because we are."

"Let me. Okay?" Rafe tapped Zack on the shoulder. *"Muévelo."*

Zack rolled his eyes and vacated the chair.

Rafe turned the chair to face Mallory and sat. "So, look. Zack picked Ellie up early from her book club and told her everything."

"Everything. But why?" Mallory twisted the heart pendant on its chain.

"Because we don't think it's safe for you and your daughter to stay here," Max said. "And now it's not safe for *Tía* Ellie either."

"Oh, my god. I never meant for this to happen. Ellie, I'm so sorry." Mallory put a hand over her mouth.

"No te preocupes." Ellie put a piece of pie in front of Zack. "Really. Don't worry. I trust my nephews. And you need help. And that means we're going to have to move out of here tonight."

"Tonight." Mallory shook her head. "This is all happening so fast. I don't understand. All I know is that I've caused you all enough trouble." She stood. "I'll get Justine and go."

"No!" came the chorus of voices.

Stunned, she turned to Rafe. He'd known all along and yet behaved like nothing was wrong throughout dinner. "How could you have acted so normal? How could you just…just…just… The entire evening you never let on." Mallory began to shake. Her anger quickly turned to rage, and she pummeled Rafe on his chest. "Why? Why didn't you tell me the minute you walked in the door?" Her hands slapped at his chest for all the times she didn't get to stand up to Blake. For the pain she'd put her daughter through. For the trouble she'd caused this family. She finally collapsed against his chest and sobbed. The warmth of Rafe's arms as they encircled her made her cry harder.

"By the time I left the office, I didn't have all the information. While you were putting Justine to bed, I got a call from Max."

"I...I...put you all in jeopardy. This can't be right." Tears began to stream down her face. Rafe held her tighter, and she buried her face in his chest.

Ellie sat. "Mallory. Mallory. Please sit. Please."

Rafe released her, and Mallory wiped her face with the back of her hand.

"I know this is hard." Ellie pressed her lips into a tight line. "Hell, it's not something I've ever been involved in. But here we are. And there's not a person related to me who would let you go through this alone without giving our best shot at helping you get out of it. So, my nephews have a plan. And I'd like you to listen to it."

After a moment, Mallory sat and nodded.

"Mallory, we pulled out the latest tech we had, and it took some doing, but we finally got into the laptop." Max crossed his arms over his chest.

Mallory almost stopped breathing.

"You never would have gotten into it, even if you'd tried a thousand passwords," Zack said. "It had encryption the likes of which we see being used only by government agencies. So, whatever is on there must be important to the people who are chasing you." He held up a hand. "Before you say anything, no we don't know what's on it."

"But didn't you just say you got into the computer?" Mallory asked.

"Yes. We did," Max said. "We also tripped some sort of signal."

"What?" She couldn't believe what she was hearing.

"Don't panic." Rafe put a hand on her forearm. "They were able to dismantle it within fifteen seconds, so we think we're okay. But no sense in taking chances. That's why we have to get on the move tonight."

"What we did see," Max continued, "were a lot of numbers on a spreadsheet that don't mean anything. At least not on the surface. We think it's a second encryption."

Mallory perched at the edge of her chair. "So, what you're saying is we're back to where we started." She pursed her lips. "I should give them the damn thing and tell them I don't know anything."

Rafe scratched the back of his head. "Well, about that. We think—" he looked at his brothers "—that if you give it to them now with the first encryption breached, they'll think you must know something."

"But I don't." Mallory raised her voice.

"We know that." Rafe squeezed her hand. "But from what we could discover, we think with your training, you can probably decipher those numbers and figure out what's put your life in jeopardy."

"How? I don't know anything."

"Because you were a forensic accountant," Rafe said.

"And how does that help?" Mallory furrowed her brow. She was trying to keep up with what they were saying, but the rising panic was making it difficult to concentrate. She dug her nails into the palms of her hands and forced herself to focus.

"This goes beyond cybersecurity and what we typically deal with. From the information we're able to see, that second encryption is what we would call a trick. You look at it, and you see nothing but a sophisticated general ledger. To the naked eye, it looks like it could be Blake's bank accounts or stock portfolio. But if you put your cursor on the last column, which is blank, it asks for a password. It begs the question, why encrypt it if all the information is already on the spreadsheet?"

"To keep me from getting his money?" Mallory said.

Zack tapped the table with his hand. "No. Because it's not real."

Mallory shook her head several times. "I'm not following."

Rafe let out a breath. "There's something more to it than meets the eye. In cybersecurity terms, it's called steganography."

"Steno—what?" Mallory squinted, trying to understand.

"Steganography. It's when something appears as one thing but is something altogether different. Like, in this case, a seemingly innocuous general ledger, but is actually concealing something else. Something your husband didn't want anyone to find out about. It's like a puzzle, only we don't know how to unlock it."

Mallory raised a hand. "Please, let's not call him my husband or my ex. I have a name for him, but I can't say it in front of Ellie."

"Oh, I've heard worse," Ellie said. "Believe me. And right now, I could probably go one better than what you're thinking,"

"For now, let's refer to him as Blake." Mallory crossed her arms forcefully over her chest. She didn't think she could ever feel this much hate for one person. "So what do we do now?"

"That's where you come in," Max said. "With whatever knowledge you have of Blake, together with your forensic accounting background, you may be able to decipher what the steganography is hiding."

Mallory didn't know what they were talking about, but it appeared they were counting on her for the next move.

This family she'd once been close to was willing to help her, despite the danger. She closed her eyes for a moment and felt a sense of strength she hadn't felt in too long. Maybe it was the Ramirez family in the room, willing to help. Maybe she'd had enough. Running scared wasn't going to save Justine. Right now, her daughter needed her to be strong. She sat up straighter. "I'm ready. What do I need to do?"

"For now, let's get you and Justine packed and out of here," Rafe said.

"Do you think they'll find us?" Mallory looked at the kitchen door.

"We're going to take every precaution so that doesn't happen. But the first encryption was government-grade. For that reason, we don't think getting the authorities involved is safe. So, we need to be super cautious, particularly since we have no idea who's involved. For now, we'll keep it among the family." Rafe nodded toward his aunt.

"My sister Claudia's kids are in law enforcement in Manhattan. We can trust them." Ellie put her hand on Mallory's shoulder.

"We contacted them and had them check the area." Max put his cup down and stepped up to the table. "At this point, there's nothing suspicious or out of the ordinary in Hollow Lake or the surrounding area. But these guys are smart, and it's only a matter of time before they figure out Blake purchased a Tesla, and you drove it off the lot."

"When they do figure it out, we do not want to be in the same town with that vehicle," Rafe said. "And to hedge our bets, Zack contacted Chip, the owner of the garage, and told him if anyone asks, they found the car vacant on the side of the road."

"Where will we go?"

"From what you told Rafe, there are men at your father's office. He moved to Rochester, correct?" Max asked.

Mallory nodded.

Rafe took Mallory's hands in his. "Well that's west of here, so we'll be heading north. First, we'll drop Ellie and Justine at our *Tía* Claudia's house. Then you and I will head farther north to Zack's lake house."

"I'm not dropping Justine off with anyone. Sorry." Mallory pulled her hands away.

Rafe raised his eyebrow. "Let's go into the living room and talk."

"I don't need a conversation. Justine comes with me, or I'm not going anywhere. And that's final."

"Mallory." Rafe's voice was firm. "We know what we're talking about. And if you want to keep your daughter alive, this is how it has to be done." Rafe placed his hands on her shoulders and put his face inches from hers, forcing her to look at him. "Are we good?"

There was a long silence, and Mallory lowered her gaze. "Yeah," she finally said, but down deep, where Justine was concerned, regardless of what Rafe said, she would make the final decision.

Chapter 10

Rafe turned on his blinker and took the Saratoga Springs exit. They were ten minutes out from *Tía* Claudia's house.

"You're sure your aunt is expecting us at this time of night?" Mallory bit her lower lip.

"Yes. Everything's fine." Rafe put his hand over hers to still the nervous tapping. "Really, we got this."

"I'm anxious about leaving Justine."

"Staying with my aunts is the best alternative. *Tía* Claudia's sons, Jack and Andres, were able to get emergency leave from the NYPD. They'll be here in a few hours. Don't worry. They'll make sure Justine is safe."

Mallory pulled her hand away and shifted in her seat.

Sensing she was upset at having involved his relatives, there was no need to stress Mallory any further by telling her there were other family members helping.

Given the time pressure and the way in which Blake encrypted his files, the Ramirez brothers needed reinforcements. Even now, Rafe knew Zack was on his mobile with Ellie's kids, Carlos, Javier, and Marisa, who owned a small software development company and had provided many of the apps RMZ Digital Fortress used. Max decided to ask them to look into the encryption. The more eyes on this, the better.

"It's not that much farther." Rafe kept his focus ahead, following closely behind Max's BMW. With its hairpin turns, the two-lane back road was nearly impossible to navigate at night unless, like the Ramirez brothers, you practically grew up here, driving this road thousands of times. Only long-time residents ventured on this road at night. Everyone else took the highway. By taking the back roads, they hoped to arrive at *Tía* Claudia's house completely undetected.

Twenty minutes later, Rafe pulled into the driveway of his aunt's home. He put the car in Park and turned off the ignition. The living room lights went on, showcasing a sleek structure of wood and glass. The large front door opened, and there stood *Tía* Claudia in her white silk robe. Her long black hair cascaded over her shoulders. The youngest of his mother's sisters, she was in her late fifties, a statuesque figure with carved features and a Roman nose.

"You made it. I was beginning to worry. *Ven aca.*" Claudia held her arms out.

Ellie was the first to climb the four wide steps to the front door, embracing her sister.

"*Ay mija*, you must be exhausted," Claudia said.

Max and Zack followed with hugs for their aunt, while Rafe picked up a sleeping Justine from the back seat. He wrapped her in a blanket, shifted her to his left arm, and put his right arm around Mallory's shoulder. He leaned in and whispered, "It's going to be okay." He pulled her in close.

"*Hola, Tía Claudia.*" Despite their reason for being here, he smiled. As a child, she always made him feel safe and loved.

"*Ay, pobrecita.* The poor little girl. Come, come. Hurry." She planted a kiss on Rafe's cheek. "Put her in the first bedroom, second floor. She and her mother can sleep there."

Claudia embraced Mallory. "Welcome to my home. Please, please come in. I'm so sorry for your troubles."

"Thank you," Mallory said.

Rafe stepped into the large open living room and smiled. Claudia's husband, Gene, an architect, had died suddenly five years ago. He'd been so young. It had shaken the family to its core. He'd built this home for Claudia as a wedding present. It had been an homage to his architectural inspiration, Frank Lloyd Wright. The open plan, low lines, the vast expanse of glass, natural woods, and muted tones gave the home a feeling of being one with the nature surrounding it. It sat ringed by woods, giving the impression it was part of the hillside.

"Okay. It's late," Claudia said in a soft voice. "I'm glad you're all safe. If you're hungry or thirsty, you know where the kitchen is. Help yourself. I'm going to bed, and we'll talk in the morning." Claudia locked arms with her sister. "*Vamos a dormir*, Ellie." And the two women marched through the living room toward the back of the house, where the primary bedroom was located.

Rafe knew no matter how tired his aunts were, they were going to grab a whiskey and talk. And this time, there was a lot to say.

"Okay then. Everyone knows where they're headed?" Max asked.

The cousins had spent many summer vacations and holidays at their *Tía* Claudia's house with its eight bedrooms. Over the years, they'd each unofficially claimed a room. And now as adults, whenever they visited, they stuck to the room they'd chosen when they were kids.

"Come on, Mallory, I'll show you where you're sleeping."

"I'll get the bags," Zack offered.

They climbed the suspended staircase to the second level and headed toward the bedroom on their immediate left. Rafe pressed a button on the wall, and the recessed lights along the perimeter of the room gave a soft glow to the muted tones in the room. With the press of another button, curtain sheers slid across the wall of glass, providing privacy. On the opposite wall, the queen-size bed held several pillows and a matching duvet in various shades of yellow and eggplant.

Mallory pulled the covers back, and Rafe carefully laid Justine in the bed.

"Mommy?"

"Yes, Punkie?"

"Where are we?" Her voice was sleepy.

"We're visiting Rafe's aunt."

Justine rubbed at her eyes. "Ellie?"

Rafe shook his head. In the last seventy-two hours, Mallory and her daughter had slept in three different places. No wonder Justine was confused. She'd gone to bed in Ellie's house, and in the middle of the night, she found herself in a different town, in a different bed.

The soft light reflected Mallory's anguish, and Rafe stared as she nervously played with the pendant around her neck. The only consolation was that they were doing this for Justine's safety.

"Sleep, my little Punkie." Mallory brushed a lock of hair from Justine's forehead, leaned in, and kissed her on the cheek.

Justine yawned and stretched. "Goodnight, Mommy. Goodnight, Rafe."

The corners of his mouth lifted into a smile. In such a short time, this little girl had grown on him, and he would do everything in his power to make sure she stayed safe.

"Come on," Rafe whispered. "She's fine. She's asleep already." He led Mallory out of the room, turning off the lights and silently closing the door.

They headed down the stairs.

Like the rest of the house, the kitchen area was sleek in design. Rafe tapped a button, and again, recessed lighting around the perimeters of the room glowed. "Want something to drink?" Rafe asked.

Mallory sat on a stool at the stone-topped island that separated the kitchen from the dining room. "I need something to calm my nerves. Uh…does your aunt have any herbal tea?"

"Yeah, I'm pretty sure you'll find that in this house." With a gentle push, the pantry door slid open, and Rafe walked into a spacious room with shelving on three walls filled with glass containers holding pasta, oats, rice, and dozens of other nonperishable goods. On the middle shelf to his left, he found the coffees and teas. "What's your pleasure?" he called from inside. "Chamomile, lavender, lemon balm, or passion flower?"

"I'll have the chamomile. Thanks."

He reappeared, putting the small canister of loose tea on the stone countertop. He filled the kettle with water and placed it on one of the burners. "I didn't take you for a tea drinker. I've only ever seen you drink coffee." He opened the cabinet above the stove and pulled out a transparent teapot.

"The last thing I need right now is caffeine. I've enough nervous energy to light up an entire city. I think it's better if I stay alert but calm."

Rafe filled the filter chamber with tea leaves. He turned to find Mallory's eyes wet with tears. He went around to the other side of the kitchen island and gently held her shoulders. "Listen to me, please. You've made it this far. None of us will let anything happen. *I* won't let anything happen." His voice was forceful, but his hands were gentle as he placed them on either side of her face. "Look at me. Mallory. I promise you. Justine will be safe. I'll do whatever it takes to make sure of that." He leaned in, pressed his lips to her forehead, and whispered, "I promise." He breathed her in and kissed her temple, then her cheek, then softly pressed his lips against hers. When she parted her lips slightly, it was all the invitation he needed, and he deepened the kiss. Sliding his arms around her, he lifted her from the stool until they were pressed against each other, and his hands were wrapped around her waist, pulling her in even closer. When Mallory sighed, he was lost to her.

At the unexpected blast of the kettle's whistle, Mallory jumped back.

Rafe rubbed at his jaw. "Sorry," he half muttered to himself. He walked back around the island and yanked the kettle off the stove. After all these years, his desire for her hadn't lessened, but the timing and circumstances were all wrong. Mallory's cheeks were flushed, and he sensed she, too, wished the timing were different. He poured the boiling water into the teapot.

"Are you going to join me?"

Rafe shrugged. "I'm in the mood for something…a little stronger." He went into the pantry, pulled out a bottle of bourbon, and poured himself a thumb full. He silently raised his glass in a mock salute, then drained it. He lifted the bottle to pour himself another shot but thought better of it. After placing the bottle back on the counter, he walked toward the glass wall on the dining room's south side and pushed back the curtain an inch. In the daylight hours, the view was spectacular, looking out over the valley and the lake beyond. Rafe sighed and moved over to the west wall, again parting the curtain ever so slightly. The full moon amplified the eeriness of the surrounding forest.

"Looking for something in particular?"

"Nah, just checking," Rafe said and turned to face her.

"You want to tell me what's going on?" Mallory's voice was low. "You want to tell me why the hell we're acting almost normal? That kiss? Drinking tea and bourbon? And now, you're casually looking out the window as if everything is fine. You and I both know nothing about this situation is normal. When we left Ellie's, you promised to tell me when we got here what happens next. I've been patient, but time's up. Please, Rafe. I can tell there's something you're not saying. Stop trying to protect me."

Rafe put his hands in his pockets and let out a sigh. "My cousins Jack and Andres did some checking and called in some favors with people they know in Rochester. From the intel they got, there are men still hanging around your father's place of business and his home."

Mallory gasped and let out a sob. "My father's home?"

Rafe rushed to her and held her hands. "I'm not finished. My cousins' friends are watching both places. Making sure nothing happens to him." The tears flooding Mallory's eyes tore at him. He had to help her end this nightmare.

"We can't waste any more time. I need to see that laptop." Mallory pushed Rafe away and paced.

"You will."

"No. I mean now." She slapped a hand on the counter.

Rafe shook his head. "It's not possible. At this moment, Max is working with Marisa, Carlos, and Javier, trying to clone the laptop."

"Ellie's kids are involved, too? Why?"

"When Zack told you it was government-grade encryption, he wasn't using the term lightly. It's going to take all of us to try and figure this out. They want to run a couple of newly developed apps that may get us past the fake wall. But they needed to clone it first. We can't take any chances. You were able to try hundreds of password combinations in order to log into the laptop. But now we're at the encryption wall, and there may be a limit to how many times you can put in a wrong password before it either sends out a signal or permanently shuts down."

"You should have told me that in the first place. You've been holding back a lot of information tonight. I don't like it."

"It's complicated." Rafe rubbed the back of his neck. "Can you please stop pacing and sit, and I'll explain?"

Mallory raised an eyebrow. "All right." She sat on the edge of the stool. "Start talking."

Rafe told her about the software company his cousins owned. Over the last two years, they'd helped RMZ develop proprietary apps, keeping them ahead of the competition. Tonight, they were using a new software that would hopefully clone the computer remotely and then try to get past the encryption.

"What happens if it doesn't work?" Mallory asked.

"Well, that was plan B. If it doesn't work, we'll have to go back to the original plan, which is using your forensic expertise. We'll know in the morning."

It was nearly midnight, and Mallory was past exhausted. Her body and mind felt numb. Stealing away from Hollow Lake in the middle of the night, coupled with the flood of information from Rafe and his brothers, seemed to have shut down her ability to feel anything. Even fear.

As exhausted as she was, she knew she wouldn't be able

to sleep until she found a way to contact her father and re-assure herself that he truly was safe. She trusted that Rafe's cousins, Jack and Andres, were looking out for him, but she had to be certain.

A year ago, desperate to see the only family she had, she secretly booked a flight to Rochester during the same week Blake would be away on business. While waiting to board, Blake unexpectedly appeared at the gate, and instead of going into a tirade, he smiled and kissed her on the cheek. He picked up Justine and hugged her, and for one foolish moment, she thought he would board the plane with them. His smile broadened, and in a calm voice, he said, "Listen, Mal, if you need to see your father that badly, go. But you're leaving Justine with me."

His words hit her harder than a smack across the face. There was no mistaking the underlying threat. He had the money and the connections to take Justine away from her. And that's when she created a way to get in touch with her father without Blake knowing.

"Rafe, I need to reach out to my dad."

"How? Is that even wise?"

"I have a special way. All I need is a computer. Surely, your aunt has one." Mallory wasn't about to let anyone stop her. She needed to know her father was okay. "Look, when that bastard of a husband wouldn't let me visit my father or let him come see me, I created a secret email account at the local library."

Rafe scoffed. "Well, that's hardly safe."

"You have another idea?" Her voice was rising.

"Come on, Mallory, keep it down." Rafe shoved his hands in his pockets. "Let me think."

Less than a minute later, Rafe grabbed Mallory's hand,

took her out of the kitchen, and past the floating staircase to the back of the house. A small hallway led to two rooms, one on either side. Rafe put an index finger over his lips in the universal sign for quiet. Then he mouthed the word *aunts* and pointed to the closed door.

Across the hall from where his aunts slept, he opened the door to a home office with built-in bookcases and another wall of glass looking out toward the front walkway of the house. The left side of the room held a built-in desk with an open laptop.

Rafe pulled out the chair and sat at the desk. Mallory watched as his fingers flew across the keyboard. Several screens popped up and then disappeared. The screen went black, and green fluorescent numbers and letters wrote themselves onto the screen.

Screen after screen popped up and then disappeared. It was taking too long, and she was about to say something when he stood and, with a wave of his hand, indicated she should sit.

She gave him a questioning look, wondering what he'd done.

He whispered, "I created a VPN."

"A what?"

Rafe put his hand up. "Shhh. A virtual private network. It encrypts your internet connection and hides your IP address. Makes it so you can't be traced. I'll give you some privacy. I'll be back in a few."

Mallory sat, heard the door close, and stared at the screen. What would she say? She bit the inside of her cheek, thinking of what to write. "Don't think. Just do it." She had to know if he was okay. With her knee bouncing under the table, she logged on to her account and thought of how to word the message. Not knowing whether the people look-

ing for her had the capabilities to break through the encryption Rafe set up, she purposefully kept the message
almost indecipherable.

Dear All Care Printing—
Punkie and I we are needing invitations of five.
Boxes of blue if you think that will work. Please use box
letters, okay? Nothing flashy, cause we love plain. If there's
a problem, you can provide a different option.
Thanks, M. Kane.

The note would appear strange to anyone but her father, who excelled at puzzles. The fifth word in each sen-
tence, when put together, would reveal the message-*Are you
okay? Love you.* The answer would tell her if anyone was
still watching him and waiting for her. Using her maiden
name would get him to read the message and know it was
from her.

Mallory re-read the email one more time and then hit
Send. She cleared the cache and was closing the browser
when she felt a hand on her shoulder. Her heart sped, and
she stiffened.

"Sorry. Did I scare you?" Rafe whispered, his breath
sweet and warm.

Mallory turned and looked up at him. "If near heart
failure counts, then yes, you scared me. I didn't even hear
you come in," she said in a whisper. The constant fear of
being found by the men who were after the hard drive was
taking its toll.

"You should go to bed. If my cousins can't break
through, then we'll have a long drive tomorrow," Rafe said.

Mallory rose and reached for his hand. A tingling sensation shot through her, and even though she knew it would be reckless, she wanted to be with him tonight.

"You go ahead. I want to double-check that the cache is fully cleared." He gently squeezed her hand before sitting at the computer.

"Rafe?"

"Yeah?"

"How much time do you think we have before they find us?"

He turned, and their gazes locked. "Let's not think about that now."

Mallory had no doubt Rafe would do whatever it took to protect them all. But she sensed there was something he wasn't saying, and that scared her more than anything.

Chapter 11

"Good morning, everyone." Rafe kissed both his aunts as he entered the kitchen.

"What about me?" Justine said, dropping a chocolate chip onto a half-cooked pancake in the pan.

Rafe patted her on the head and kissed her forehead.

"We're making pancakes. And they're going to be delicious," Justine said.

Rafe wiped some batter from Justine's cheeks. "I have no doubt. And I want to be the first customer."

"Okay." Justine tugged on Claudia's sleeve. "Rafe wants to eat first."

"I bet he does," Claudia smirked. *"Vaya, él es mandón."*

"I am not being bossy. I thought I'd be a test case." Rafe slid into the chair beside Mallory at the dining table and whispered, "We'll leave after we eat." His hand caressed her cheek. "We want to make sure Justine feels at home so she'll be okay when we go."

Mallory nodded her understanding. "Where's Max and Zack?" She poured herself a coffee from the thermal carafe on the table. "Want?"

"Yeah. Thanks." His gaze went to the ceiling. "They're upstairs on the phone with Marisa. Their app didn't work. She and Max are talking through what we'll need to take with us so you can work on getting past the steganographic wall."

"Hey, Mommy, look. I made a cow." Justine giggled. "This one can be for you."

"Ay, que bonita," Claudia said. "You make a fine sous chef." She gave Justine's shoulders a squeeze. "Ellie, *mira*. Look what our little *chiquita* made."

"Excellent. A culinary artist in the making," Ellie exclaimed.

The attention her daughter was receiving from these two women warmed Mallory's heart. This is what she'd hoped for when her daughter was born. A large extended family who would love and care for her. She could only hope that this was what Justine's future would be like. Mallory remembered how confident and content the Ramirez brothers seemed in school. Their many family members filled the bleachers, cheering them on for the school basketball and baseball games. Her own family had always been small. And now it was just her dad and Justine. She had to keep them both safe. They were all she had.

"Mommy, look at my cow."

"That's great, Punkie." But Mallory didn't get up to look. Her mind was on her father. With Rafe's help, she'd checked Claudia's laptop first thing, but still no answer from her dad.

"Mommy, look."

"That's nice, Punkie." Mallory chewed on her bottom lip. What could be keeping her father? He checked his emails as often as most people checked their social media. It didn't matter what time of day. She was certain she would have heard from him by now. His lack of response only managed to allow her mind to paint horrific images that something bad had happened.

"No. Come here and look," Justine urged.

"Okay." Mallory forced a smile and stood, coming

around the breakfast bar. She peeked over Justine's shoulder and immediately saw why Justine had been excited. "Wow. That really is a cow. You're an artist, Punkie."

"That she is indeed," Ellie said, mixing more batter in a white bowl.

"Thanks," Justine said, grinning from ear to ear.

Mallory heard the pride in her daughter's voice and couldn't help but note—despite their being on the run—her daughter, surrounded by encouraging people and not the suppressive traits of a maniacal bully, had become noticeably confident.

The sudden chiming sound had Mallory looking for her phone before remembering she'd sent it out west. She looked up to find Rafe fishing his phone from his back pocket.

"I think you got a message." His voice was soft.

"How do you know?" Mallory tilted her head, straining to hear his words over the constant chatter of Justine, Ellie, and Claudia.

"I set my phone up to alert me if an email came in."

Mallory nodded. "Punkie, I have to go check on something. I'll be back soon, and we'll eat all your pancake cows."

"Okay, Mom. This one right here—" she pointed to the one in the pan "—I'm making it special for you."

Mallory couldn't help but genuinely smile. In the middle of all this madness, her five-year-old, who'd been dragged through it all, was still a ball of sunshine—standing on a step stool in a too-big apron, enjoying herself. It was another reminder of why she needed to get into that computer and find out what Blake had hidden.

The home office looked different in daylight. The room featured light gray and soft cream colors against blonde wood. The wall of glass looking out on the walkway was alive now, with the sound of birds flitting between the bushes and trees that lined the intersecting stone paths. The architecture was extraordinary, and she imagined the three families spent many a wonderful holiday here. She yearned for a life like that. If only she could go back and do things differently. She'd missed out on so much. Mallory released a heavy sigh. This was no time to dwell on what wasn't. What couldn't be. She had to focus on getting out of the situation she was in.

Rafe stood at the desk, opened the laptop, and typed a series of keystrokes, and her email popped up. "Have a seat." He pulled out the chair.

Mallory sat and positioned the laptop's cursor over the email from All Care Printing and double-clicked. She leaned forward. She felt the blood drain from her face as she read her father's response.

Hello, Ms. Kane-The item you requested is still out of stock. It's a popular item and people are here waiting for it. They inquire daily.

There's no need to follow up. I'll contact you directly when we have it.

"Look at this." Mallory turned the screen to face Rafe. He rested his hands on the desk and leaned in.

"What does it mean?" Rafe asked.

"It means you were right. No one has found me because they're camped out at my dad's place, waiting for me to come there. Shit. My poor father."

"Mommy, you said a bad word."

Mallory turned to find Justine in the doorway.

"Why'd you say a bad word? What's wrong with Grandpa?" Justine fiddled with the strings on her apron.

"What are you doing here? I thought you were making pancakes." Mallory deflected with a weak smile.

"They're ready. The aunts told me to come and get you. But what's wrong with Grandpa?"

She didn't want Justine worried. "Nothing's wrong with Grandpa. Remember I told you we couldn't move there yet because of the asbestos?"

"I think so."

"Well, the people who were supposed to help him aren't there yet. So, he's been doing a lot of the work himself. That's all. He's fine, though. Don't worry."

"Can we make him a card?" Justine asked.

"A card?"

"You know, like a get-well card, so he feels better about having to do all that work."

Mallory smiled at Justine's genuine kindness. "That's a great idea," she said, feeling terrible about lying to her daughter.

"Come on, Mommy." Justine rocked against the door jamb. "Let's eat before the cows get cold."

Mallory closed her eyes and tried not to scream because that was the only release that would give her a modicum of satisfaction. "I'll be right there." Her father's email made it crystal clear that he was still being watched, and time was running out.

From Claudia's back deck, Mallory watched Justine and Zack. They were fishing in the lake at the bottom of the hill. Justine seemed so happy, and it was nearly crushing Mallory to leave her, but she had no choice. Rafe's cousin Marisa hadn't been able to break the second encryption.

It was now up to Mallory to try and decipher the puzzle. She could almost bear leaving her baby, knowing she was being looked after by Rafe's family.

She pushed the heart pendant up and down her chain, willing herself to stay strong.

"I know it's hard not to worry, but she's in good hands." Rafe handed Mallory her large travel tote, along with a shopping bag. "I packed your things."

Her eyebrow raised. "You didn't have to do that."

Rafe took a step back. "I see that look in your eyes. I'm not him, and I wasn't trying to control you. I wanted to give you extra time with Justine before we left."

Mallory relaxed her face. "Thanks. What's this for?" She held up the shopping bag.

Holding an identical shopping bag, Rafe pulled out a fake beard.

She furrowed her brow.

"Check out yours."

Shrugging the straps of her tote onto her shoulder, she opened the shopping bag to find a blond wig and sunglasses. "Are you serious with this?"

"As serious as a heart attack." Rafe began putting the fake beard on his face.

For a moment, she couldn't find the words. This wasn't a joke, and that scared her more than anything. "I thought you said no one followed us."

"I did say that."

"So...so..." Mallory scoffed, "What's this all about?"

"It's called being safe. We're driving a long distance, and we don't need anyone on our tail." Rafe pointed to the trees on the west side of the house. "You see that mini forest over there?"

Mallory nodded.

"About a mile from here, Jack and Andres left us a car. We can walk through the woods to where it's parked."

"Why didn't they come to the house?" Mallory asked.

"They're doing their surveillance thing at the moment."

Mallory nodded that she understood, but she didn't.

She leaned against the deck railing and turned her head to gaze at her daughter. Her heartbeat ticked up a notch. If she were being honest and took a step back from her life, she would have to admit that the last few days resembled a bad TV movie. Was she doing the right thing?

Blowing out a breath, she rubbed the side of her face, still trying to make sense of it all. "I'm not trying to be difficult. I know how much you and your family are working to protect us. But I don't understand the need for the disguise. I thought your cousin Marisa said we weren't being tracked. And how does she even know that?"

"Marisa's ex-military. She knows a thing or two about trackers and tracing people. So far, she says we're in the clear. But she's as cautious as the rest of us because it involves Blake Stanton."

Mallory's eyes widened.

"Come on. Can you blame her? Or any of us? The family is out in full force on this, and we're not taking any chances. Especially if this goes as high up as we think it does."

It took a moment, but it finally dawned on Mallory why they all insisted she go farther north. How could she have been so dense? It wasn't only about having the quiet time to decipher the code. They wanted her away from the aunts. Sure, the brothers and cousins would look after Justine. But they were also here to make sure nothing happened to Ellie and Claudia. She'd put their lives in danger just as much as her daughter's. The realization hit her in the face like a bucket of ice water. This wasn't a choice. She had to leave. To protect these people. She closed her eyes to keep the tears from spilling.

Rafe's arms were around her before she could pull away, and she didn't want to resist. With his musky scent and his strong arms wrapped around her, it was like coming home. It felt safe.

She allowed herself a moment in his arms before she pushed back and wiped her face with her hands. "I'll go put this on, and then we're out of here." Her steely determination came from the hatred she felt for Blake Stanton, and she would focus on holding onto that feeling until this bad dream of a life was over.

Chapter 12

With their new looks firmly in place, they began walking. Claudia's house was fairly secluded, surrounded by two acres of woods. With a compass in hand, Rafe led them for a little over a mile until they came to a nondescript dark gray SUV parked in a small clearing at the side of a dirt road. "Here's our ride. The fact that they think you might be headed west to Rochester to see your dad and we're going north gives us a little time to figure out what we've got." Rafe hoisted the backpacks with the laptops, his software case, and Mallory's travel bag into the back seat.

"Let's hope," Mallory said, climbing in on the passenger side.

Rafe reached under the driver's seat and pulled out a soft-sided case. Placing it on his lap, he unzipped the case to reveal two burner phones and a set of walkie-talkies. "Take these." He handed Mallory a phone and a battery. "Don't attach the battery unless you have to make a call. And then be quick." He unstrapped the walkie from the case and handed it to her. "Don't turn it on for any reason unless we're separated."

"Rafe, you're scaring me. Do we really need all this? The wigs, a different car, burner phones?"

He noticed the tremble in her hand as she held the

walkie. "In a word, yes. We don't take any chances, and we stay safe." Rafe pressed the ignition button. "You ready?"

She chewed on her inner cheek and nodded.

He wanted to tell her it would be all right, to stop worrying. If only he could. In truth, he wasn't exactly confident everything would work out. Not since Zack and Marisa called at seven in the morning with their data mining search results on Blake Stanton's missing plane.

"Okay. We're off." Rafe put the car in gear and pulled out onto the dirt road. His mind stuck on the conversation with his brother and cousin.

It gnawed at Rafe that Zack and Marisa had a more difficult time than usual getting any information on the last flight Blake Stanton had taken. The man seemed to have covered his tracks well, which was in and of itself suspicious. Due to Marisa's unrelenting tenacity, they'd finally managed to get a hit through a backdoor channel and into the private airport's manifest. The document revealed the first names of the other passengers on board. With a little more data mining, they were able to come up with the surnames of the other three passengers on the doomed flight. The information, while startling, didn't come as a big surprise, knowing the circles Blake traveled.

On board was a prominent aide to the head of national security. Oddly, there had been no mention of his name in the news or online as being on the same ill-fated aircraft as Blake Stanton. The aide seemed to have mysteriously disappeared, just like the black box. The other two were executives from the Mason Corporation. The Ramirez brothers were very familiar with the company that had government contracts to manufacture long-range missiles. It was a passenger manifest that reeked of possible unsavory dealings. This new revelation put the family on high alert.

The idea of keeping all this information from Mallory seemed wrong. She had a right to know. But Max and Zack thought she had enough to worry about. They needed her to focus on getting the information from the laptop.

"You've been awfully quiet for the last half hour. What are you thinking?" Rafe asked.

Mallory sighed. "I miss my daughter. And I'm worried about her." She faced him. "I know she's in good hands, but I still miss her. I can't help it. I'm a mother."

The fake beard was itchy, and he scratched the side of his face. "Look, I've never been a parent, but I know how worried my mother was when they sent me to prison. It almost broke her. The only consolation was that she lived long enough to see me released." The words had simply tumbled out. That part of his life he didn't share with anyone but his family. What possessed him to tell her now? To make her feel better? It no longer mattered. The words couldn't be taken back. The only sound was the tires slapping against the road. Keeping his gaze straight ahead, he waited for her response.

"Are you joking?"

The tone of her voice cut him. Instead of being offended, he let out a wry, single syllable laugh. "I wish I were. But I'm as serious as a judge's gavel."

"What did you do?"

Now her tone infuriated him. The question hit him square in the chest. It told him that she didn't really know him if she could believe he'd done something to deserve prison time. It felt like all the air in the car was sucked right out. "Mallory, I know it's been years since we've seen each other. But do you honestly believe that I could commit a crime for which I would have to go to prison?"

"I don't know what to think." She threw up her hands.

"I only know what you tell me, and this is the first I'm hearing of it."

"Well," Rafe scoffed, "I thought you should know. I mean, we are spending all this time together. Until now, it's not like we've had much time to get reacquainted. We've been dealing with your issues."

"Exactly. My issues. And my issues are because I was married to an awful human being, who I'm sure committed enough crimes to put *him* away for years. I'm sure that's what's in that laptop. His crimes and anyone who colluded with him. And that's who's after me." Mallory hit the passenger window with the side of her hand. "So, forgive me if I'm a little curious. If I'm asking what in the world they put *you* away for. Being involved with one criminal this lifetime is quite enough. Thank you very much." She let out a huff.

"I was framed." Rafe delivered the words in a matter-of-fact way. There wasn't a hint of defensiveness in his voice. He was done defending himself.

"You going to tell me what happened?"

He heard the tremble in her voice and hated that he scared her.

"It's complicated."

"So, *un*-complicate it."

What the hell? He drew in a sharp breath. He didn't expect to be on trial. Not again. He shifted in the driver's seat, working to tamp down a sense of rage coupled with injustice. He'd volunteered the information, and now she was grilling him. He hadn't expected that from Mallory. He understood how wounded she was by her marriage, but he was the wrong target. She shouldn't be on the attack with him. "You wouldn't understand."

"Rafe—"

Silence followed. He waited for her to say something

more, but nothing came. The unspoken questions hung in the air. What happened? Who did it, if you didn't? Why were you the target? The same questions he and his brothers had asked dozens and dozens of times. Each time, coming up empty. No matter how many leads they chased. The fact that he'd been cleared wasn't a true vindication, not without finding the person or people who framed him. Without that, he didn't think he could ever be free. Without that, living a normal life was out of the question. He would forever be looking over his shoulder. So he knew exactly how Mallory felt. He also knew regardless of his feelings for her, he couldn't act on them. There was no future for them. Once this was behind them, she'd move on. And rightly so. In his current situation, he could offer her nothing but more looking over her shoulder.

Gripping the steering wheel, he quickly glanced in Mallory's direction. Her eyes seemed to bore into him.

"Rafe. I don't want to play games. I don't want to be afraid. And I don't want to pull out of you what you should have already told me. I just want you to tell me what happened."

Rafe let out a slow breath. "It's a long story."

Mallory scoffed. "Start at the beginning. We have a long drive. I'm a captive audience and all ears."

Her sarcasm cut, and Rafe could have done with a bit more empathy. Whatever he felt, he knew she was hurting, and her life was upside down. This was another hit she clearly wasn't expecting. He let out a long breath. "About twelve years ago, I worked as an IT analyst at a state agency in Albany. You know. All the perks, short working hours, good vacation time, health benefits, and pension. My parents were happy I finally settled down."

Mallory frowned. "What do you mean finally settled down?"

"Oh, man. We've got a lot of catching up to do." Fifteen years was a long time to be out of touch. So much had happened it would be difficult to fill in all the gaps. It almost seemed ludicrous being on the run and telling her his life story after she left Hollow Lake. Well, they did have a long drive, and part of him wanted her to know if only to cement the fact that they had no future.

"I finally stopped messing around and went back to college. I spent my senior year as an exchange student in Prague. I got mixed up with a group of people I should have stayed away from. They were...well...let's just say they didn't like playing by the rules and operated on the outskirts."

"Outskirts of what?" Frustration rang through in her question.

"We skirted around what was legal, what wasn't. Fooled around in the dark web."

"You?" Mallory's voice held astonishment. "You were senior class president. You were the guy who went to the library and the nursing home to help with their computers for free. I mean, you were like a model high schooler."

"Things changed." Rafe gave a one-shoulder shrug. "My dad, you remember him. When you knew him, he was a lawyer."

"Yeah."

"Well, he got bumped up to county judge. And the higher up the judicial system he went, the more play-it-by-the-book he got. I guess I rebelled."

"You got involved in the dark web?" She sucked in a breath. "I'd say that was a bit dissident."

Rafe gave her a sideways glance. He didn't blame Mallory for her flippancy. She'd been lied to by her dead husband, and now he was confessing things he'd never intended for her to hear. "I never thought we'd get caught. But we did and I was sent home."

The memory of what he'd done brought back old feelings of shame. He could feel his cheeks flush. "We pirated movies and games and sold them." The words rushed out. "It was wrong. I knew it was wrong. My father wanted to kill me. I never finished my last year of school. He kicked me out of his house and refused to pay for the education of a criminal. He unceremoniously handed me all my student loans and told me I was on my own."

While neither spoke for several minutes, he could almost sense Mallory's mind whirring with a hundred questions. He checked the highway mile marker. They were another seventy-five miles from Lake Placid, and dark clouds hung low ahead. They seemed to match his mood.

"That can't be the end of the story. What does Prague have to do with being framed and going to prison?"

"I was sent to prison for cyber theft. But that was years later. And I was innocent. But the fact that I had a prior record didn't make my case an easy one." He paused. "I don't like reliving the past, so I'm going to say this fast." He held up a hand while keeping his eyes on the road. "Don't say anything or ask any questions until I'm done."

"Okay."

Rafe glanced at Mallory, who was staring straight at him. He would tell her his story, and either she would believe him or not. His hope was that she still had faith in him. "My first offense, which was really my only offense, was hard on my father. My mother tried talking to him. Tried convincing him I could make amends. That one bad thing shouldn't affect my entire life. But Judge Ramirez is a proud Puerto Rican. Came from nothing, worked his way up, and he expected his sons to do better. So, he wasn't exactly in a forgiving mood."

Rafe shifted uncomfortably in his seat.

"At my father's insistence, I did community service. Became a part of the Big Brothers program. And I got a job in Albany working for an IT company developing software. I was good. It's the one area in life where I've always excelled. You know, all those zeros and ones, the programming, the software. Without an actual degree, I started at the bottom, but it wasn't long before I was promoted. I would come in early and stay late to help fix bugs and develop new software, and before long, I started climbing the ladder."

Rafe stopped talking and put on his blinker, pulling into the exit lane.

"Why'd you stop talking? Are we here already?" Mallory looked around.

"Not yet. Soon. This is the last exit with any food. We can go to a drive-through. Grab a coffee and a sandwich. Then we're about an hour away."

"But why stop at all?" Mallory rubbed at her eyes. "You're confusing the heck out of me. I thought we were in a hurry to get to the lake house. Not to mention we're in the middle of a very heavy conversation. What is going on?"

Rafe pulled off the exit and checked the rearview mirror. "I spotted a dark blue pickup that I think may be following us. If it follows us off the exit, then we may have a problem."

Mallory turned in her seat.

"Please don't do that. Just keep your eyes ahead and act normal."

When they were through the toll, Rafe turned left. He rechecked his mirrors but saw nothing. "We're in the clear."

Mallory sat back. "I don't know how much more of this my heart can take."

"Since we're off the Thruway, let's grab something quick, then be on our way." He looked over at Mallory. Squeezed her thigh. "You going to be okay?"

"I'm not going to lie. I'm feeling uncomfortable on a number of levels."

Her words weren't a surprise, but he'd handle her feelings later. Right now, his gut told him to be on the lookout for a blue pickup.

As they pulled away from the drive-through, Mallory placed both coffees in the center console cup holders. Then reached into the paper bag and retrieved an aluminum-wrapped egg sandwich, pulled back the corners, and handed one to Rafe. "Here."

"Hold on to it for a sec."

Mallory furrowed her brows but didn't comment.

Rafe made a U-turn and drove in the opposite direction from the Thruway. By the looks of it, they were headed into town. "Where are we going?"

"I know a place where we can stop and eat," Rafe said.

"But I thought this was going to be a quick pit stop?"

"It still may be. I'm being cautious. I want to make sure we're in the clear."

Mallory turned and looked out the rear window.

"I wish you'd stay seated and not look back." They drove a few more miles into the center of town. "We'll park for a few minutes." Rafe pulled the SUV into an open-air municipal parking lot containing about a dozen available spaces.

"Why here? And why are we stopping?"

With the SUV now parked, they faced Main Street. "See across the street, over there?"

Mallory turned and looked at the one-story brick structure. "Why in heaven's name are we parked across from a police station?"

He took the sandwich from Mallory and bit into it. "Seems like this is the perfect place to park in case anyone's following us. Let's sit and eat for ten minutes." He chewed and then swallowed. "Looks like rain anyway."

"Are we seriously going to talk about the weather now?" Mallory stared at him. The energy running through her nearly made her body vibrate. She was like a coiled spring about to pop. She needed answers, and Rafe was being way too nonchalant. She wanted—no, she needed to know two things: Why was he sent to prison? And were they really being followed? In no particular order because both unanswered questions were freaking her out.

"I'm not going to discuss the weather with you. I'm going to tell you what happened and why I served time," Rafe said.

When he turned to face her, she saw the fatigue in his eyes and dark shadows under them that weren't there two days ago. With the realization that she was responsible for his exhaustion, and that her situation put his family in peril, the pent-up anger and frustration she'd been feeling dissipated. "I'm listening. No judgment." She held up her hand. "Promise."

"All right. Then I'm going to give it to you straight up, no chaser."

About time, she thought. She had to know what kind of man Rafe had become. But once she knew, would it matter? She was miles away from her daughter. She was carrying a laptop with what she imagined held highly incriminating information. Damaging enough that her life was in danger. All things considered, she was well and truly at his mercy.

Besides, once this ordeal was over, and she hoped like hell that would be soon, she'd be on her way to live with her father and probably never see Rafe again. To her surprise, the thought produced a pang of sadness. It had to be the lack of sleep and too little to eat in the last forty-eight hours. She took a healthy gulp of the coffee, nearly burning her tongue. But she said nothing. She needed to hear what he had to say.

"Where was I?"

"You were moving up in the company," Mallory said.

Rafe nodded. "Yeah. So, as I moved up, I started working on bigger projects. Without getting too technical, I helped create personalized antivirus programs for our clients. I got really good at it until one day, one of my programs was compromised, and I had to figure out why, which led me to find out about cybersecurity. It was way more interesting than developing antivirus software. Anyway, as technology got more sophisticated and more companies began using cloud-based systems, there was a need for my services." Rafe took one last bite of his sandwich and wiped his mouth with the paper napkin. "One thing led to the next, and I thought, why should I make money for someone else? Why not start my own business? So I did."

She smiled to herself. Her mother had been wrong about him. He had been ambitious. "So, what happened?"

"I quickly became in demand, and in a few months, there was more business than I could handle. I hired a couple of technicians, some analysts, and a receptionist. It was proving to be a real business." Rafe turned toward her. The glint in his eye was unmistakable.

"I was on top of the world. My father actually invited me to Sunday dinner. My future was bright, and the past was behind me."

She could hear the *but* coming before it was out of his mouth.

"I got too big, too fast. There were too many balls in the air. It was hard to keep track of every project. Next thing I know, the FBI marches into our offices, and I'm arrested for crypto-jacking."

"Crypto-what?" Mallory's brow raised.

Rafe scoffed. "The short answer is stealing someone's cryptocurrency by hijacking their computer."

"And did you?"

Rafe hit the steering wheel with the palm of his hand. "Oh, man! Mallory. Not you, of all people." He clenched his jaw. "Of course I didn't do it. I was set up." He paused and pressed his lips together. "Look, me and my brothers tried to find out for the better part of a year who was behind it and why they would want to frame me."

Mallory didn't understand what he was trying to say. How could he know he was framed when they couldn't find out who framed him? She didn't want to doubt him. But she also didn't want to be with yet another man who was a liar.

Crack!

She jumped at the sound of the unexpected thunder. People on the street began scurrying into the various shops to get out of the sudden driving rain. Across the street, a woman with a purse over her head rushed into the bakery that butted up against the police station. Mallory wondered if the woman led a normal life. Or was she, too, carrying the weight of the world? She sank back into the leather seat, concentrating on the downpour. Within seconds, the rain on the windshield was like an open fire hose on full blast, obliterating any view.

"What are you thinking?" Rafe's voice was hoarse.

She fixed her gaze on his face. She'd ask him the question, and his eyes would tell her everything she needed to know. "How'd you know you were framed if you can't find out who framed you?"

Rafe nodded. "Logical question. And an easy one to answer. I wasn't the only person accused of the theft. In fact, several other companies around the country, like mine— small, individually owned cybersecurity firms—were in a similar situation."

He didn't look away. His eyes were clear, the kind, honest eyes she remembered.

"The FBI thought we were a ring of hijackers. But we weren't. I mean, for the most part, we'd known of each other's existence. But that was it."

Mallory couldn't believe it. "Were you all arrested?"

Rafe nodded. "Eight of us."

"Oh, my god." Mallory put a hand to her chest. "How did you prove you were innocent?"

"We hired good lawyers. But mostly, it was Max and Zack. They believed in me, and they were unrelenting. They coordinated the investigation. They didn't work for me at the time. But they are my brothers. They wanted to help. And with Zack's legal background and Max's knowledge of securities trading, they were able to poke enough holes in the government's theory so that the case could be reopened on appeal."

The Ramirez brothers always seemed to be there for each other—a quality she admired. Even in high school, they stuck together. As an only child, she didn't have that luxury. She looked at him with a mix of regret and envy. Regret over what they once had and envy of the life he had with his family. "So, what did they find out?"

"There was no physical or cyber evidence that the eight of us collaborated. But they did find a virus in each of our systems. A company in Chicago sent all of us a request for a proposal. It was for a two-million-dollar contract. The information needed to create the proposal was sent on a link. We all downloaded it within days of each other."

"Why would you download a link? Don't they tell you never to do that?" Mallory thought there was a flaw in his thinking.

"This was a reputable company." Rafe made air quotes and took a swallow of his coffee. "The fact is, that link put a worm in our system, and that was it. It siphoned off money from people's accounts. People we didn't even know."

Even though she knew Rafe would never commit a crime, try as she might, it was difficult to wrap her mind around what he was saying.

"The FBI had no case against us. But it took a year to prove it, and I spent that year in prison. The currency was never found. Poof. Into the ether."

Another crack of thunder, and the rain came down harder.

"Looks like we'll sit a bit longer. I don't want to drive in this."

Mallory agreed.

"All this time, my brothers and I have been working to find out who framed me."

"Why, when the charges were dismissed?" Mallory turned her whole body to face him.

"Because I can't rest until my name is cleared. I don't feel I can fully be free if I'm not one hundred percent exonerated." Rafe looked away. "It kills me because breast cancer took my mother before I could prove it. My dad went back to forbidding me in his house. It stings because I lost both of them." Rafe sucked on his teeth. "But my brothers are by my side and committed to helping me find the truth. They're also committed to helping me repair the relationship with my father. But that's for another time." He let out a long, exaggerated exhale. "So. Now you know."

The sadness in his voice pierced her. She remembered his parents well. And if she were being honest, his family was another reason she'd fallen for him—his big, boisterous, loving family. Sunday dinners at his house were a big affair, and she cherished her invitations to join the aunts, uncles, and cousins at a table filled with plates and plates of food. His parents' home was bursting with life, music, and oftentimes spontaneous dancing. But it was that desire never to be far from his family, to never leave Hollow Lake, that eventually split them up. Now, she ached for him, knowing the many hits his life had taken over the last fifteen years. His business troubles, his mother's death, and his father disowning him.

"Looks like the rain's letting up. Maybe we should head out."

Mallory repositioned her seat belt and stared out the passenger window but wasn't really looking. Her mind was otherwise occupied by thoughts of Rafe and her feelings for him. The truth suddenly overwhelmed her. They could never go back to what they had. Her life was nothing but uncontrolled chaos. And when this was over, she'd leave and give him a chance to find someone with a clean slate and no baggage.

Rafe started the car and turned on the wipers. It bothered him that Mallory hadn't said anything after he'd filled in the missing pieces of his life. He wished he knew what she was thinking. But right now, he'd have to put his feelings for her on the back burner. His attention was focused on making sure no one was following them.

The SUV eased out of the parking spot, and Rafe didn't turn on his blinker. He didn't want to signal which way he would turn. He rechecked his rearview mirror. All clear. He headed straight for the Thruway.

Twenty miles from Zack's lake house, they stopped at a local grocery store for provisions. Only three days ago, he'd been at this very store for a coffee on his way back from his fishing vacation. So much had happened since then that it seemed like another lifetime.

Rafe exited the car, pulled a cap from the back seat, and pushed it down over his forehead. "Be sure to keep your sunglasses on. And never look up. There are probably CCTV cameras in the store. Keep your head down and be as quick as you can."

He held the door open for Mallory and pulled the bill of his cap lower. The market was small, with only four aisles and two registers. Rafe pulled a cart from the stack while sizing up the few customers milling about in the aisles. "Honey, I'll get us some steaks for dinner. Why don't you pick up some potatoes and salad stuff." His voice was loud enough to be heard. If anyone were listening, they'd have to assume they were a married couple shopping for dinner.

Rafe's attention was pulled toward a man a bit taller than six feet, with a couple of days' worth of stubble, dark sunglasses, and an expensive Barbour jacket. The loafers on his sockless feet screamed money. Immediately, his antennae went up, and his gaze frantically searched for Mallory. He bit his tongue, trying not to call her name.

The man headed over to the register with a loaf of bread. "Hey, Maureen. How's it going?"

"It'll be better once my shift ends," the thin redhead said.

"I hear that." And they both chuckled.

Rafe took in a deep breath and tried to slow his heart

rate. It appeared the guy was a regular. But the incident had him looking over his shoulder for the duration of the time spent in the store. He'd feel safer once they were inside Zack's lake house.

By the time they arrived at the house, Rafe was stiff from the long drive. They climbed the slate path, and under the mat by the large mahogany door was the spare key. It took three trips to get everything into the house, and when Rafe locked the door behind him, he let out a breath. "Well, we made it."

Zack's house was the perfect retreat; over the years, Rafe had come here for long weekends to forget his troubles. He never dreamed he'd be here with Mallory. The large open floor plan seamlessly connected the living, dining, and kitchen areas. The one bedroom was off to the right of the living area. He felt his face sag when he remembered there was only one bedroom.

"What's the matter? Is someone out there?"

Rafe pulled off the fake beard and, took a step down into the living room and stood inches away from her. "No. Sorry, didn't mean to scare you. It's...well, I was so busy trying to get us up here and away from Hollow Lake, I forgot there's only one bedroom."

Mallory opened her mouth, presumably to say something, but Rafe heard no words. Nervous himself, he scratched the back of his neck. Yes, he was still attracted to Mallory, and he wanted her with an intensity he'd never had with any other woman. But now was not the time. Was he crazy for even thinking that? Their lives were in danger, and he needed to get himself in check. "Li-listen... uh..." Rafe stumbled over his words. Nerves getting to him. "I'm going to take the couch and sleep out here. So please don't worry."

Mallory's response was a high-pitched laugh. Rafe thought it bordered on the hysterical.

"Rafe. For goodness' sake. I'm not even sure we're going to get any sleep. We have work to do." Mallory slowly turned three-hundred and sixty degrees. "Why don't you set up the computer and software on the dining room table while I unpack the groceries? Then we'll switch places. I'll start working on the computer, and you can make dinner." She paused and tilted her head. "You do know how to cook?"

Rafe nodded as the heat of embarrassment crept up the sides of his neck. "On it." He walked to the backpack, pulled out the burner phone, put in the battery, and sent a text to Max. Here. The response was swift with a simple thumbs-up emoji. The entire transaction took less than fifteen seconds. He removed the battery and put the phone away.

"Everyone back at *Tía* Claudia's is fine." He looked around and swallowed hard. A strange sensation pricked at the back of his neck. His instincts told him time was running out.

Chapter 13

Forty minutes passed, and Mallory was still staring at the laptop screen. The spreadsheet Zack told her about had dozens and dozens of numerical entries. The sheet was divided into four columns, with the fourth column blank. When she moved her cursor to that column, a pop-up would request a password.

The spreadsheet, with its various numbers and letters, appeared to be a jumbled mess. Nothing related to anything else. That would be so unlike Blake, who was anything but disorganized. This was the steganography she was told about. This was the puzzle she needed to crack in order to get answers.

Cautiously, she scrolled down the sheet, studying each number, looking for a clue. Anything she could start with that would tell her what type of puzzle this was. The answer was here, even if it was proving to be a bigger challenge than she had imagined. Mallory rubbed her temples hoping to release some of the tension crawling up from her shoulders to her neck like a web. There had to be a way to approach this problem.

"Hey, Mallory," Rafe called from the kitchen area. "I know we're not on vacation. But we do have to eat. So, the potatoes are almost ready. I'm going to cook these steaks on the grill."

"Uh-huh." Mallory heard the sliding doors to the deck open but was too engrossed in what was on the screen to look up.

"Be right back," Rafe said.

"Sure." For several minutes, she stared at the screen to see if a pattern would emerge. When that didn't work, she moved her index finger across the trackpad, highlighting each row one by one in an attempt to find similar sequences. Some rows began with letters—others with numbers. So far, she hadn't been able to make sense of the randomness with which the numbers were placed.

When she thought she might have spotted a pattern, she grabbed a notebook from the backpack and drew lines on the paper, mimicking the columns on the screen. She wrote, erased, and wrote again. She continued, hunched over her notebook, adding and subtracting numbers. Nothing seemed to make sense. She ripped the paper from the notebook, crumpled it, and threw it on the floor. She started from the beginning, drawing columns on the notepad, writing, rewriting, and writing again. Each time, she returned to the screen, checking her numbers against those in her notebook. In frustration, she kicked the leg of the table. *Come on, Blake. What's in here? There's something. I know I'm close*— She jumped when she felt hands on her shoulders.

"Sorry. Didn't mean to scare you."

"Rafe!" Mallory put her hand over her heart. "You can't keep coming up behind me like that. I didn't even hear you come in."

He squeezed her shoulders in response. "Sorry, but I made enough noise opening and closing the deck door that

I thought you heard." Rafe didn't take his hands away and instead began massaging her shoulders. "You're tense."

"You should be worried if I wasn't."

"Ah, there's that sarcasm I've grown so fond of."

"Really, Rafe, stop." She put her hand over his. "One more squeeze, and I may just fall unconscious." She groaned. "And we need me awake."

Rafe began massaging her upper back, ignoring her. "Simply providing a little relaxation," he said.

It felt delicious, and for a moment, she could imagine him caressing her entire body, but they were treading on dangerous ground, not to mention they had other priorities. She needed to change the course of where this was headed. "I don't know what it is, but when it comes to numbers, especially puzzles, I go into a… I don't even know what to call it. I shut everything else out."

"I believe the phrase you're looking for is *in the zone*." He continued kneading her tight shoulder muscles.

"Huh. Maybe you're right." Mallory looked up at him. "I do tend to shut it all out." She placed her hands over his and stilled his motion. "I'm good. Thanks." She patted his hands and pushed her chair from the table.

"Well, whether you realize it or not, you've been sitting here for two hours."

"Are you serious?" Mallory turned her head and looked up at him. "That can't be."

Rafe smirked. "Told you—in the zone. Anyway, I stopped cooking the steaks as soon as I saw that concentrated look on your face. But it really is time to take a short break and eat something."

Mallory hesitated. So much was riding on her. She rubbed at her eyes, stood, and stretched. "Maybe a short break."

"I didn't want to disturb your papers, so I set us up outside. It's a nice night, and I've put the heat lamp on. We're not facing the road, so I think we'll be safe." Rafe pointed to the deck where the outdoor table was set with plates and silverware.

Reluctantly, Mallory agreed. Between sitting in the car for hours and sitting in front of the computer, her body was feeling the strain. And the aroma of the grilled steak made her stomach rumble. "I suppose I'm hungry after all."

Rafe slid open the deck doors, and Mallory stepped outside. This far north the late summer air was crisp, and the glow of the lights from the houses across the lake reflected in the water. This would be a nice romantic setting if she weren't running for her life. But that was so far from what they were dealing with it made her laugh out loud.

"What's funny?" Rafe asked as he took a seat beside her.

Mallory shook her head. Embarrassed to even be thinking such thoughts. "Nothing. Let's eat." She cut into the steak, took a bite, and moaned. "Amazing." She closed her eyes and chewed.

They ate their meal in silence, and the quiet agreed with her. When she finished her last bite, Mallory's gaze settled on the lake, and her mind seemed to still of any thoughts.

"Did you get enough to eat?" Rafe asked, invading the void in her mind.

"Yes. Thanks. It was very good. This is the first moment I haven't thought about Blake or that stupid laptop, even for only a few minutes. Being out here is almost soothing. I wish… I wish…" Mallory waved her hand. "Oh, never mind. I have no right to want anything. Not until my life is normal again. Whatever that is."

She paused, thought for a moment, then twisted her mouth and slammed her hand on the table. "Actually," she glared at Rafe, "I know exactly what normal is. Me and Justine living a life without fear, without anyone telling us what to do and how to be." She blew out a heavy breath. "Oh, god. Rafe. Sorry, I didn't mean to direct that at you. You've been nothing but… Without you, I'm not sure Justine and I would still be safe." She put her head in her hands. "Thank you. If I haven't said it before, I'm saying it now. Thank you."

His hand touched her shoulder. "No need to thank me. Besides, we've got a little way to go yet."

"Yes, and I need to get back to it." Mallory groaned. "My body doesn't want to move. What's waiting for me seems insurmountable. I don't know if I can solve it."

"I'm betting on you. I know you'll get there." Rafe began clearing the table.

She pursed her lips and looked at the shining lights in the distance when, out of nowhere, the hint of an idea popped into her mind. "Wait. Don't go. When I was young and couldn't figure out a puzzle, it helped if I talked about the different possibilities for a solution with my dad. It helps if I can talk through what I'm thinking."

In one fluid motion, Rafe put the dishes down, turned his chair, and straddled it, resting his chin on his arms. "I'm all ears."

With that simple movement, once again, Rafe showed her what kind of man he was. Interested. Concerned. Willing to be there and help. He stared and calmly waited for her to speak. While his gaze was intense, she didn't look away. Nothing about Rafe was threatening, and it was something she'd have to get used to. Not every look was disapproving.

In fact, she could see now there was a distinct difference. Her husband's glare had the purpose of intimidation. Whether it was showing his displeasure over the way she cooked his dinner or his annoyance that Justine was still awake. Or unhappy with the way the house or she looked. Or a million other things.

The difference between Rafe and Blake made it impossible to think of the two of them in the same breath.

When she was dating Rafe, he would always listen to whatever problem she had. At this moment, the kindness on his face reminded her of what they once had. It was more than love; it was mutual caring and concern. That's what she'd been missing all these years. She stared into his eyes.

"You okay?" Rafe asked.

Mallory felt the tears in the back of her throat for what she'd lost, but now was not the time for regrets or should-have-beens. There was work to do. A relationship wasn't in the cards for her. *Focus, Mallory. Focus.*

She cleared her throat. "Okay. So, all this time, we've been thinking about how to crack the password and the second encryption."

"Yeah. So?"

"Well, I don't want this to be a conversation about Blake, but there's something there. I know it."

Rafe reached for her hand, and she forced herself not to pull away.

"Tell me."

"I was thinking that when Blake and I started dating, he would spend hours asking me about my job. At the time, I honestly thought he was interested in what I did. He said understanding how I spent my days made him feel closer to me. He said it was important that, as a couple, we could talk to each other about our work. He reasoned that most couples drift apart when they aren't interested in what the other person does. I found his attentiveness attractive. You know how the beginning of a relationship is? You want to know everything about each other."

Rafe gave a half nod, encouraging her to go on.

"But it was pretty much one-sided."

"How so?" Rafe leaned in.

"After each question about my family or my childhood, he'd always ask about my work. At the time, I was rapidly moving up at the firm and working in some capacity on high-level cases. Blake would specifically ask me about cases involving securities fraud and embezzlement. I was the one forensic accountant at the company who had a thing for puzzles, and it somehow made me faster at solving cases. Maybe because I didn't just look at the numbers, I viewed each case like an intricate maze that needed to be navigated. Puzzles and math are my favorite topics to tackle. Remember how I never let you finish the Sunday crossword, and I always helped you with your calculus homework?"

Rafe smiled. "How could I forget? Sunday afternoons were my favorite, and you won the regional math competition, so why wouldn't I ask you for help with math?"

She wondered if life had ever been that simple and shook away the thought. Dwelling on her past with Rafe wasn't going to get her any closer to solving her problems and keeping her daughter safe. "Anyway, I told him countless stories of my 'brilliance—'" she made air quotes "—and how I discovered hidden money trails and mistakes the perpetrators made." Mallory tilted her head and looked up in thought. "Funny, he'd always ask me how I would do it differently if I wanted to get away with it. And I always had an answer."

Rafe let out a breath. "Oh, man. So, without knowing, you inadvertently taught him how to hide a money trail."

"Exactly." Mallory shuddered. She closed her eyes at the sheer stupidity of her supposed whirlwind romance with Blake when she realized he'd used her from the start. First, to gain the knowledge she had. And later, by holding on to her and Justine as props for photo ops. Always presenting the picture-perfect couple at the latest political fundraiser, charity ball, or any number of events he insisted she attend. Her presence afforded him a respectability he didn't have on his own. "What an idiot I was." She spat out the words.

"Don't be so hard on yourself. You were dealing with a pretty evil guy."

"Well, that's over. I'm going to beat him at his own game." Mallory sat up straight.

"Tell me how."

"I was thinking of all the passwords I've tried on the first encryption—birthdays, anniversaries, graduations—" Mallory ticked each one off on her fingers "—and none of them worked, and they probably won't work on this second encryption. And you know why?"

Rafe shook his head.

She took a moment to answer. When she did, her words were halting. She was still working out how everything fit together. "Blake knew everything, I mean, he knew every-thing about me. I…I had no…secrets from him. At least not at the beginning. You know?"

"I suppose so." Rafe cocked an eyebrow.

"Well, it was as far from a two-way street as you could get because I knew precious little about Blake or his fam-ily. Even after six years together." Mallory scoffed. "After Justine was born, that's when he changed. He got mean. He was gone a lot, and when he was home, he was annoyed and impatient. Nothing I did was right. He became jealous of the time I spent with my father and was even jealous of the time I devoted to our daughter. Stupidly, I attributed his horrific behavior to his heavy workload and the important people he was working for." Mallory gave a wry chuckle and looked toward the sky. "Who was I kidding? I made excuses—one after the next, after the next. For the longest time, I refused to see what was right in front of me. I ignored the news reports of his alleged illegal dealings."

Rafe reached out and put his hand over hers.

Mallory stopped talking. The warmth of his hand made her close her eyes. "Don't," Mallory said. "Let me finish." She abruptly got to her feet and began pacing the deck.

"I'm telling you all of this because, during our marriage, we barely spoke to each other. About anything. Except for one thing, and that was his father's suicide. And that wasn't even a conversation. It was mostly a rant about how his stockbroker father took his own life because of the big bank failure of 2008." She stopped pacing and looked at Rafe. "You remember when the government bailed out the banks for trillions of dollars?"

"Yeah, I remember." Rafe furrowed his brow. "Why?"

"Well, every couple of months, Blake would get on a jag about it. He'd start off talking about how deceptive banks were, and within minutes, he'd work himself into a fury."

"And what does this have to do with passwords?" Rafe asked.

"I know it sounds crazy, but I think that Blake's father's death in 2008 has something to do with getting past the second encryption and opening up some of these folders."

"You think the password is two, zero, zero, eight?" Rafe said.

"Not all of it, but a piece of it." With that, Mallory marched back into the house and sat in front of the laptop. She picked up the pencil and wrote the year on the tablet.

"Think, Mallory, think," she said aloud. Tapping the pencil on the notepad, she tried to come up with more numbers that stood out from her time with Blake.

Rafe was right behind her now, pulling up a chair to the dining table. "Can you remember the date of his suicide?"

Mallory put her head in her hands. "I'm thinking. I usually tried to block him out during his fits—wait. October! Yes. His father died in October because I love that time of year, and Blake always made me feel bad for being happy in the fall." She wrote the number ten next to the year.

"Can you remember anything else?"

Mallory shook her head.

"Let's try what you have," Rafe said.

Mallory took a deep breath. "I'm afraid. Zack said we only get a few tries before the computer either sends up a signal or we are permanently locked out."

Rafe bit his lower lip. "We have to start somewhere."

"Okay. Here goes." She leaned forward, studying the spreadsheet on the desktop. She clicked on the first row in the fourth column, and a pop-up box appeared requesting a password. Carefully, she typed in 102008 and hit Enter. Nothing. Perspiration began to form on her upper lip.

"I really hoped that would work. Too much to ask for." Mallory slumped back in her chair.

"Wait." Rafe pointed to the screen. "Try not typing in the whole year."

"Huh?"

"Try 1008," Rafe said.

Mallory took another breath and typed in the numbers. When she hit Enter again, nothing happened. She could feel more sweat collecting at the base of her neck. She had no idea how many times they could type in a wrong password before they were locked out. They needed to be cautious.

"We have a month and a year. We've got to be missing the date. I don't know when he died. If only we could try all 31 days of the month of October." Mallory kept her fingers hovered above the keyboard.

"Yeah. If only," Rafe said. "Can you think of any possible date that would make sense?"

Mallory laid her head on the table. "I hate him. I hate him. I hate him." Mallory sat up and looked at Rafe. "His cruelness lives on." She took in a breath. "So. What would an evil person like him do?"

"You're scaring me. You have a strange look on your face."

"Because I think I've finally beaten him at his own game. If I were Blake Stanton, and I didn't want to create an obvious password like the exact date of my father's suicide, but I still wanted a reminder, what date would I choose?"

Rafe pursed his lips. "I'm clueless. You tell me."

"Halloween, of course." Mallory laughed, then quickly typed in the number 10312008. She expected nothing to happen when she hit Enter. To her surprise, up popped a swirling rainbow-colored ball. In seconds, the spreadsheet transitioned into a checkerboard pattern that disappeared, revealing three folders.

"That worked!" Rafe slapped his hand against his thigh.

"Hmm. Let's not pop the champagne yet. I don't know what I was expecting, but I have no idea what this is." Mallory ran her index finger over the trackpad. "I guess I'll start by opening each folder and see what I find."

Two more hours passed while Rafe watched Mallory at the computer. It seemed as if her expression never changed, and her eyes never left the screen as she opened each folder, one after the other. He did what he could, offering her something to drink and eat. But she refused each time, barely noticing him. Her laser concentration never left the screen.

Rafe wasn't sure what he expected, but he didn't think it would take this long to find something that would give them a clue. The nervous energy pulsing through his body had him pacing the length of the living room. Twenty steps in one direction and then twenty steps back. Each time he reached one wall, he checked the time on his phone.

The pacing wasn't helping; all it managed to do was leave Rafe alone with his thoughts. Thoughts that were becoming dimmer by the moment. He could no longer deny that he'd become attached to Mallory and to Justine. His feelings for Mallory weren't just rekindled; they were on fire. Regardless of the mess she was in, he wanted to be with her. The whole thing added up to an impossible situation. He couldn't ask her to be with him because he needed to clear his name. Any type of relationship outside of the friend zone was off the table. Besides, he rationalized that when this was over, she was going to live with her father. Sadness enveloped him like a heavy overcoat. He tried pushing through it by pacing from wall to wall faster.

When he couldn't take it another moment, he stopped at the head of the dining table. "Did you find anything?"

"Lots of numbers and letters," Mallory replied without looking up.

"Looks like this is going to take a while," Rafe muttered to himself.

"Uh huh," Mallory said as she scribbled something on a pad.

Once again, he paced. There was nothing else to do. Like a metronome set at a steady pace, he walked back and forth for what seemed like hours, but when he checked his phone, only ten minutes had passed. He didn't know how much longer he could continue to do this. He was either going to pass out from fatigue or lose his mind waiting for Mallory to decipher the spreadsheets.

"I'll be right back," Rafe said on a long breath.

"Where are you going?" Mallory asked, looking up for the first time.

"Outside, check around."

Mallory half stood as if she were ready to bolt. "Is everything okay? Did you hear something?"

"No. No. Nothing's wrong. I'm sorry. I didn't mean to frighten you," Rafe said, walking to the kitchen area. He opened a side drawer and pulled out a flashlight.

"What's that for?"

"Truth is, I'm a little antsy. There doesn't seem to be anything I can do to help you decipher the spreadsheets." Rafe shrugged. "I just want to take a look around. I need to do something."

"Why not rest? You must be exhausted."

"Not yet. I'll rest once I have a look outside."

"You think that's wise?"

Rafe waved the thought away. "If someone were following us, we'd know by now. And if someone were tracking the laptop, Max would have alerted us." At least, that was his sincere hope. While he didn't want to worry her, he also wanted to check the area to ease his own mind.

"All right. But please, don't be long, and don't go far," Mallory said.

"I won't."

"And be careful!"

The look in her eyes and the concern in her voice warmed him. Made him feel wanted. He hadn't felt that in a long time. "I'll be back soon."

The night air held a chill. He zipped his jacket closed and

headed toward the wooded area on the side of the house. The tall trees surrounding the property allowed only a sliver of moonlight to reach the path. He pulled the flashlight from his back pocket and let the slender beam of light lead him as he walked a wide perimeter around the cabin. He couldn't see much, so every few feet, he stopped to listen. It was dead quiet, and yet a cold shiver traveled up his spine. He couldn't shake the feeling someone was watching him. Tightening his grip on the flashlight, he pointed it in several directions when a slight rustle in a bush to his right got his attention. Rafe held his breath and slowly walked toward where he'd heard the sound. A twig snapping beneath his own feet echoed in the silent night and stopped him dead in his tracks. Whoever was behind the bush knew he was coming in their direction. The leaves in the bush rustled once more, and he wished he had more than a flashlight in his hands. Inching closer to the sound, he lifted the flashlight above his head, ready to use it as a weapon, when a large buck burst forth, knocking Rafe to the ground as it took off. "Holy mother of…" Rafe's heart was in his mouth.

He lay on the ground for several minutes, trying to catch his breath. Over the years, he'd seen plenty of deer, moose, even bears. And not once had he been this afraid. His teenage years spent at his aunt's house had been filled with dozens of dares by his cousins as they traipsed through the woods at night. But tonight had been different, and until now, he hadn't realized how wound up he was. Mallory, her daughter, and his family were all at risk.

Dusting himself off, he took in a heavy breath and searched for his flashlight. Retrieving it from a nearby fallen log, he picked it up and realized his hand was shaking. It took two more walks around the perimeter of the cabin to still the whooshing sound of blood rushing in his ears.

Before going in, Rafe stood at the front door surveying the area, again pointing the flashlight in several directions. It was a few minutes before he sensed a stillness within himself and around the cabin. Only then was he satisfied they were alone and went inside.

Quietly, he hung his jacket on a nearby hook and bolted the door behind him. "How's it going?" Rafe asked as he raked his hands through his hair.

"I'm still looking," Mallory said.

Rafe saw worry etched in the furrow of her brow.

"Do you need anything? Coffee?"

"God, no. No more caffeine, please." Mallory arched her back and stretched.

"Maybe you should take your own advice and get some sleep," Rafe said.

Mallory shook her head, unconsciously tapping the tip of the pencil on the paper and jiggling her knee up and down. "There's no time. I'll rest when this is over. It shouldn't be much longer. I feel like I'm getting close."

"Really?"

"Yeah." Mallory picked up the pencil and wrote on the pad.

Rafe came closer and put his hand on Mallory's shoulder. "Don't let me keep you. But if you need anything, I'm right here."

"Thanks," Mallory said, and went back to the papers in front of her.

Rafe dug his hands in his back pockets, wishing he could help, but there was nothing for him to do but keep watch over her. It wasn't safe to call Max or Zack. He needed to stay off anyone's radar. He was edgy and bored and needed something to do. Glancing around the one-bedroom house as if it were his first time there, instead of his hundredth, including just a few days ago under very different circumstances, his gaze finally settled on the shelves in the corner. Running his fingers across the books on Zack's shelf, he picked out a mystery, perched himself on the couch and attempted to read. After reading the first paragraph a dozen times, he tossed the paperback onto the coffee table and focused his attention on Mallory.

Hunched over the laptop, she chewed on her lower lip. He smiled, remembering that same look whenever she took a math test. They'd been so in love back then. What would have happened if they'd stayed together? The memory of her soft lips and her small, firm breasts gave him a warm sensation. He wanted her despite all the craziness since she'd stumbled back into his life. He wanted her.

Rafe gave himself a firm mental shake. They had things to take care of right now. She hadn't pushed him away, but she hadn't encouraged him either.

He continued to study her. She looked tired. But she was still as beautiful as ever, and he was as attracted to her now as he'd been all those years ago. Rubbing his eyes with the heels of his hands, he stifled a yawn, willing himself to stay awake. The need to protect her was strong.

Coffee, he thought. Caffeine would keep him awake. He rose from the couch and, as unobtrusively as possible, he made a fresh pot. Rafe paced some more, then finally perched again on the edge of the couch and watched and waited until his eyelids grew heavy and fluttered closed.

"Rafe, I think I found something!"

Chapter 14

"Rafe! Wake up."

Mallory's voice sounded distant, and Rafe realized he'd fallen asleep. He opened his eyes, sat up, and regrouped. He stamped his foot on the ground to rid it of the pins and needles sensation. "What did you find? What time is it?"

"It's three o'clock."

"In the morning?" Rafe wasn't sure how long he was out.

"Rafe? Wake up. Come here. I found something."

He gave a grunt and stood. His legs felt heavy, and he was a bit unsteady on his feet as he walked toward the dining area. Scrubbing a hand over his face, he walked up behind Mallory and squinted at the laptop screen.

Mallory turned toward him. "Turns out my suspicions were correct. Blake paid very close attention to everything I said about my job and how to hide money. He even took it a step further. It's all right here in black and white." She tapped the edge of her pencil on the papers.

Rafe picked up one of the spreadsheets she'd printed out and glanced over the rows of numbers. "Mallory, I'm not an accountant. Hell, you know I wasn't that good at crossword puzzles. Please tell me exactly what you've found. Step by step." Rafe pulled up a chair to the table.

"Sit. I'll show you." Mallory took the paper from his

hand. "Each line represents an account. But the numbers aren't account numbers. They represent something else."

"Something else? They look like numbers and letters to me."

"Stick with me. I'm about to explain. Each one of these initials represents a country: GC is for Grand Cayman, SC is for the Scottish Isles, OK is for Okinawa, and so on."

"How do you know that?" Rafe asked.

"Because these are all places where you can store money offshore."

"But as far as I know, that's not illegal."

"No, it's not. Not unless you're using these accounts to launder money, and that is illegal." Mallory put her pencil down and sat back.

"How can you tell this is a money-laundering scheme?" Rafe asked.

She let out a heavy sigh. "That's where I'm stuck. I can't prove it. There's a missing element. If I'm right, there's a key that opens these folders and shows the next layer of encryption. The key must be the drive. They must be one and the same. And on it is the information that could prove the money has been laundered, where it went, and who benefited. It could put important people behind bars. I'm sure of it."

"How can you be so sure?" Rafe asked.

"Remember, I'm trained to find the one mistake in a million. Look at this account here." Mallory pointed to a line on the spreadsheet. "This account number is eight digits long." She picked up another page. "This account here is five digits long—nothing out of the ordinary. But the account with the eight digits was the longest on any of the pages, so it was easy to spot. As I looked through the sheets, there were other accounts with eight digits. Again, no big deal. Except each of those accounts looked similar in some way, but I couldn't place my finger on exactly how. And when I took a really close look, I realized they all held the same numbers but in a different order."

"I'm totally not following you," Rafe said.

"Look, here. This account is 71228903." Mallory turned the page. "And here, it's 12289037." Using her index finger, she moved further down the page. "And here it's 22890371. And look here—28903712." She turned to Rafe. "What do you see?"

He studied the sheets for several minutes. "They're the same numbers, only each time the first number listed moves to the end of the sequence," Rafe said.

"Exactly. It's too much of a systematic coincidence not to be the same account. I tracked this one account through pages and pages, and each time it appears, the amount decreases from five million to three million two hundred and fifty thousand dollars."

"So that means one million seven hundred and fifty thousand dollars is missing." He stopped to think about it. He was a cybersecurity expert. Not a money-laundering expert. But in his mind, criminals were criminals. In the last ten years, he'd dealt with so many different nefarious schemes in his line of work that he'd learned to think like them. He folded his hands on the table and looked at her.

"What? What are you thinking?"

"Mallory, what you've managed to uncover is amazing. But does it prove anything? To the naked eye, it could appear that whoever owns these accounts simply decided to cash in."

"No." She slammed a hand on the table. "How could it? Look." She pointed to the sheets. "The missing amount appears here in a totally different account. Each time there's a withdrawal from an eight-digit account, the exact amount appears in a different account. That's moving money from one account to another in smaller amounts, so no one knows where it comes from when you buy things like, say, arms to finance a terrorist organization. It's money laundering 101."

"You know this for sure?" Rafe asked.

"No. Not for sure. It's a hunch."

Rafe pushed back from the table. "We can't go on hunches."

"You're right, but it's more like an educated guess. Right now, all I have are a bunch of numbers and initials that I believe are offshore accounts that are part of a money-laundering scheme, with initials that belong to the names of people and corporations. But these files, by themselves, prove nothing. The missing drive is the key that will unlock the whole system. I'm sure of it. Once that's unlocked, we'll know exactly what Blake did that has me and my daughter running for our lives."

Mallory looked drained. Rafe pulled his chair close and took hold of her hands. "You did a great job. You've found out a lot tonight."

"Come on, you and I know the truth," Mallory said. "The men after me aren't going to stop until they get what they want. They probably already have this. What they don't have is the drive that opens the next layer of folders. Those folders will be the most incriminating. That's the evidence. Because I'm positive the next layer names the names."

"We need to find that drive," Rafe said.

"I know you're right, but I have no idea where it could be. I tore my house apart looking for it. When I found the hidden laptop, I thought that was the drive. It's the only thing I could find. Believe me, I looked." Mallory rolled her head from side to side, trying to ease the tension from her shoulders and think.

"I know you did. Or at least you think you did."

Mallory whirled around. "What's that supposed to mean?"

"Please don't get upset." Rafe waved his arm over the spreadsheets. "I only meant that clearly your husband—"

Mallory stamped her foot. "Can we stop calling him that? Please."

"All right," he said quietly. "Look at all the work Blake went through to hide his money-laundering scheme. He would have done the same thing with the hard drive."

"But maybe he had the drive on him when the plane went down," Mallory suggested.

"Maybe." Rafe shrugged. "But not likely. From everything you've told me, he's not the type to be careless. From what we know in those spreadsheets, it looks like he was dealing with some pretty scary people who wouldn't think twice about taking Blake out. I've been up close and personal with men like that in prison. The only thing that keeps you alive when you're dealing with scum like that is an insurance policy. And that drive was Blake's insurance policy. If they're still looking for it, then it's got to be hidden somewhere."

"So where does that leave us?" She blew out a breath and threw her pencil on the table. "I need a break." She put her hands on her hips, leaned back, and stretched her torso.

"If we can think outside the box for a minute and be as devious as Blake, maybe, just maybe, the key isn't a separate disc, or hard drive, or anything but another puzzle already stored in those folders."

Mallory shook her head. "Honestly, I'm having a hard time wrapping my mind around any of it." She stifled a yawn. "I can't think anymore. I need to close my eyes, only for an hour or two." She raised her arms over her head and gave a long stretch. Her T-shirt rose, exposing the smooth skin of her waist.

Rafe knew he should look away but couldn't. There was no denying he'd like nothing more than to curl up in bed with her and make love. But Mallory needed sleep. They were both running on fumes, and it was affecting her ability to think. He could see the fatigue on her face. Rest was what she needed. Not him or his desires. That would make him as selfish as her dead husband.

"You take the bed. I'll sleep on the couch."

Mallory shook her head. "Don't be silly. You barely fit on the couch. I can sleep there."

"No." He took hold of her hands and felt the jolt of desire. "You've been working nonstop." He put his arm around her shoulder and led her to the bedroom. "Get some rest." He gave her a gentle push over the threshold. "See you soon." He closed the door before he had time for second thoughts.

The couch didn't look half as inviting as the bed in the other room. But that ship wasn't going to dock tonight. Flopping down, he found he was wide awake and frustrated with thoughts of Mallory. A warm sensation flooded his groin, and he shifted his position on the couch and groaned.

Rafe opened his eyes and blinked. It took a few moments for his mind to register where he was. Streaks of sunlight slanted across the wood floor, and he bolted upright and frantically searched the room.

The dining table held the laptop and papers, but no Mallory. He rushed to the bedroom and stopped short at the threshold. In the center of the king-size bed, Mallory slept, fully dressed, curled in a ball. Glancing over to the bedside table, he checked the time on the alarm clock—barely seven in the morning.

They'd slept for four hours. Had he given her enough time to rest? The woman lying in the bed looked peaceful, so at odds with their situation. In the last three days, he hadn't seen a relaxed look on her face. As much as he didn't want to wake her, time was not on their side.

Backing out of the room, he left the door open and began loudly rummaging through the kitchen cabinets, prepping breakfast, in the hopes the noise would wake her and she'd have a moment to herself before coming into the kitchen.

He poured coffee beans into the grinder. The rich cocoa aroma gave him something familiar to hold on to. It reminded him of his mother. This was her morning ritual. God, how he missed her.

Rafe spooned the freshly ground beans into the coffee maker basket and pressed the start button. Absently, he stared at the machine and lost his thoughts in the drip, drip, drip, of the rich brown liquid into the glass carafe.

"Wow. I was out."

Rafe turned to find Mallory rubbing the sleep from her eyes. "You didn't sleep that long. Only about four hours."

"No wonder I feel like a truck ran me over. Then backed up and hit me again for good measure."

"Here. Have some of this." He poured coffee into a mug and placed it on the kitchen island "You'll feel better."

"Thanks." Mallory took the steaming mug in her hands.

"You've been hunched over that laptop for hours, poring over numbers. That might have something to do with how you feel."

"Maybe." Mallory shrugged. "But I think it has more to do with not being able to figure out if we're missing a drive, or a key, or a puzzle or whatever it is we need to open those folders and get the evidence." Mallory sighed and focused on the countertop. "Truth is—I'm a bit distracted. I miss my baby girl." She chewed on her lip. "You think I could speak with her?"

The plaintive tone in her voice hit him in the chest. The look on her face told him she was hurting. While he was empathetic, he couldn't risk having her make a call. "Mallory, I'm sorry. But that's a no-go. We can't take the chance."

"But why?" Her tone was a half plead, half whine.

"It's not safe. But more importantly, we don't want anyone to track Justine or my aunts, and making a call for any length of time could put everyone in jeopardy."

Mallory slammed her mug on the counter. "Okay. What you're telling me is, if I don't find this damn drive or whatever it is we need, we could be stuck here? Or worse, running for the rest of our lives?" She put her hands on her hips. "Oh, hell no!" She stomped over to the sliding glass door, pushed it open, and stepped out onto the deck.

Rafe came up behind her and put his arms around her. He could feel her body shaking. She was crying, and it nearly broke him. "Mallory, I know we can get out of this. I believe in you."

She turned to face him, and the pleading look in her eyes was all he needed. He pulled her tighter and pressed his mouth on her lips, taking her in hungrily. He'd wanted her since they kissed two nights ago. He pressed up against her, and she felt as good as he remembered. His tongue greedily entered her mouth. Her moan was all he needed to put his hands under her T-shirt and cup her breasts. He was breathing heavily and wanted to take her right there when she abruptly pushed him away.

"Please, Rafe. We can't do this."

He dropped his arms and took a step back.

"It's not that I don't want you…" She turned away. "The timing is off. I'm sorry if—"

Rafe put his hand up. "Don't. I get it." He let out a breath. "Look, I'll give you some space. Why don't you shower? I'm going to walk a couple of laps around the perimeter of the house. Get some fresh air. I'll be right outside."

She stepped forward. "I didn't mean to—"

"Really. We're all good. We are. I won't be gone long."

Frustration coursed through her, and Mallory wanted to scream, cry, and throw dishes. Instead, she picked up the burner phone, put the battery in, and pressed the number 1, programmed to call Claudia's house. The phone rang twice before Claudia answered.

"Hi. It's Mallory." She held the mobile phone in a tight grip.

"Is everything all right?" Claudia asked.

"Yes. Yes. I can't be on the phone long. Can I please speak with Justine? Please."

Claudia didn't say another word. There was silence, and Mallory checked the screen on the phone to make sure they were still connected. When she put the phone back to her ear, she heard her daughter's voice.

"Mommy. Mommy. Where are you? When are you coming back?"

Justine didn't sound sad, but her questions still pierced Mallory's heart. "Soon, baby. Soon."

"Mommy, where's Teddy? We can't find him anywhere. I can't sleep without him."

There was a rustling in the background, and Mallory heard Claudia telling Justine to say goodbye. The next thing

Mallory knew, the phone went dead. She threw the phone on the bed.

Her world was crashing in on her. She'd alienated Rafe, and her daughter was in a strange place without her and the security of her teddy bear. She sat down on the bed and put her head in her hands. Minutes passed before she knew the only solution was to pull it together and get some answers. Maybe Rafe was right, and the key to everything was still in that laptop.

A fresh start was what she needed, and she'd begin by taking a shower and changing her clothes.

The hot water felt luxurious and was doing the trick in reviving her senses. When she was done, she turned off the taps and wrapped herself in a towel. She felt marginally better. The travel bag Rafe packed was sitting in the corner of the room. When she opened the bag, she smiled. Her clothes were folded in neat piles. A pair of jeans sat on top, followed by her white button-down blouse. She dressed, and before leaving the room, she pulled out her jean jacket from the bottom of the bag, and with it came her daughter's teddy bear. "So that's where you got to. How did you get wrapped up in my jacket?" Then Mallory remembered they'd been playing dress-up with the stuffed animal and Justine put him in Mallory's jacket. In his hurry to pack Mallory's things, Rafe must not have realized that Teddy was still wrapped up in her clothes.

She picked up the scraggly bear and hugged it. She froze when she heard the front door open.

"It's me. I'm back," Rafe called.

"Coming." She walked into the living room holding the teddy bear.

"Where'd you get that?" Rafe asked.

"Accidentally packed with my things."

"Oops. Sorry." Rafe pointed toward the bedroom. "You all done in there?"

Mallory nodded and put the bear on the dining table.

"Okay. I'm going to take a quick shower and then make us something to eat. Are you feeling lucky?"

She raised an eyebrow. "Lucky?"

"I mean, lucky that you'll get what we need from that laptop. Looking for the key within the key, so to speak."

"I'm going to give it my best shot."

Rafe smiled, and Mallory appreciated that he was keeping the atmosphere light. If only things were different.

By mid-afternoon, Mallory still hadn't found the answer. Fatigue threatened to take over, and she pushed away from the table. "I need to stretch. Get the kinks out."

Rafe pulled out a stool from the kitchen island and sat while Mallory walked around the dining table several times. She picked up Justine's teddy bear. The feel of the stuffed animal in her arms gave her the odd sensation of being closer to her daughter, which was where she wanted to be right now—with Justine, living a normal life. Not holed up in a remote lake house working out how to stay alive. This entire situation was all too surreal.

"Want some water?"

Mallory shook her head and continued pacing, squeezing the bear to her chest. She stopped. Eyes closed, she tilted her head toward the ceiling, hugging the bear as if it were her daughter. *Stop it. Wake up. The sooner you find a solution to this mess, the sooner you'll see Justine.*

Pulling out the dining chair with her foot, she slumped back down and wiggled the trackpad, waking the screen with the same spreadsheets. Nothing had changed since she took a stroll around the dining room. She placed the teddy bear on the table next to the laptop, facing her, and gave it a weary grin. "Teddy, you and me. We're going to figure this out."

"Are you talking to me?" Rafe asked. The tired smile on his face told her he was suffering the same anxiety and mental fatigue.

"No. Why don't you rest? You didn't get much sleep last night. I'll give this another go. There's got to be a way in. Right, Teddy?" She patted the bear on the head and froze. "Hold on." Patting the bear on the head again, she leaned forward, examining it more closely. "Rafe, hand me a sharp knife," she said, staring at the stuffed animal as though it would get up and walk away if she took her eyes off it.

"What for?" Rafe inched closer to her.

"Please, just get me a knife." She held out a hand, waiting.

His hesitancy had her slapping a hand on the table in frustration. The stuffed animal fell over. "I think there may be something in Teddy."

"Seriously?"

Mallory made a wriggling give-it-here motion with her hand. "Please. The knife."

Rafe opened the kitchen drawer and handed one over.

The paring knife weighed next to nothing in her hand. The steel of the blade was sharp, and she pointed the tip of the knife directly at the top of the teddy bear's head and drove it straight in.

"Whoa. Hang on, what are you doing?" Rafe was by her side in a second. "What are you doing?" he repeated.

Without raising her head, Mallory looked up at Rafe. "I think the key we're looking for has been right here the entire time."

"You mean inside Justine's stuffed animal?"

"That's exactly what I mean." Mallory pulled the knife out and rotated the handle between her forefinger and her thumb. "It's got to be in here somewhere, and I'm going to find it."

"What makes you so sure?"

A sound between a one-syllable laugh and a scoff escaped her mouth. "I've been so stupid. It was right here the entire time." She shook her head in disgust. "This is the only gift Blake personally bought for Justine. All the rest—birthday, Christmas, Easter Bunny surprises, just-because presents, you name it, every single gift my daughter received was because I made all the purchases. It never occurred to him, not even when she was born, to buy her anything. Except for this stuffed animal right here." She placed the tip of the blade at the center of the worn plaid bowtie around the bear's neck.

"Don't." Rafe sat kitty-corner to Mallory and leaned in close. "Think about it. If, and I'm saying *if* the key to Blake's crimes is hidden in the bear, then we need to carefully dismantle the bear so as not to destroy what we're looking for. If it is a drive, we don't want to damage it."

The white-hot rage inside her was bubbling to the surface. "You don't get it." She looked into Rafe's eyes. "He gave her this as a gift, but the way he made her keep track of it was almost maniacal. If he came home and found she wasn't playing with the bear, he'd ask her to stop what she was doing and go get Teddy." Mallory scoffed. "It was strange. Heck, it was even crazy, but so much of him was strange and crazy. He was a cruel man in so many ways. It got to the point that I made up a game for Justine. When I knew Blake would be home, which thankfully, as the years went by, became less frequent, I would tell her to find Teddy because he, too, wanted to say hi to Daddy. How messed up is that?" Mallory put an elbow on the table and rested her forehead in the palm of her hand. She wanted to go back in time and spare Justine from all the madness. She wanted to be stronger for her daughter. At that moment, she made a mental vow if she ever got out of this, she would be a better mother. She would protect her daughter at all costs, and most importantly, she'd never let another man run their lives.

An overwhelming urge surged through her. She wanted to stab the stuffed animal in the chest repeatedly until there was nothing left but shreds. Looking down at her hand, she could see her grip on the knife was tight enough to turn her knuckles white. She dropped it and pushed away from the table. "Okay, Rafe. You do it."

Rafe pushed his chair in closer and turned the bear to face him. Using his right hand, he squeezed each ear and all four paws. "Feels crinkly. Like old stuffing."

Mallory nodded. "Are you prepping for surgery, or are you going to get down to business?"

"Here goes." Laying the bear on its side, Rafe reached for the knife and began ripping the side seams out, one by one. Some stitches were harder to remove than others. But he took his time, forcing himself to be patient, not wanting to take any chances that would damage whatever it was they were meant not to find. Maybe it was the missing key. Maybe it was something else. Maybe it was nothing at all.

"Are you really going to take out one stitch at a time?" In a rhythmic beat, she tapped the pencil on the table.

Rafe stopped and stared at her hand. "What are you doing, beating out Morse code?"

"Oh." She put the pencil down. "Sorry. Nervous."

"In answer to your question. Yes. I'm not deliberately

trying to drive you mad by going this slow. We need to do this right. No mistakes."

"Okay." Mallory stood. "I'll go make some coffee. You want some?"

"Uh-uh." He went back to ripping each seam until the furry material could be pushed away, revealing some sort of off-white polyester fiber fill. The stuffing that once made up the shape of a child's teddy bear was now a pile of loose strands and small cotton bags. Rafe first examined the cotton bags located where the paws would have been. "What have we here?" He turned toward the kitchen. "Mallory, there's a flashlight in the top right-hand drawer by the stove. Would you please hand it to me?"

"Sure." Mallory pulled open the drawer and fished out the flashlight, handing it over to Rafe.

With the flashlight in one hand, he separated one of the cotton bags with the knife from the rest of the pile of what was once a teddy bear. Shining the light, he leaned in closer.

"What do you see?" Mallory asked.

He turned to find her looking over his shoulder. "Not sure. Could be nothing. But we're about to find out." He handed Mallory the flashlight. "Shine it on the bag."

Carefully slitting the bag open, dozens of small plastic pellets scattered over the table.

"What in the world are those?" Mallory asked.

"Nothing." Rafe scooped the pellets back into one pile. "Looks like they were used to add weight to the bear's paws. I mean, they aren't anything that will help us."

"Yes, but there are four bags. Try them all."

One by one, he cut through the bags with the same result. Each as innocuous as the last.

Mallory let out a heavy sigh.

"Let's not give up yet. We still have the filling." Cautiously pressing against every single square inch of the fiber filling, Rafe's finger stopped at the center of where the bear's belly had been. He pulled away the individual layers of fibers until he found what he was looking for—a silver nano drive the size of a small child's thumbnail. "And there we have it." His voice was calm yet flooded with expectancy.

"What is that?"

"I think we've found what Blake was hiding. Whoever is after you needs the laptop, but they also need this." Rafe held up the thumb drive. "This, my dear, I believe is the key to the information on the laptop."

Chapter 15

"Give me the drive. I'll put it in." Mallory's fingers nearly trembled with excitement.

"Wait! Don't do that." Rafe closed his hand over the drive. "We don't know what this is. It could be something that wipes out the entire computer." He walked over to his backpack. "Max gave me this laptop, just in case. We'll make a duplicate file of what you've already uncovered. We don't want to lose what we have."

Mallory was hesitant. Her fingers itched to put the drive in now and not wait. "How long do you think it will take?" She watched as Rafe began setting up another laptop and USB transfer cables.

"We can't use the internet, which would be the fastest. So, unfortunately, this is going to take a while." Rafe plugged the cables into a connecting box. "I know you don't want to wait, but better safe than sorry. There's too much on the line."

Mallory knew he was right. They'd come this far, and her gut told her there was information on that drive that would likely save all their lives. She had to tamp down her anxiety.

"Hand me another USB port from my backpack."

Mallory rummaged through his bag and held up a silver square. "You mean this?"

"That's the one." Rafe made the final connections and fired up the second laptop. Within a few keystrokes, the copying process began. "Well, you may not like this, but according to this computer, it says it will take four hours to transfer all the materials."

The scream lodged in the back of her throat nearly choked her. A tantrum was wholly unnecessary, but that's precisely what she felt like doing. Throwing things. She clenched her jaw and balled her fists.

"Mallory, please breathe. Your face is turning an unhealthy shade of red."

She took in a deep breath and relaxed her jaw. "I'm trying not to scream."

"I see that. And I understand your frustration. But this is necessary. We need to take this precaution. Trust me. Let's just be happy that we're close." He looked at the clock over the kitchen cabinets. "I'll tell you what. It's nearly dinnertime. I'll make us something quick and easy. We can eat while the computer cooks away."

It wasn't as if she had any choice. So she agreed.

"You like omelets?"

"Sure. Anything's fine. It's not like I have a big appetite." Mallory sighed. "I'm going to sit out on the deck."

"Turn on the heat lamp," Rafe called out. "It's getting toward dusk, and the chill will move in fast."

Out on the lake a pontoon boat silently slipped across the water. Probably the last ride of the season before they docked the boat. She smiled. People were living their lives, going about their business, unaware that someone living right down the road from them was digging into money laundering and who knew what else. "Ahhhhh." She tilted her head toward the sky and rubbed her hands over her face, wanting to erase the last few days from her mind.

"Mallory. We're about to eat. There's nothing we can do until the computer is ready. Please, difficult as it may be, try to relax." Rafe set down two plates and went back inside.

She hadn't thought she could eat anything. Her stomach was twisted into one big knot. But the beautifully cooked omelet and the aroma of melted brie, basil, and scallions filled the air and made her stomach growl.

"I thought we could use a little wine. We have some time before you have to go back to work." He placed two wine glasses and a cold bottle of Chablis on the table.

"Uh… I don't know."

"Yeah, yeah. I know you need to stay sharp. You don't have to have any if you don't want."

Mallory considered that one glass over a four-hour period wouldn't hurt. And if she needed to take a nap after dinner, she had plenty of time. "Okay. One glass."

Dinner was peaceful except for the worried look on Mallory's face.

"You okay?" Rafe asked.

"How I feel is all relative."

"Relative to what?" Rafe frowned.

"The moment. The minute." Mallory sighed. "Whatever stray thought pops into my head. I'm okay one second, and the next, I remember what's happening, and my heart pumps faster, my body fills up with adrenaline, and I start doing the mental fight-or-flight dance."

Rafe reached for her hand, and this time, she didn't pull away. "I'm so sorry for everything you've been through."

"Thank you." She leaned in closer and kissed him. It nearly took his breath away.

When she kissed him with more intention, he whispered,

"Mallory, if you're not ready to take this to the next level, then stop."

When she deepened the kiss, that was all the answer he needed. He scooped her up in his arms, and without taking his eyes off her, carried her to the bedroom.

As he gently lowered her to the bed, her arms wrapped around his neck, and her legs encircled his waist. He hovered over her. Kissing her mouth, her chin, her neck. Her body pressed against his hardness.

"Your jeans?" she whispered.

He didn't need to be asked twice.

She helped him with the buckle and slipped her hand inside and held him. He thought he'd lose it right there. He gently removed her hand. He wanted this to last longer than a minute. He slowly unbuttoned each button on her shirt, and when he saw the lace of her bra, he smiled. His teeth moved the fabric to the side, and his mouth descended onto her breast.

She moaned and arched her back, giving him better access. His hand traveled to the center of her core, gently stroking.

"Condom," she whispered.

Forcing himself to break away, he rolled over to the other side of the bed, reached inside the bedside table, and pulled one out. "My brother keeps a stash. Don't ask."

Mallory giggled, and her eyes softened.

"You're so beautiful," Rafe said, and those were the last words he spoke.

Mallory opened her eyes and turned on her side to find Rafe gone. She must have fallen asleep. She stretched, feeling relaxed, before she remembered about the computer. Making love with Rafe had been blissful. But also dangerous. She'd forgotten how tender and exciting it was to be with a man she cared about. Rafe always had a habit of making her forget where she was. And tonight was no exception. For a time, her mind had been completely wrapped up in him. She smiled, then internally admonished herself for losing her edge or even forgetting why she was here in the first place. She needed to stay sharp and keep focused.

After throwing the covers off, she quickly got dressed and went into the living room.

"There you are." Rafe smiled wide.

Mallory looked at her feet, feeling the blush creeping up her face. "I must have fallen asleep."

"Don't worry. There's another eleven minutes before the transfer is complete." Rafe kissed her on the cheek. "Want something to drink?"

"Water. Please." She walked over to the table and took her place in front of the computer. Tapping her foot on the floor, she kept her gaze glued to the screen while the progress bar inched down second by second until the transfer was complete.

When he set the water glass down beside her, Mallory avoided his gaze, embarrassed she'd let things get so far. She was aware she was withdrawing but was physically and mentally incapable of stopping it. They had no future together. Trusting any man, even Rafe, was asking too much of her emotionally. After years of living with abuse, it was the only way she knew to protect herself. Rafe would never understand. How could he?

The computer chimed, bringing her back. "I think it's done. Do I wait for you to unhook the cables?" Her words were clipped and emotionless. She didn't want him to get the wrong impression that what they'd done was a forever thing.

"Uh, yeah." Rafe reached over her shoulders to get at the cables, leaning his chin on top of her head.

Mallory wiggled out from under him and stood. "I'll get out of your way." She saw the hurt in his eyes. If there was time, she would have explained what she was feeling. But that wasn't a luxury they had. They'd already wasted four hours.

Rafe stepped away from the table. "All yours."

Mallory sat. "Thanks."

It took a few more minutes to unhook the connections, for Rafe to check the backup computer, and for Mallory to confirm that everything had been copied. Once she was satisfied, Rafe shut down the backup laptop and placed it in the backpack.

They'd finally arrived at the moment they'd been waiting for. "Here goes." She held her breath as she pushed the tiny nano drive into a slot at the side of the laptop. A rainbow-colored circle appeared and began spinning. Mallory moved in closer, and Rafe was leaning on her chair, looking over her shoulder.

The swirling ball stopped, and the computer screen went black. Mallory gasped. "No. What happened? No, no, no," Mallory yelled. She was about to hit the enter key when the screen came back to life, and a single document appeared. She put her fingers on the trackpad and began to scroll. There were hundreds and hundreds of sequences of letters and numbers.

"Well, he didn't make it easy," Mallory said.

"What do you mean?" Rafe asked.

"This may, in fact, be the key, but it doesn't spell anything out. I'm going to have to do some digging back in the original folders."

"I don't get it," Rafe said. "I thought this would be the answer."

Mallory held up an index finger and shook her head, her eyes never leaving the screen.

"The bastard." Rafe shoved his hands in his pockets.

"Apparently, the key works if you know what you're looking for," Mallory said.

"Of course," Rafe said and punched his fist against the doorjamb of the bedroom.

"Please, let me think. I need a minute. I have to put myself into Blake's mind and see how this all comes together." Mallory looked up. "Maybe you should wait outside."

Rafe looked surprised, but Mallory didn't have the patience for explanation or civility. "Out. Now. Seriously, I need quiet. I have to concentrate."

Rafe didn't move, but his reluctance was no match for her stare. He finally turned, grabbed his jacket, and left.

Mallory picked up a pencil and the spreadsheets she'd been working on earlier. Moving her gaze from screen to spreadsheet, she had to push away the feeling that this was an impossible task. She went through the same procedure as before—writing down numbers, checking the screen, and then going back to the beginning of the column and checking again. Twenty minutes had passed when Rafe stuck his head in the door.

"Out!" Mallory demanded without looking up.

Forty more minutes crawled by before she finally put the pencil down and pushed her chair away from the table. To the casual observer, it looked as if she were thinking. But Mallory's hands were shaking, her throat was dry, and her heart was racing.

She'd not only cracked the code, but she almost wished she hadn't.

What she had in front of her were account numbers, the location of billions of dollars in various offshore accounts, and where the money had been transferred. Mallory stared at the names on the accounts, barely able to breathe. In her wildest thoughts, she never could have imagined that Blake would be involved in such an enterprise.

In her possession was concrete evidence of dozens and dozens of names of known arms dealers, terrorist organizations, and several government officials who were responsible for the disruption of foreign governments, bombings, drug smuggling, human trafficking, and cybercrime. A ripple of fear crawled up her spine. These were the kinds of people who would have no trouble getting rid of her, and anyone she had ever known, without a moment's hesitation.

Mallory nearly jumped out of her seat when the door opened.

"You okay?" Rafe hung his jacket on the peg and walked toward her. "What did you find?" Rafe knelt in front of her and grabbed her hands. "You're ice cold. Mallory, what's happening?"

Mallory physically shuddered and took in a breath. "I am not okay. None of us is okay. What's on there—" she nodded toward the laptop "—is evidence of money laundering and criminality that goes as high as you can possibly get in government. And right now, I'm in so deep, and I don't think anyone can protect me if they found out what I now know. In fact, I'm not sure who we can trust."

"Mallory, start at the beginning. What did you find?" Rafe said.

"I cracked the code. Once I did that, the documents became accessible. And…well…have a look." Mallory stood and motioned to the laptop.

Rafe leaned over the table and passed his fingers over the trackpad waking the screen. Mallory leaned against the wall, watching his expression as it went from non-comprehension to shock and then to what she was sure was disbelief. Those had been the gamut of emotions she'd experienced when she went through the documents.

"Son of a bitch." Rafe slammed his hand on the table. "This is…this is…this is…"

"*Extraordinary? Unbelievable? Criminal?* Are those the words you're looking for?"

"Actually, there are no words," Rafe said.

"Well, I've had a few more minutes to digest this, and I have a few thoughts." Mallory moved closer to Rafe. "I think we're in more danger now than we were before we broke into that laptop." Mallory raked her hands through her hair and let out a defeated sigh. "The fact that some-one from our government is involved… Well, I think we have a situation. And I personally have no idea how to get out of it. None."

"Take it easy, Mallory. It's not the entire government. It's one person." He wrapped his arms around her.

She pushed him away. "Do not tell me to take it easy! And please, do not try and comfort me. Right now, that's an impossible task." Mallory chewed on her thumbnail and paced the length of the room. Everyone in Rafe's family and her daughter were in danger. Any one of the people listed on those spreadsheets could be after her. The thought was terrifying.

"Listen, let's take a moment to think," Rafe said.

"If you have a suggestion that gets these criminals be-hind bars until they die and keeps us safe, without having to hide in witness protection, I'm all ears. Because I'm thinking that's the only way we get out of this alive." Mallory's voice took on a shrill quality, and Rafe went to her.

"Don't, Rafe. Don't try and comfort me. Please. If anything, this is a time to stay alert and be ready for anything. I don't need your comfort. I need solutions. Last week, this felt like a bad dream, but I know better now. This is a living nightmare. And I feel as if I'm never going to wake up." Mallory rubbed at a burning sensation in her chest. "We are dealing with very, very bad men. Men who will stop at nothing to get at what we have. We've stepped into some deep—"

"Shh." Rafe looked around. "Do you hear that? How could a phone be ringing?"

Chapter 16

Following the sound, Rafe ran into the bedroom. He threw the covers to the floor in search of the muffled ringing. Kneeling, he looked under the bed and spied the phone. Reaching with his fingers, he pulled it toward him and pressed the talk button.

"Get the heck out of there now! You've been tracked." Max's voice came screaming through the receiver. "Don't say anything. Get out. Call me when you get to where you're going." The call went dead.

With quick precision, Rafe dislodged the battery. He'd turned to find Mallory in the doorway, hand over her mouth.

"Did you use the phone?" His voice was steely.

She nodded.

"They've found us. No time to discuss now." He stormed past her and into the dining area.

"I'm sorry," Mallory cried. "I...I...had to speak to Justine. I forgot to take the battery out."

"We need to pack up now!"

"That's all you're going to say?" Mallory asked.

Rafe practically bit his tongue, suppressing his rage. Anything he said now would be cruel. He'd told her not to call her daughter. It wasn't safe. Maybe he could forgive that. But to leave the battery in the phone—that was careless, bordering on reckless. It was the kind of disregard that might lead the criminals directly to them.

"Please. Rafe, say something. It was a mistake."

Rafe remained silent, moving with speed and determination throughout the house, gathering the equipment and spreadsheets, and unplugging the laptop. He grabbed the two backpacks and shoved everything inside. "Don't bother to pack. Just put on your sneakers." Mallory didn't move, seemingly frozen in place. "Mallory, go. Now."

The look on Mallory's face telegraphed her fear. He wasn't sure if she was afraid of him or the situation. Either way, there was no time to dissect feelings. He needed to come up with a plan.

Within minutes, Rafe had the backpacks stuffed and ready, as Mallory walked back in from the bedroom.

"Grab one." Rafe strapped a backpack onto his shoulders. He picked up the phone and reinserted the battery.

"What are you doing?" Mallory asked.

"Insurance," Rafe said, placing the phone on the table. "Whoever traced us will still think we're here. Let's go."

Mallory headed toward the front door.

"We're not taking the car. We're on foot." Without waiting for her response, he opened the sliding doors to the deck. It was nearly two in the morning, the quarter moon providing little light. "Stay close behind me."

Mallory nodded.

They made their way up the path, away from the lake and toward the surrounding woods. The wilderness seemed to swallow them instantly, and Rafe turned on the flashlight. "We need to get to Saranac. It's about nine miles west. We can get help there."

"Help?" Mallory said. "But we don't know who we can trust."

Rafe couldn't read her face in the darkness, but he could hear the tremble in her voice. As angry as he was, the situation called for them to work as a team. At least until they could get some help. He let out a deep breath and, with it, some of his anger. "We can trust my brothers and my cousins. That's who we'll call. They'll help us figure this out. For now, we need to stay two steps ahead of whoever has tracked us."

Within thirty minutes, they were in the dense forest on a steep rise. Mallory was having difficulty keeping up with Rafe. Given that she'd put them in this mess, she wasn't about to tell him to slow down. Gritting her teeth, she matched him stride for stride as they made their way up the seemingly endless incline. Rafe asked her if she wanted to stop and rest. But she waved him off. "I'm good."

They continued upward, and her breath came in raspy gasps that seemed to echo in the forest. They passed towering pines and birch trees that looked like ghosts in the dull moonlight. The shriek of an owl sounding so much like a human cry made her stumble.

"You okay?" Rafe whispered.

"Yes." She bent over and placed her hands on her thighs. The sweat dripping down her back against the cool night air made her shiver. "I need a minute." Mallory took in a deep breath, telling herself these nocturnal forest sounds were normal. The fact that she happened to be on their turf at this time of night wasn't comforting. But she needed to buck up. It was imperative they get to Saranac no matter what.

"I'm ready. Let's keep going." She took hold of Rafe's hand and continued upward. The thin sneakers she wore were no match for the forest floor. It felt as if she were barefoot, stepping on every rock, pine cone, branch, seed, stone, and nut. Her jaw tightened in determination, and she continued forward. She would not be the reason they didn't make it to Saranac.

They hiked for what seemed like an hour before Rafe abruptly stopped.

"I can keep going. We don't need to stop." Mallory was breathing heavily.

"I think we may have veered off course slightly." Rafe pulled back the sleeve of his jacket and checked the compass on his smartwatch. "Looks like we're going a bit more north than west. We need to double back a few hundred feet."

In the distance, they heard twigs snap, and they both froze. Rafe grabbed Mallory's hand and put a finger over her mouth, signaling they should remain quiet. Another snapping sound and her heart caught in her throat. The forest seemed to be an echo chamber. She couldn't tell what direction the sound came from or its distance. She looked around, but the dense foliage made it impossible to see anything.

Rafe tugged on Mallory's hand. Without warning, he shoved her under some nearby underbrush and huddled beside her. Her heart hammered in her chest, and she put her hand over her mouth to stifle the sound of her ragged breath.

They waited without moving for what seemed like an eternity. More minutes passed, and the silence was all-consuming except for the whooshing sound of blood in her ears.

She wondered if maybe they'd imagined someone was there, or it was an animal in the woods. And then, to prove her wrong, came the unmistakable sound of human feet walking on the forest floor. From a distance, she saw a flashlight beam. She closed her eyes in the childlike hope that no one would see her. Rafe held her hand, and she held her breath.

They waited. Slowly, she opened her eyes. From her vantage point, Mallory couldn't see anyone, but she could feel him—a malevolent shadow inching closer, her heart rate accelerating with each passing second. It took every ounce of willpower not to bolt and run. Rafe's steadying hand was the only thing keeping her grounded.

Sitting on the back of her legs was becoming uncomfortable, and her feet were beginning to fall asleep. She desperately wanted to get the blood circulating, but a movement of any kind might alert whoever was out there.

When she spied the worn hiking boots of the pursuer, about fifty feet away, she held her breath. The flashlight beam seemed to be circling the area, and she prayed they were far enough into the underbrush not to be found. Rafe's hand on hers was a lifeline of sanity because she was sure she was about to go crazy with fear. Squeezing her eyes shut, she thought about Justine. About getting back to her and holding her and smothering her with motherly kisses.

When she opened her eyes, the beam of light seemed to be moving up the mountain, away from them. She could still hear the pursuer's receding footsteps. Rafe's arm went across her chest to hold her in place, sensing she was about to bolt.

Another eternity passed before Rafe whispered in her ear. "Follow me and do what I do."

Mallory nodded and watched as Rafe got on his side and silently rolled out from the underbrush. She followed suit, and when he grabbed her hand to help her up, her legs collapsed. The numbness of pins and needles was the only feeling. She lay there trying to massage some life into her right leg.

Rafe knelt and massaged the other leg. Together, they worked without saying a word. Her gaze darted around, making sure they were alone. When she could feel a sensation in her toes, she gave Rafe a thumbs-up, and he helped her to her feet. This time, she remained standing.

Once again, Rafe checked the direction on his compass. He took hold of Mallory's hand, and they wordlessly traveled west. This portion of the forest was a dense canopy of trees with barely a sliver of moonlight coming through. There were no trails, and they were forced to push the branches out of their way while the undergrowth grabbed at their ankles. Without any real tread on the soles of her sneakers, Mallory slipped several times on the mossy ground.

When they finally reached the top of the hill, they could see the glow of soft lights in the distance.

"That's Saranac." Rafe spoke low. "Another four miles or so, and we're there. It's all downhill now."

It didn't matter what direction they were going, uphill or down. Every one of Mallory's muscles screamed in protest.

For the last mile, the backpack had begun to feel like it was filled with a hundred-pound weight instead of a spare laptop. She could feel a wet ooze in her sneakers. She couldn't see in this light, but she was certain it was blood. Regardless of how battered she felt, she would not give up. She would not slow Rafe down. Not until they were safe. If she could hang on, and make it down the hill, then there would be time to tend to her aching body.

The forest was denser on this side of the hill. As they continued their descent, she found she was battling low-hanging branches that scratched the sides of her face, tangled in her hair, and snagged on her jean jacket. Just as she was getting the hang of the rhythm and pace of the descent, Rafe came to a sudden stop, and she nearly toppled him over. They both stood still and remained quiet until she heard it. Footsteps coming from behind.

Rafe grabbed her hand and pulled her along as they took off running. They ran over roots and ducked under low-hanging branches that ripped at her clothes. Mallory's heart beat like a war drum as they raced down the mountain.

The sound of their assailant's footsteps getting closer, adrenaline spurring her on. She turned her head to see how close he was, and without warning, she tripped over a rock. Letting go of Rafe's hand, she fell and rolled over on her side. The searing pain seemed to travel from her ankle to the top of her head.

"Come on, Mallory," Rafe whisper-shouted.

"I can't. I think it's broken." She cradled her foot, willing herself not to cry, but the intensity of the pain was almost unbearable. She pressed her lips together, forcing herself not to scream.

With no time to waste, Rafe scooped her in his arms and carried her. His heart hammered in his chest as he ran. Before long, he knew he couldn't keep the pace needed to outrun their assailant. Not with Mallory and the two backpacks. He needed to find a place to hide.

Veering off to the left, he charged back up the treacherous slope. He had to lose whoever was chasing them.

"Where are you going?" Mallory asked.

Rafe couldn't speak, so he shook his head. She seemed to understand he could either carry her and run or stop and talk.

He continued for several yards until he came to a small ridge that appeared to be flat ground. The trail was going in the opposite direction from the town, but he needed to find some shelter until he could assess if Mallory could walk. Hopefully, their assailant wouldn't guess they were no longer headed for Saranac.

He traveled the ridge for several more yards until it came to an abrupt end with two enormous boulders sitting in the middle of the path, halting any further progress. They were co-joined at the top, with a cavelike opening at the base. It wasn't passable, but it could serve as a place to hide until he could figure out their next step.

He set Mallory down inside the makeshift cave.

"I'll be right back."

"Where are you going?"

Rafe looked around. "You can't make it down the hill, and we're too exposed out here. I need to find something to conceal us until I can figure out our next move. I won't be long."

He didn't have to go far before he found several large rocks he could roll into place, building a blockade in front of them but leaving a little more than a foot at the top to ensure they didn't suffocate.

Putting the last rock in place, he sat back and turned on his flashlight.

Mallory covered her eyes, and he lowered the beam.

Gingerly, he pushed back the pant leg and saw the swelling and discoloration. "I have no idea if it's broken or if it's a very bad sprain."

"While you were building this fort, I moved my ankle. It's painful. No question. But if I can wrap it, I think I can make it the rest of the way. We have to try."

Rafe raised an eyebrow. "Wrap it with what?"

She pulled the bottom of her blouse out of her jeans. "Does that flashlight come with a Swiss Army knife?"

Rafe shook his head. "No, but I actually have one of those." He reached into the inside of his jacket and pulled out a knife.

"Cut the bottom off. We'll use it as a wrap."

Rafe did as instructed and now held a long strip of material in his hand. "You know if you take your sneaker off, that things going to blow up like a balloon."

"What choice do I have?"

"You'll never get that sneaker back on, and you'll need it to get down the hill." Rafe tried to think. He needed her to be able to walk. There was no way he could carry her the rest of the way. "We'll wrap it with the sneaker on. It will at least give you some support."

The flashlight beam caught the skepticism and fear in Mallory's eyes.

"I promise. We're going to make it to town. We're going to get help. You'll see Justine again. And we are going to get out of this mess."

"That's a lot of promises, Rafe."

"And I intend to live up to them." He lifted her leg onto his lap and began wrapping the material around the sneaker.

Mallory gasped.

"Sorry." Rafe stopped for a moment. "Hang on, I need to get this tight, so it'll support you."

Mallory closed her eyes and took in a deep breath.

Rafe wrapped the material around the sneaker a few more times and gently placed her foot back on the ground. "There. Finished."

"Thanks."

Their hiding place wasn't tall enough for Mallory to

stand, so they had no way of knowing if she could walk. Rafe prayed it would hold.

"Now what?" Mallory asked.

"I think we wait until dawn. I have a feeling whoever is pursuing us doesn't want to be seen in the light of day." Rafe pulled back his sleeve and looked at his watch. "It's four o'clock. Sun should be up in another two hours. Why don't you get some rest?"

"Rest?" Mallory scoffed.

The sudden spine-chilling scream startled them into silence. A second primal scream reverberated through the air.

"What is that?" Mallory's gaze darted around.

"Bobcat," Rafe shouted to be heard over another hair-raising scream by the predator right outside their makeshift barricade. "At least, I think so."

Rafe stiffened at the sound of something climbing the rocks toward the small opening at the top. In a moment, two hazel eyes glared back at him, and a claw swiped into the opening several times.

"What do we do?" Mallory backed as far away as she could as the growls grew louder.

"Stay still. Do not look at him. Bow your head and force yourself to slow your breathing. If we play dead, maybe he'll go." Rafe only hoped that was true. He had zero experience being up close to a bobcat. He only knew what they sounded like, and right now this one was too close for comfort.

At first, the snarls and growls only grew louder and more exasperated. Rafe could almost sense the animal's frustration. In time, the growls became guttural purrs. But Rafe didn't dare look up and barely took a breath. He had no idea how much time had passed, but eventually, there was only silence. "Don't move," Rafe whispered under his breath.

There was no telling what was beyond the rocks—was the animal gone, or only playing a cat-and-mouse game, ready to pounce as soon as they poked their heads out?

Streaks of dawn peeked through the opening as Rafe slowly lifted his head. Despite the uncertainty of what awaited them, man or beast, he knew they had to take their chances and leave the cave and make it into town. By removing one of the rocks at the top, he was able to peek through the opening. With no way of knowing if it was safe or not. He opted to trust his gut that, for the moment, they were alone, and all nocturnal creatures had decided to rest, leaving them the opportunity to get down the mountain.

One by one, he removed the rocks forming the barricade until the opening was cleared. The early morning daylight streamed in, magnifying the weariness in Mallory's eyes and the dried blood on the side of her face, evidence of their fight during the night with the naked tree branches as they ran through the woods.

"Are you okay to go on?"

She nodded. "I have to be." Her tired smile didn't reach her eyes.

"Come on. Let's get you out of here." He crawled out, then reached in and helped her slide out of the cave. He helped her stand. "Lean against the rock for support. I'll be right back." Without giving her the opportunity to say anything, he stepped away from their temporary shelter and walked a few feet into a wooded area, searching the forest floor for a branch of some kind that could serve as a crutch. Within minutes, he found a fallen tree, some of its branches scattered around. He selected one that appeared sturdy enough, about four inches in diameter and over five feet tall. Too tall, he thought; she could accidentally poke an eye out with a misstep. Resting his foot on the tree trunk, he placed the branch across his knee and tried to snap off about twelve inches of the branch. The veins in his neck bulged as he asserted more pressure until the piece finally snapped off.

When he returned, he found Mallory leaning against the wall. Her eyes drooped. "Mallory. Wake up. Come on. Use this as a crutch." He placed the branch in her hand. "Here, put your other arm around my shoulder. This will give you the support you need. It's a steep slope."

As they made their way slowly down the mountain, Rafe checked behind him every few yards to see if they were being followed. Something was amiss. There had to be a reason whoever was trailing them had vanished.

"Look, Rafe. The village. Oh, thank goodness."

Early morning smoke rose from several chimneys, and Rafe could see cars traveling on the road. Relief flooded through him. He could almost taste safety. "We'll head straight for the police station and call my brothers from there."

When they finally made it to the police station, Mallory collapsed onto a bench just inside the door. The large clock against the opposite wall indicated it was barely six thirty in the morning. Patches of the gray linoleum floor were still wet with bleach, and the smell permeated the air. The waist-high wooden partition separated the five utilitarian desks from the small waiting area. Only one desk was occupied. The nameplate read Jenna Bower, Receptionist. The look of alarm on the round-faced woman told Mallory everything she needed to know.

Covered in dirt, with visible scrapes and bruises, she and Rafe appeared more like fugitives on the run.

"We need help." Rafe stepped forward, his voice urgent.

Jenna flinched. Her gaze moved from their hands to their backpacks. Without taking her eyes off them, she picked up the phone and pressed a button. "Sheriff, you need to come out here. Right now."

From the back of the room, a frosted glass door opened and a burly, bald-headed man over six feet tall hurried toward them, his hand resting on the butt of his gun. "What the hell is going on? I'm Sheriff Michael Mitchell. Who the hell are you two?"

The sensation they'd stepped from one bad experience and into another nearly had Mallory in tears. Mentally, she recoiled from the lawman with his finger inches from the trigger. This place felt anything but safe. She would provide only the essential details, enough information so they could quickly get back to Justine and Rafe's family. She relayed the details of their harrowing night in the woods and explained they had no idea who their assailant was but needed to get back to Saratoga Springs so she could pick up her daughter.

The sheriff's wrinkled forehead and pursed lips told her he was skeptical.

Mallory didn't care what he thought or what she had to endure as long as he hurried up and helped get her back to her daughter.

"I'm gonna have to see some ID. And I'm going to have a couple of my deputies take a ride over to that mountain. Take a look around the trails." The side table against the wall held two-way radio equipment. He issued instructions through the handset and when he was finished, replaced it back on the receiver. "Now, why don't you hand over a driver's license or something that tells me who you folks are."

They did as they were told.

"Jenna, please run these." He turned back to Rafe. "Real gentle, take off the backpack, and slide it right over here."

Rafe did as instructed.

The sheriff turned to Mallory. "Now, your turn."

Rafe went toward her to help.

"Nuh-uh. Stay right there," the sheriff said.

Mallory saw the glint of mistrust in his eyes. She hurried to remove the backpack. In too much pain to stand, she kicked it over with her good foot.

"All right now," he said to Rafe, "you sit over there by your girlfriend while I have a look."

The expression on Rafe's face mirrored how she felt—trapped and anxious.

Without ever taking his eyes off them, the sheriff placed both backpacks on one of the empty desks. He pulled out a laptop and opened the cover. Mallory took in a sharp breath. "Hey—"

Rafe put a hand on her forearm and shook his head.

She sat back, pressing her lips firmly against each other. While she understood the need for the sheriff to be cautious and in control, she couldn't afford for him to mistakenly press the wrong button on the laptop and erase anything or damage the information they had.

"Sherriff, I think you want to see this." The receptionist peeked out from behind her desktop computer screen.

"Can it wait?" He pulled the spreadsheets from the backpack.

"It most certainly cannot." Her voice was urgent.

Mallory squeezed Rafe's hand and turned to him.

His furrowed brow communicated he hadn't a clue what was happening.

The sheriff took two quick steps to his receptionist's desk and looked over her shoulder. Mallory watched as his expression turned from annoyed to surprised, his eyebrows raising a considerable inch.

The sheriff cleared his throat. "Uh, Mr. Ramirez. You need to call your brother Max. It's urgent. The FBI's with him. You can use the phone on that desk."

"What the hell is going on?" Mallory stood, and instantly, her leg buckled. The pain shot through her.

Rafe turned to her. "Mallory."

She waved him off. "I'm okay. Call Max now."

"Sheriff, do you have any first aid back there? Her ankle's pretty bad off."

The sheriff nodded and headed to the back. Rafe raced to the phone on the desk but didn't lift the receiver.

"Rafe, what in God's name are you waiting for?" Mallory slammed her palm down on the bench. "Call now."

He scrubbed his face with a hand. "I call up favorites on my phone. I don't know Max's phone number by heart."

Perspiration formed on Rafe's upper lip. What wasn't the sheriff saying? He looked over at the receptionist, whose frown only reinforced that something wasn't right. "What is going on? What's on that computer screen of yours?" He took a step toward her, and Jenna pushed back, the wheels of her chair moving her a foot away.

"Hey, hey. What's going on?" the sheriff said as he approached with what looked like a first-aid kit. "Step away from there, Mr. Ramirez." He put his hand on the butt of his gun.

The sheriff had used that intimidating move before, and Rafe thought it did the job. He backed up. "Listen. I need to know what you saw that has made both you and your receptionist jumpy."

"Call your brother."

"I'd really like to do that, but I don't know his number by heart."

"Oh damn. Smartphones make everyone dumb." Sheriff Mitchell gave his receptionist a weary look. "Give them the number here. Tell them to call." He passed through the swinging Dutch door and settled next to Mallory.

"Why not just tell me," Rafe demanded.

The sheriff didn't answer. Calmly, as if he had all the time in the world, he lifted Mallory's leg and placed it across his lap. After removing the dirty makeshift bandage, he cleaned the area with rubbing alcohol. Then he cracked open an instant ice pack and placed it on her ankle.

The ring of the phone startled Rafe, and the sheriff nodded.

Rafe picked up the receiver. "Max, what's going on? Is everyone okay?" Rafe listened, and the blood drained from his face.

"What? What's he saying?" Mallory yelled.

Rafe held up a hand, then held it over his ear so he could hear Max more clearly. The call lasted only a few minutes. When he hung up the receiver, he turned and went to Mallory. Taking both her hands in his, he looked straight into her eyes. "Blake kidnapped Justine."

Chapter 17

"What are you saying? Blake's dead." Mallory's voice had an eerily calm quality.

"Apparently, he's not. And now he has your daughter. You get her back when you give him the drive."

Her eyes filled with tears, and she covered her mouth with her hand.

Rafe could see she was trying to process what he said.

"How? How did this happen?" Tears streamed down her face.

"At the moment, there are a lot of unknowns. The FBI's still trying to figure it out. But he left a note. He directed Max and Zack to get back to Hollow Lake, and he'd give further instructions once we arrived."

"How did the FBI get involved?"

"This is a kidnapping case, and it involves Blake Stanton. They had to be called in."

The far-off look in her eyes told him she might be in shock. He put his hand on the back of her neck and pressed his cheek to hers. "We're going to get her back. I promise."

They were driven to an empty field ten miles out of town where an FBI helicopter took them back to Hollow Lake.

The moment Mallory and Rafe stepped off the elevator at the RMZ offices, they were greeted by Zack and Max.

"Oh, thank god you're here," Zack said, pulling them both into a hug.

"Never mind about us. Tell me exactly what's happening. Any word on Justine? How long has she been gone?" Mallory's words came out in a rush.

Zack gently put his hand on her forearm. She saw the concern in his eyes and understood the entire family was upset.

"*Tía* Claudia put her to bed at around seven thirty. She checked on her around nine, and that's when she discovered Justine was gone. A note was left with the demands you already know about." Zack shoved his hands in his pockets. "Jack and Andres were there, and they called the FBI."

With a house full of adults, including Rafe's detective cousins, she had a hard time understanding how this had happened. And as quickly as she had that thought, she remembered that her dead husband wasn't dead. He was as devious as ever. If he'd managed to have an entire plane and its black box disappear, then he could get past several adults and take her sleeping daughter in the night.

"So what happens now?" Mallory took in the scene. The low hum of at least a dozen men and women talking on phones, typing on tablets, all stationed around the common office area beyond the reception desk. Some wore badges that hung on chains around their necks, identifying them as agents. Others were dressed in dark blue T-shirts with the unmistakable yellow letters *F-B-I* emblazoned across their chests. Mallory stiffened. "Why so many?"

"This is Blake Stanton we're talking about," Max said, as if his simple explanation were enough to warrant what appeared to be over a dozen agents. "They've been here for hours."

"Let's head back." Zack nodded toward the conference room. "The head of the investigation is going to fill us in.

All we know right now is they're setting up wiretaps on the phones."

"Wiretaps?" Mallory asked.

"According to the FBI, this is a hostage situation. The next move is Blake's, and he'll make demands on where to drop off the drive. They're hoping to have the tap on the phones up and running before his next call," Max informed them.

Mallory took a step to follow the brothers but nearly fell. She put a hand on the wall and lowered her head, squeezing her eyes shut, waiting for the pain to dissipate.

"Mallory?" Rafe stepped in front of her and cupped her chin in his hand. "What's the matter?"

"My ankle. It's…"

Rafe lifted the hem of her jeans. "It's still pretty badly swollen." He put his arm around her waist. "Lean on me."

"I'll get some ice." Zack headed toward the kitchen.

"I don't have time for this," Mallory complained.

"I get it. There's a lot going on—" Rafe spoke in a hushed tone "—but take a deep breath. Come on. Let's go in and find out what they know."

They entered the conference room, the smell of stale coffee already filling the air. Two FBI agents were set up at the head of the table. Rafe settled Mallory in a chair.

"This is Agent Robert Byron," Max said, pointing to a tall, thin man wearing an open-collared light blue button-down shirt and jeans.

Agent Byron nodded and turned to a red-headed woman wearing dark-framed glasses. She barely acknowledged them as she continued talking on the phone. "That's Agent Shore. She's the lead on the case and will fill you in." He went back to typing something on his tablet.

Zack came in with a fresh ice pack. "Here you go."

"Thanks." Mallory rested her ankle on the seat of a nearby chair. "Can you please place it right on top?"

"Sure thing." Zack rested the ice pack on the outside of her ankle and took a seat next to Max. The four of them waited.

Mallory settled back in the seat and tapped her other foot on the wood floor, waiting anxiously for the agent to end her call. When it appeared the agent wasn't in a hurry, Mallory began drumming her fingers on the table one after the other. The gentle touch of Rafe's hand on her forearm stilled her.

She followed every movement Agent Shore made as she rose from the chair, turned, and faced the window, continuing her phone conversation in whispered tones. Her trim frame had the physique of an athlete. Mallory thought she couldn't be more than thirty years old. If that. She looked so much younger than Agent Byron or, for that matter, any of the agents Mallory passed in the office common area.

She chewed her thumbnail raw, not sure how much longer she could wait to get answers.

Max checked his phone while Rafe peppered Zack with questions about Justine.

But Mallory had already been told about how Blake managed to take Justine and the ransom note he left. There wasn't any more information that Rafe's family could tell her. Justine had been gone for over twelve hours. She wanted to know what the authorities were doing now, in the present. From where she sat, it looked like a lot of nothing, and no one had given her any information since she arrived. Minute by minute, she was losing hold of her patience until she could no longer wait for answers. "Excuse me." Mallory slammed her hand on the table. "Agent Shore, are you ever going to get off that phone and tell me what the hell is going on with my daughter and how you plan on rescuing her?"

The room fell silent, and within seconds, the red-headed agent ended her call and turned to face Mallory. "I'm Agent Taylor Shore." She placed both hands on the table and leaned forward. "I understand you're very concerned, but we are doing everything we can."

"Concerned?" Mallory scoffed. "How 'bout Out. Of. My. Mind. This is my daughter."

Agent Shore held up a hand. "I get it." She pulled out a chair and sat. "Here's what we know and what, in all probability, will happen next."

"I'm listening." Her lower lip trembled.

"Blake said he knows you have the drive and is demanding it in exchange for your daughter. So, before we go any further, we want you to hand over that drive and tell us what's on it that would make Blake Stanton mysteriously rise from the dead and orchestrate a kidnapping." She leaned back, crossing her arms over her chest. "Please understand we have no intention of giving him what he wants. The bureau, along with several other organizations, has been watching him for years. That is before he quote, unquote died in a plane crash. We know what he's capable of. We just don't have concrete evidence. So, we're aware if he took your daughter, there's some pretty damning evidence on that drive. And we want it."

Mallory's mouth went dry, and she gave Rafe a sideways glance. Should she tell them what was on the drive? Could she trust any of them?

While she thought, a dissonant hum coursed through her body and settled in her bones. It was the hum of rage. Six years with an abusive husband, days on the run, discovering heinous crimes committed by people in power, a treacherous hike through the Adirondacks, and her daughter's kidnapping. She'd had enough. It had to stop now, or she was certain it would never stop.

"No." Mallory shook her head. Her voice was firm. "That's not how we're going to play this." The words were out of her mouth before she knew what she was saying. "First of all, I don't know what's on the drive. I wasn't able to open it," she lied. "Secondly, it's the only bargaining power I have."

Both agents looked astonished.

"How?" Taylor Shore asked.

"As you said, there must be some pretty damning evidence on that drive, and if I turn it over without getting my daughter back, I've lost everything in the world that means anything to me."

"But—"

Mallory raised a finger. "Hear me out, Agent Shore. You plan on giving Blake a fake drive anyway. Correct?"

The agent nodded.

"So. I'll keep the real one until I know that Blake is caught and that you'll protect me and my daughter. Then I'll turn it over." Mallory stared straight ahead, settled back in her chair, and crossed her arms over her chest. "Deal?"

Taylor Shore peered over the top of her glasses and glanced at Rafe.

"Don't look at him," Mallory said. "He doesn't know anything." Avoiding the agent's eyes, Mallory studied her clenched hands in her lap, willing herself to keep a neutral expression.

"Do you honestly believe he would hurt his own daughter?" Agent Byron asked.

"Without a doubt." Mallory's voice was devoid of emotion.

Agent Shore stood. "Seeing as time is of the essence—" she paused "—we have a deal."

Mallory let out a breath. She had to hold on to the hope that the FBI would catch Blake. She had to hope the people listed on the folders on the drive believed she knew nothing. Only then did she have a prayer of living a normal life with her daughter.

A broad-shouldered, dark-haired man stuck his head into the conference room. "We're ready."

Taylor Shore nodded. "Thanks, Agent Cain."

"Ready for what?" Mallory asked.

"Blake's note said he'd call Rafe's cell phone."

"Mine?" Rafe raised his eyebrows. "How does he even know my number?"

Agent Shore waved Agent Cain back in and held out her hand. She took hold of the slim black mobile phone. "This is yours?" she said to Rafe, holding up the case with his initials on the back.

Rafe nodded. "How did you get my phone?"

"Before you took off, you left it with your brother Max so that you wouldn't be tracked. Smart move."

"But why is Blake calling me? How does he even know me?"

"All good questions." She pushed the phone to the center of the table. "In fact, those are questions we were going to ask you."

Rafe frowned. "I haven't a clue." He looked over at Mallory as if she might have an answer.

Mallory shook her head. She was as astonished as Rafe looked.

"Hmm." Taylor Shore turned her attention to Mallory. "Mrs. Stanton. Do you know how your husband got Rafe's number or why he asked to speak to him?"

A brisk knock on the door stopped the questioning.

Agent Cain was on the other side of the glass, giving a thumbs-up.

"Okay. We've got the phone taps ready, so at least we'll be able to pinpoint his location when he calls." Agent Taylor sat forward. "If it comes to it, we'll need to show him something."

Mallory nodded.

Agent Byron placed a square canvas case in front of her and zipped it open. Inside were dozens of drives in all shapes and sizes. "Take a look. See if any in here matches what you have."

Mallory scanned each slot. "This is it." She pointed to an identical silver nano drive.

Rafe's phone buzzed on the table, and the room went still. Both agents put on headsets. The words *Unknown Caller* appeared on the screen. "It's him," Rafe said.

Agent Shore looked at her partner and then nodded for Rafe to answer.

Rafe grabbed the phone and swiped open the call. "Yeah."

"I'm going to assume the FBI has a trace on this call," came Blake's voice over the speaker.

An icy chill spread like branches of a tree across Mallory's back and shoulders. She never thought she'd hear that voice again. Thinking rationally was off the table. The white-hot rage nearly blinded her, and she wanted to leap into the phone and kill him with her bare hands. "Give me back my daughter," she screamed, hurling herself across the table and grabbing the phone.

"Ahhh. Darling. How are you?" Blake's voice, saccharin sweet, was eerily calm. "Have you recovered from your fall? How's your ankle?"

"You son of a bitch. I want my daughter now. She has nothing to do with this."

Rafe pulled her back into her seat and held on to her trembling shoulders.

Blake's cruel laugh echoed in the room. "Much as I'd like to spend time chatting, we have business to discuss. As I was saying, I'm sure you're with the FBI right now, and they're listening in."

Mallory shifted in her seat and looked at Agent Shore, whose expression was unreadable. She hadn't moved a facial muscle since the call began.

"I would expect nothing less," Blake continued. "I know your friends at the bureau are trying to trace this, but I've got this call bouncing off several different satellites, so it's not likely you'll be able to pinpoint my location. I didn't get to where I am by taking stupid chances, so I'll make this fast." A sound between a laugh and a sneer came through the phone.

Mallory cringed. That was the noise he made whenever he was about to "prove" to her he had the power.

"Turns out I have a few things to put into place before I'm ready for the exchange. I'll phone you tomorrow at nine a.m."

The line went dead.

The shocked silence reverberated in the room.

Mallory leaned her head back and let out a cry. Rafe turned her chair to face him and held her in his arms.

"What does this mean?" Zack asked.

Agent Shore took off her glasses and rubbed the bridge of her nose. "He's stalling."

"For what?" Max asked, leaning forward. "What kind of game is he playing?"

Agent Byron stood and paced the length of the table. "If

I had to guess, it sounds like what he needs to make his getaway hasn't fallen into place yet."

Agent Cain came back into the room, a sour expression on his face. He shook his head.

"Damn!" Agent Shore said. "We didn't get the trace."

Mallory tried to clear her head. Think the way Blake did. She was married to him for six years. He was always covering his tracks. His ability to lie convincingly was an art form.

"What if he disappears?" Zack said.

Mallory sat up and wiped her eyes. "That's not going to happen."

"How do you know that?" Zack asked.

"Because he doesn't have the drive. That's the whole point here. With that drive, he holds the power." Mallory cleared her throat. "With that drive, I have to assume he has enough ammunition to keep powerful people doing his bidding and keep himself alive." She squeezed Rafe's hand. "He'll call back. He needs us."

Agent Shore smiled. "I appreciate your candor and your confidence. And let's face it. You know him better than anyone."

"Yes. And I wish I didn't."

"So, now what?" Rafe asked.

"You've both had a rough couple of days." Agent Shore stood. "Let us continue to work on tracking him. Maybe we'll get lucky and catch him before he calls tomorrow. In the meantime, you should all go home and get some rest."

"Ha!" Mallory slowly rose from her chair. "I won't be able to rest until I have my daughter back." She looked at Rafe. "But I would like to take a shower. Can you take me back to Ellie's?"

Rafe nodded.

"We'll send some agents with each of you. Station them outside your homes," Agent Byron said. "Although, I don't think Mrs. Stanton should be on her own."

Mallory turned. "It's Ms. Kane."

Agent Byron coughed. "Understood."

"Don't worry. I'll stay with her tonight." Rafe inched closer to Mallory. "And I'll have my phone if you need to reach me."

Zack and Max stood. "We'll drive you."

Mallory and the three Ramirez brothers left the offices and drove the four blocks to Ellie's house.

Rafe held Mallory's hand in the back seat of Zack's car. The eerie silence unnerved him. But he couldn't think of what to say that would allay any of their fears. Mercifully, the ride to Ellie's house was short. When Zack pulled up, Rafe got out of the car and helped Mallory onto the curb. He leaned into the passenger side window. "Thanks, guys."

"Oh, we're coming in with you," Max scoffed.

"Nah, man. I got this." Rafe said. *"No te preocupes."*

"Don't worry?" Max clicked open his seatbelt. "We're way past that. Move out of the way."

Rafe stepped aside, knowing this wasn't the time to argue with his brothers.

Zack turned off the ignition and got out of the car. "We stocked Ellie's refrigerator before you got here. We're going to stay long enough to make sure you eat something and get some rest." He looked over at Mallory. "Well, as much rest as you can get, considering we're waiting on a madman to get back to us with his instructions." Zack marched up the porch steps, took the key from his front pocket, opened the door, and waved Mallory in.

Rafe came up behind Mallory, who stood in the foyer,

not moving. He walked around, facing her. Her glazed-over eyes worried him. She looked slightly catatonic. "Mallory. You okay?"

"Hmm."

Her response wasn't encouraging. "I know you're worried." Rafe looked at his brothers. "We all are. I'm not sure there's more we can do until Blake calls back."

"I know." Mallory's voice was barely above a whisper. She dropped her backpack onto the floor.

The concern for Mallory's state of mind was beginning to grow. Rafe never imagined he'd ever see Mallory this defeated. He raised his eyebrow and glanced once more at Max and Zack, silently asking them for help.

"Hey, bro." Max put his hand on Rafe's shoulder. "You both need to eat something. We'll get it ready. But first, why don't you help Mallory upstairs? I'm sure she'd like to get cleaned up."

Max was right. Maybe that's all she needed. They were both a little worse for wear after their flight through the mountains. "Come on, Mallory. Let's get upstairs, and you can take a shower. You'll feel better." He knew the words were wrong the moment they were out. She wasn't going to feel better until her daughter was safely back in her arms. "I mean—"

"I know what you meant." Her tone was lifeless. Dull. "I'm sure I smell. I'll wash up so I don't offend anyone."

"Here." Rafe handed the backpacks to Zack. "Don't let them out of your sight." He turned and climbed the stairs behind Mallory.

She went into the room she'd stayed in at the beginning of this ordeal and sat on the edge of the bed.

Rafe wanted to go to her but stopped himself. He'd been sitting on a question since they left the FBI at his office. Why had Mallory decided to keep the real drive? Why had she lied and said she hadn't opened it and that he didn't know anything about it? Clearly, she had her reasons. But he wasn't sure she was thinking straight. She probably needed a minute to herself—alone with her thoughts. She'd been through so much in the last few days. It was a lot for anyone to take in. The fact that his head hadn't exploded was a miracle. He couldn't imagine what she must be going through. Before this night was over, he was going to find out what she was thinking.

For now, there wasn't much any of them could do but wait for Blake to make his next demand. Rafe let out a heavy sigh and headed into his cousin's old room, where there were several pairs of jeans and some shirts hanging in the closet. Ellie kept clothes for Rafe and his brothers to change into whenever they did work around her house. Of course, they never needed to change. They'd simply perform whatever chore needed doing, then head home to change because they all lived so close to one another. He suspected Ellie liked the clothes hanging in the closet because it made her feel less alone. For whatever reason, he was happy to have something clean to change into. He pulled a pair of black jeans from a hanger and a dark blue shirt. As he was closing the closet, he saw the tip of a boot at the back. "What have we here?" Bending down, he reached into the back of the closet and grabbed the tip of the boot by the laces, knocking over a couple of shoe boxes in the process. "So this is where you got to." In his hands, he held his old work boots. He smiled, remembering he'd done some repairs on the back porch and needed more than sneakers as protection for his feet in case a hammer or heavy board slipped from his hands. What he couldn't remember was leaving them here, but he was glad of it.

The sneakers that took him through the mountains and to safety were fairly destroyed.

He grabbed a towel from the linen closet and stepped into the bathroom. He stripped off his belt and emptied his pants pockets, pulling out his phone. One look told him the battery was nearly dead. They needed it in case Blake called. He ran down the stairs to the kitchen.

Max was at the stove and turned. *"Mano, ¿qué pasa?"*

Rafe held up his phone in his hand. "Battery dying."

"Give it here," Zack said. "I'm charging mine. But yours is way more important."

Rafe handed him the phone. "Thanks."

"How's she doing?" Zack lifted his brow toward the ceiling.

"Not great." Rafe dragged his hand over his face. "I mean, can you blame her? She told me horror stories about him. But I never really got it until that phone call." Rafe shuddered. "His voice sounded like pure evil."

"Totally," Max said. "Even if you never heard his voice, what kind of man kidnaps his own daughter? *Bestia.*" Max spat out the last word.

"Hey, man," Zack said, pointing to the ceiling. "I don't hear any water running. You sure she's okay?"

Rafe flew out of the kitchen, taking the steps two at a time. He turned the corner and found Mallory still sitting on the edge of the bed, staring straight ahead, her gaze not following him when he walked into the room. "Mallory? You haven't moved from this spot." He knelt in front of her. "Come on. Let me help you."

Mallory didn't respond.

Rafe felt helpless. But he had to do something. He needed her to be strong. "Listen to me. Now is not the time for you to fall apart. Your daughter needs you." Rafe squeezed her hands. "I need you. Please."

Her eyes filled with unshed tears. Rafe didn't move. A single tear fell down her cheek, and he took her in his arms.

Mallory sobbed into his shoulder. She needed the release. When she backed away, his shirt was wet with her tears. "Sorry." She wiped her nose with the back of her hand. "I needed that." She looked down at her feet. "I don't know what I'll do if he does anything to Justine."

Rafe grabbed her by the shoulders. "Don't even think like that."

"But he's a crazy person." Mallory walked toward the window. She huffed out a breath. "Justine's innocent. She shouldn't be a pawn in his vicious game. And it's all my fault. I married him."

Rafe came up from behind and rested his hands on her shoulders. "Don't think that way. Come on. Dim thoughts won't bring her back."

Mallory stepped out of his arms. Her eyes were no longer dull. There was a fury, an inner rage.

"You and I both know what's on that drive. We know the kind of people that bastard Blake was dealing with and who he was helping. We know what horrific crimes they were and are committing. Do you imagine, for one minute, Blake gives one damn for Justine? To him, she's a pawn." Mallory let out a sob and clasped her hand over her mouth. "Somehow, I will make this right. And I will get my daughter back."

"We're all here to make sure that happens. We will get her back. There are no other options. Now, let's get cleaned up. And something to eat. You need your strength." He turned her by the shoulders and marched her into the bathroom.

Rafe pushed the shower curtain back and turned on the

faucets. "You're going in for a nice hot shower. If it doesn't make you feel better, at least you'll be clean."

She let out a small laugh.

"And after that, we'll get you fed and some rest. Tomorrow will be here before you know it, and you'll have your daughter back."

"I'm okay. I don't need any more coddling. I'm over my shock."

"Happy to hear that," Rafe said, noticing the room was beginning to fog up.

"I do, however, need help with taking off this bandage and this sneaker," she said.

Rafe knelt before her. "Put your foot up on my knee." He gently unwrapped the bandage, untied the shoelace, and began to ease off the shoe.

Mallory hissed.

"Does that hurt?"

Mallory's eyes were squeezed shut. "I think this needs to be quick." She gripped the side of the sink. "Yank it off and get it over with."

"Are you sure?"

Mallory's face tilted upward. "Uh-huh. Just do it."

He pulled the sneaker off and heard the gasp that escaped her lips.

"Are you all right?"

"I will be." She lowered her head and faced him.

"Breathe," he said.

She took in a deep breath and slowly blew it out through her mouth.

"Well, it's turning an interesting shade of purple. I'll give you that."

"Thanks." Mallory rolled her eyes. "Listen, Rafe, I need a favor, and I really hate to ask you, but I don't think I can get into that shower by myself. I don't think I can put any weight on my ankle."

Rafe raised an eyebrow.

"That wasn't an invitation," Mallory said.

"No?" He tilted his head.

Mallory paused. "Well, maybe. I don't want to be alone." She swallowed. "Stay with me."

"You don't ever have to be alone." He lifted her up. "Lean against the wall." He pulled her shirt out of her jeans and ran his hands down her waist to her hips. His fingers gently released the top button at the waistband, then slowly slid her pants down.

The fog in the bathroom continued to build as he slid his hand up her legs and unbuttoned each button on her shirt and helped slip it off. Reaching around the back, he unhooked her bra, letting it fall forward. His hands made their way to her waist as he slipped her panties down and helped her step out of them. "Wait right there."

Rafe pulled his shirt over his head and stepped out of his pants and underwear. He was hard. And he wanted her.

In one movement, he scooped her into his arms and lifted her into the shower, placing her gently under the showerhead.

She leaned back, and the warm water cascaded down her face.

Rafe thought she was the most beautiful woman he had ever seen. Old feelings and new ones emerged. They'd been through so much together these last couple of days. He loved her strength, her mind, her determination. If he couldn't take away her anxiety, at least he could make her feel better.

He reached behind her and took hold of the shampoo bottle. Placing a small amount in his hand, he rubbed it into her hair, massaging and caressing her scalp.

"That feels so good," Mallory moaned.

When he was done with her hair, he took the bottle of liquid soap, lathered it in his hand and began to wash her back. With his fingers, he gently kneaded the muscles in her shoulders.

Her arms stretched out, and her hands pressed against the tile wall.

As she held herself upright, Rafe washed her in slow caressing motions. They didn't speak. Her sighs of pleasure mingled with the sound of running water.

Mallory closed her eyes. A deep shiver ran through her as Rafe touched every part of her body. When he was done, she turned, leaned against the wall, and watched him as he washed away the dirt and tension of the last few days. He was as magnificent as she remembered. As teenagers, they'd never been shy around each other. Making love to Rafe had always been sexy and easy. He made every part of her tingle.

When he moved toward her and pressed his lips against hers, she willingly opened her mouth and let his tongue explore hers. His kisses traveled to her breast. She felt the tenderness as he sucked at her nipple. She melted into his arms. She needed him now. Grabbing his face in her hands, she said, "Take me now. Please."

Without another word, he was inside her. As he thrust, she felt as if she would explode.

"Mallory. I love you."

She couldn't speak. Her love for him was strong, but she couldn't get the words out. Without Justine, it wouldn't be right. At this moment, her heart wasn't her own. All she wanted was to ride this feeling until she could no longer take it.

His thrusts were deeper. She grabbed onto his back and wrapped her legs around him until they exploded at the same time.

She lowered her legs, held his face in her hand, and kissed him gently on the mouth. He picked her up and toweled her off.

"You look like you could use some sleep," Rafe said.

Mallory shook her head. "No doubt you relaxed me. But I can't sleep. Not until I know what's happening with my baby."

Rafe nodded. "Okay. Well, let's get dressed and get something to eat."

Once they were changed, Rafe helped Mallory down the stairs to the kitchen.

"Hey. That was a long shower. You two should be extra clean," Max teased.

Mallory felt the flush in her cheeks. She was embarrassed. Not only had she done something so personal in Ellie's house, but her daughter was in danger. Instantly, she wanted to take back the last hour. She lowered her gaze to the floor. "Sorry," she mumbled.

"Oh, shoot. Mallory, I was only kidding." Max stood and went to the stove. "Come on. Sit. I've got some *sancocho*."

"You had time to make that?" Rafe said.

"What is that?" Mallory asked.

"It's a soup with plantains, yuccas, and chicken." Max lifted the lid and stirred the pot. "And no, I didn't make it today. It's leftovers. I cooked up a big batch before I went on vacation and froze it. And you all are the lucky recipients of my efforts."

"Max is the wannabe chef in the family," Rafe said.

"Wow. That's right. We all took a vacation. That seems like a lifetime ago instead of a few days." Zack shook his head. "So much has happened. You couldn't make it up. Or maybe I could."

The sharp look Rafe gave Zack didn't go unnoticed. "Don't mind him, Mallory," Rafe said. "He's the wannabe novelist."

Mallory gave a faint smile, sat, and kept her head down. What she'd put this family through. It was unthinkable. Here she was in Ellie's house, and Ellie couldn't even be here because of Blake and what he'd done. "I'm so sorry. I've caused you all so much trouble."

Rafe grabbed her hand. "Don't think like that."

"I'm sorry I said anything," Zack said. "We're in this now. All together. No regrets. We move forward, get your daughter back, and get to the other side of this."

Max put the spoon down, walked to the table, and touched her shoulder. "We're all here for you, Mallory."

Regardless of what the brothers said, and she knew they meant well, once Justine was safely back, she'd disappear. The information she'd found out from the drive was too dangerous. The wrong kind of people might discover what she knew. She couldn't take a chance and put this family through any more. She would get her daughter back even if she had to kill Blake Stanton with her bare hands. She closed her eyes and took in a small breath. "I'm okay. Really."

Max gave her shoulder a gentle squeeze. "All right then. Let's eat."

After dinner, they washed the dishes and cleaned the kitchen.

When Rafe checked his phone for what seemed like the hundredth time, Mallory said, "Blake isn't going to call. This is exactly how he gains control and holds the power. He keeps you second-guessing. You wonder how a man could hold his daughter for ransom. It seems unthinkable.

And maybe it is for most fathers. Not him. He was never a father." She spat the words out like something foul had crawled into her mouth. "This is how he operates. He said he'd call tomorrow. Believe me, he won't call a moment sooner—just to keep us all on edge."

Rafe put down the phone. "He's doing a really good job of it."

The sudden ringing of the house phone startled everyone, and Mallory nearly dropped the plate she was about to place in the cupboard.

The brothers froze.

Max nodded for Rafe to pick it up.

He walked to the green wall phone and lifted it from the receiver. "Yes." Rafe's face was tight, his voice brusque. Within a moment, his expression seemed to relax. *"Aún no. Sabremos más mañana."*

"Who is he talking to?" Mallory gripped the dish towel. "What is he saying?"

"It sounds like he's talking to one of our aunts. He's telling her we don't know anything yet."

She lowered her eyes. The aunts were calling. This wasn't right. The whole family was in this, and she needed to find a way to extricate them from her problems. As much as it pained her to lose Rafe, it was the right thing to do.

After they cleaned the kitchen, Zack insisted they play cards to pass the time and get their minds off the clock. Mallory went through the motions, and by midnight, she was physically weary. Knowing she would face Blake tomorrow made her insides turn, but also made her realize she needed to be strong. Being dead on her feet would not help the situation. So, she'd force herself to sleep.

Stretching her arms overhead, Mallory yawned. "It's time for me to get a little shuteye."

"Good idea." Max turned to Zack. "It's time for us to go and let them get some rest."

Mallory nodded. "Okay then. See you in the morning. And wake me if you hear anything."

"Of course," Max said.

"I'll help you up." Rafe stood.

She held up a hand. "No. I can manage." The hurt look on his face stung but keeping him at a distance was the right thing to do. She had to end this thing between them.

Chapter 18

By six o'clock the next morning, Mallory was dressed and waiting for Rafe on the porch. She knew Blake wouldn't call until nine, but she wanted to be at the RMZ offices anyway. Her formerly dead husband was full of surprises, and she didn't trust that he wouldn't do something crazy before then.

"Zack's on his way," Rafe said, as he closed the front door behind him.

"Thanks."

"You sure you want to leave this early? I mean, there's not much we can do just sitting in the office."

"There's not much we can do sitting here either." Mallory didn't look up. Her focus never strayed from the street.

Zack pulled up with Max in the passenger seat. Mallory stood and limped to the car.

"Good morning," Max said. "Did you get any rest?"

"If you call tossing and turning restful, then I got plenty." Mallory snapped her seat belt in place.

"Same," said Zack, and he pulled away from the curb. The drive to the office was silent and somber.

When they entered the RMZ conference room, they were met by Agent Shore, looking impossibly fresh and rested.

"It's early." Shore checked her watch. "What are you all doing here?"

"We're here in case something happened sooner than expected," Mallory answered.

Agent Shore let out a breath and tilted her head toward the back of the room. "Well, make yourselves comfortable. Coffee's fresh."

After several hours and many more cups of coffee, it was finally time for Blake's call. They were all in the conference room, in the same positions as yesterday.

At nine o'clock exactly, Rafe's cell phone rang, and he swiped it open.

"Write this down," Blake barked. "I'm not going to repeat it. I want the drive delivered to Hampstead Farm, off Route 23. Leave it at the entrance of the old grain elevator. Once I'm sure the drive's in working order, I'll call you with your next instructions."

"No, Blake, that wasn't the deal. The drive for Justine." Rafe's voice was firm.

"You have thirty minutes."

"That wasn't the deal." The words rushed out of Rafe's mouth. "It could take longer than that to get to Hampstead Farm."

"Rafe—" Blake's voice dripped with venom "—you and I both know your motorcycle can make it there in less than that. I expect you, and only you, with the drive. If I see another car, police vehicle, chopper, or even the local traffic cop, I disappear with Justine. You all got that?"

"That's not happening." Rafe shook his head. "No way."

"Come alone, with the drive. You've got thirty minutes, or you never see Justine again." The phone went dead.

"He's bluffing. Right?" Rafe's question was directed to Agent Shore.

Her expression gave nothing away except for the almost imperceptible shake of her head. "It's hard to know," she said. "The guy sounded amped up. Nervous people in his position are capable of pretty much anything. So it's best if we work within his request."

"Work *within* his request? What does that even mean?" Rafe asked.

"It means we do as he says, except for the part where there's no FBI presence and that we give him the actual drive."

"How does this guy know so much about Rafe?" Max asked. Until now, both brothers had remained quiet. "I mean, they've never met, so how does he know my brother owns a motorcycle?"

"And, yesterday, on the call, he mentioned Mallory's fall," Zack said. "How did he know about that?"

"We don't have time to dissect that right now." Agent Shore began typing into her phone. "But it's definitely worth investigating. I'm giving this new information to one of my agents, and they'll start digging into it. In the meantime, we need to move out fast. I take it you know where this Hampstead Farm is?"

"Yeah. It's been abandoned for years."

She handed Rafe the fake nano drive. "Where's your motorcycle parked?"

"Hold on." Mallory put up a hand. "That's your plan? Send Rafe in there with a fake drive?"

"We'll be there providing backup for Rafe. Once Blake has the decoy, he'll be surrounded by agents and we'll take him into custody," Agent Shore said.

Nothing Mallory heard instilled confidence in the FBI's plan. When she first entered the RMZ offices, she felt reassured that so many agents were on the case. Surely, they would find a way out of this and rescue her daughter. In her wildest thoughts, the plan was never this. Rafe could get hurt, and she'd lose her daughter in the process. Neither option was acceptable. Mallory put her face in her hands. "I feel sick."

Rafe was by her side. "You okay?"

"I think I need to splash some water on my face. Where's the bathroom?"

Rafe put his arm around her waist to help her up.

"I got it." Mallory stood on her own, the pain shooting from her ankle to her hip bone. "I won't be long." Gritting her teeth through the pain, she quickly made her way to the ladies' room, her mind racing. She looked in the mirror. Evidence of her harrowing night in the deep woods was revealed by the scratch marks on her face and hands. She splashed water on her face several times and then reached for a paper towel. Holding in a scream, she buried her face in the towel and worked on taking in deep breaths. She had to stop Blake, and she didn't trust the FBI to have her daughter's interest as their priority. The gleam in their eyes at the thought of capturing Blake Stanton told her everything she needed to know.

When she walked out of the bathroom, the common area buzzed with agents packing up and Taylor Shore giving orders. Keeping her head down, Mallory continued unnoticed toward the elevator and pressed the button several times. "Come on. Come on." She punched the button with her finger again. "What's taking so long?"

Finally, the elevator arrived, and she slipped in. She hit the button for the ground floor several times until the doors closed. Mallory closed her eyes in relief as the car descended.

When the elevator doors opened, Rafe stared at Mallory. "Going somewhere?"

"How did you—?"

Ignoring her dazed expression, Rafe pulled her off the elevator and to the side. "Just what do you think *you're* doing?"

"I'm scared Blake will spot the fake drive."

"That doesn't answer the question." Grabbing Mallory by the shoulders, he was inches from her face. "You're not thinking of going up against Blake by yourself—are you?"

"I can't let anything happen to my baby girl." She was breathing hard. "I thought we could give him the fake drive. But I was wrong. I spent the night turning it over and over in my mind. Who was I kidding? I know who Blake is and giving him the fake drive is too dangerous. We can't take the chance. So I'll give him the real one and tell him I never opened it. It's my only chance to get my life back and keep my daughter safe."

Rafe tried to process what she was saying. *Her life back.* A life without him. "And you thought that was a viable plan?"

"You heard Blake. He's insane, but he's smart. And I don't trust him. For that matter, I don't trust the FBI. Everyone wants what they want, leaving Justine as the pawn in all of this." Her voice was harsh. "Knowing Blake, he'll have a way to check if the drive's authentic right on the spot, and I can't take that chance. I know I'm right. The only way to get my daughter back safely is to give him the real drive." She pounded on his chest. "Please. I need to go."

The pleading in her voice nearly broke him. Rafe, too, had doubts that the authorities had the same priority. They wanted that drive and Blake Stanton behind bars. He was beginning to understand Mallory's thinking. "If people think you were never able to open it, then you're free."

"Exactly. Please, Rafe." She held up the key fob to Max's car. "Justine first."

"Where did you get those?"

"I took them off the table when Max was looking at his phone."

Maybe she was right. Maybe she was the only one who knew how to handle Blake. Rafe ran his hand through his hair and looked at the elevator panel. It was still on the ground level. No one had called for it. But there was precious little time before the agents came down. He needed to act fast. "You're right. Blake is insane. We'll give him the real drive." Rafe held out his hand. "Hand it over."

Mallory's confused look didn't stop him from leaning in close. "Give me the drive. He's expecting me to have it, and we don't want to deviate too far from the plan."

She reached into her back pocket and handed it over.

"Okay. That's it then." Rafe turned and ran out of the building.

"Rafe. Wait for me!" Mallory cried.

He didn't turn around. He knew her ankle wouldn't hold, and he could get to Justine faster than anyone. Besides, for whatever reason, Blake wanted him as the messenger. Mallory had been through so much. But it hurt knowing she wanted her life back without him. How could he begrudge her wanting to be free of any man after what she'd been through? If he couldn't have her, at least he'd rescue her daughter from a monster.

Rafe ran the four blocks to *Tía* Ellie's house, where he stored his motorcycle in her shed. By the time he reached her house, his lungs were on fire. Raising the shed door, he jumped on the bike, flipped up the kickstand, jammed on his helmet, and took off.

Mallory slumped against the wall when the elevator opened and out poured Agents Shore and Byron with Max.

"Where is he?" Max looked around the lobby.

"He took the drive," Mallory said.

"What do you mean *he* took the drive? Who is *he*?" Max asked.

"Rafe. I'm talking about Rafe. He took the real drive," Mallory said.

"Dammit," Agent Shore snarled.

"What the hell is my brother up to?"

"He's going after Blake," Mallory said, and felt as if her heart would break. What if Rafe wasn't successful? What if he got hurt? What if she never saw her daughter or Rafe again?

"*¡Temerario!*" Max followed the agents toward the front door.

"What are you saying? Where are you going?" Mallory cried. "Please, Max, what's happening?"

Max didn't stop but called over his shoulder, "I said, my brother is being reckless. I can't let him go in there alone."

Mallory felt bile rise in the back of her throat. Exactly what Blake didn't want was happening. She only hoped Rafe would get there and grab Justine before this army of law enforcement arrived. The exact thing that would make Blake do something crazy. She hobbled behind Max but came up short when he suddenly stopped outside the steps of the office.

"Where the hell are my car keys?" Max patted his front and back pockets. "Damn it. Damn it. Rafe took my keys."

"No. He didn't. I have them." She held up her hand. "I'm going with you."

He quickly swiped the keys out of her hand. "No, you're not." Max's long strides took him around the car to the driver's side in seconds.

"We're wasting time arguing. I'll ride on the hood if I

have to, but I'm going." Mallory's hand was already pulling on the passenger side handle.

Max gave her a stern look and then pressed the door release on the key fob. "Get in," he said.

Taking a shortcut through the back streets of town, Rafe made his way to Route 9W within a few minutes. The route featured one lane in each direction, winding through the mountains along the broad Hudson River. Heading north, he was going over fifty miles an hour on hairpin turns, passing cars that didn't have his urgency.

Rafe thought of all the possible ways he could trip up Blake. From what he knew about Mallory's husband, he couldn't be trusted to live up to his end of the bargain. His mind went around and around with possible scenarios, and none of them were good. Everything about Blake screamed wild card. He was a madman who had no compunction about faking his own death, terrorizing his wife and child, and then holding his daughter for ransom. What kind of sicko did that? He ached for Mallory and what she must have endured at the hands of that psycho. There was no more time to think. He needed a plan that didn't include walking straight into what could be a trap.

After all, he didn't know Blake, and yet he specifically asked that Rafe bring the drive. That alone meant he had to watch his back. He checked the time on the dashboard. He was perilously close to being late. Ignoring all road signs, Rafe gripped the throttle and twisted it toward him, increasing his speed.

He checked his mirrors and wondered where the Feds were. Surely, they were already on the road. He hoped they had the good sense to stay hidden and out of the way. There was no telling what this maniac was capable of and how far he'd go to get what he wanted.

Ten miles before the exit, Rafe jerked the bike to the right, veering off the road onto the grass and disappearing into a wooded area. He knew this stretch of land well. Growing up, his mother took them on weekly trips to Hampstead Farm for fresh eggs and homemade cheeses. While she made small talk with the owners, he and his brothers played explorer all around the property. His only advantage over Blake would be his familiarity with every square inch of the property, including the nooks and crannies where one could hide.

Instead of coming up the main road alone on his motorcycle, which Blake would expect, he'd arrive behind the grain elevator. If nothing else, at least he'd have the element of surprise. Maybe even some time to scope out the situation.

Mallory sat in the passenger seat, tugging at the chain around her neck with one hand and biting what was left of her nails on the other. "We should have caught up to Rafe by now."

Max nodded. "I was thinking the same thing."

"Where could he be?"

Max blew out a breath. "I can't believe I didn't think of it."

"Think of what?" Mallory's voice rose.

"He didn't take the interstate. He took the long way around on Route 9W."

"Why would he do that?"

"Because, on a motorcycle, he can cut through the woods and ride around to the back of the farm. It's faster."

"What?"

Max explained the alternate route and that it was only possible with a motorcycle because of the trees. "He'll be there soon."

Mallory turned her head. The agents were following close behind. "What are we going to do when we get there?" Max didn't answer. "Max, are you listening? I said—"

"I heard you. The truth is I don't know."

Mallory felt the car jerk to the right as Max pulled the car onto the shoulder. "What are you doing? Why did you stop?" She turned to find the agents pulling up behind them.

Max got out of the car.

Mallory unbuckled her seat belt and was out of the car seconds later. Clenching her fists, she ignored the pain and limped as fast as she could to catch up to Max.

She reached Agent Shore's car just in time to hear her curse.

Taylor Shore smacked the dashboard. "A shortcut to the farm? Unbelievable."

Max nodded. "Straight through the woods. And impossible for any of our cars to get through."

"Then we'll have to keep going until we get to the farm. Hope we get there in time," Shore said.

"No. Absolutely not. We can't. He'll take Justine," Mallory pleaded. "Listen to me. I know he will. He said no cops. Let's let Rafe handle this."

"It's too dangerous. This isn't how we're playing this one out," the agent said.

"We're wasting time," Max said. "We could argue all day. The fact is, Rafe is probably already there. The short-cut will take him right through to the back of the grain elevator—" Max stopped. "Wait a minute. Rafe's going to try and end-run Blake. He's going in through the back to try and sneak up on him. At least that's what I would do."

"And...?" Agent Shore said.

"Keep following me," Max said as he ran to his car.

Mallory followed and jumped into the passenger seat. She barely had time to close the door when Max peeled out onto the road.

"How do we know the agents won't call in reinforcements?" Mallory asked.

"They probably already have. Let's hope they have the good sense to stay hidden until we get Justine and Rafe away safely."

Chapter 19

The dense woods began to thin out, and Rafe sensed he was a couple of hundred yards away from the farm. He rolled the throttle back, slowing the bike while squeezing the lever on the right handlebar. He swung his leg over the seat and walked his bike toward a fallen tree, laying it on its side to keep it out of sight.

Crouching low, Rafe made his way toward the back of the grain elevator. He moved as quickly and quietly as he could.

The neglect of a decade of abandonment was evident everywhere. To his left, a rusted threshing machine sat among three feet of weeds. A large hole could be seen in the roof of the elevator that once stored grain. The barn no longer sported the vivid red Rafe remembered as a child. Instead, it looked more like a washed-out brown with a sagging back door. The sounds of a working farm were gone. No chickens clucking, dogs barking, or the mechanical sounds of the milking machine. He moved farther along, stepping over fallen trees and piles of leaves from autumns past.

The piercing scream stopped him where he stood. His heart pushed against his chest as if it wanted out. The roar of blood through his ears made it difficult to discern where the sound came from. A deep male voice yelled, but Rafe was unable to make out the words.

The grain elevator was in sight, and Rafe took several tentative steps in that direction.

"I want my mommy."

He looked at the deserted buildings but couldn't determine where Justine's cries were coming from. Getting on all fours, he crawled to the back of the grain elevator.

Justine's cries grew louder.

"Shut up, or I will give you something to cry about."

Rafe didn't recognize the voice but sensed it was coming from the barn, not more than fifty feet away. He lay flat on his stomach and inched his way around the grain elevator to get a better look. From this vantage point, it was difficult to see beyond the barn door. He was about to stand when he heard the click of a gun at the side of his head.

"Get up, slowly."

Rafe didn't move.

"I said get up!" Blake's voice sounded hoarse but no less insistent.

Slowly, Rafe raised himself up.

"Get your hands up and walk," Blake ordered.

With the gun to his back, Rafe walked into the dark barn. A shaft of light filtered through from a missing board on the side wall, illuminating the ten empty stalls. A decade's worth of dried hay lay all about. A strong smell of rotted wood hung in the air. When his eyes adjusted, he spotted Justine in the corner. His heart kicked up another notch. A tall man with bulging forearms was holding her around the waist, and his hand clamped over her mouth. He caught a glimpse of the man's hiking boots. The same hiking boots that followed him and Mallory in the woods last night.

"Stop walking," Blake commanded. "Now, slowly, and I do mean slowly, get to one knee."

All Rafe could think of was how to get to Justine. The unexpected appearance of an accomplice wasn't helping. The current situation didn't bode well for either of them.

"I said get down, now."

Justine's muffled cries clawed at this soul.

"Keep your hands up," Blake barked.

With his hands over his head, Rafe got to one knee.

"I know you have the drive. So tell me which pocket it's in, and do not even think of trying anything."

Rafe had less than a second to think. With his back to Blake, he lied and said, "Back right pants pocket."

"Don't move a muscle." Blake's tone was low and menacing.

He felt Blake behind him and knew this was his last chance. After this, he'd probably be a dead man. He placed a hand on the ground to push himself up, and instead of standing straight up, he hoisted himself backward and pushed the top of his head into Blake's jaw.

Stunned, Blake dropped the gun to the ground.

Rafe kicked it to an open stall, turned, and punched Blake in the gut.

Blake fell backward but quickly sat up and kicked the legs out from under Rafe, who went down hard. Blake jumped on top of him, pinning him to the ground, and threw a punch.

Reflexively, Rafe turned his head to the side. The punch managed to clip his ear, and the blow stunned him, giving Blake time to land another punch. This time, square on his jaw.

With adrenaline coursing through his body, he blinked, quickly shook his head, and with all his might, managed to push Blake off and straddle him across the chest, punching him in the face once, twice, and a third time before he felt a sharp kick in his back throwing him off balance and giving Blake enough time to roll out from underneath.

Each man now crouched, fists ready, walking around each other in a circle.

"Don't hurt Rafe. No. No. Let me go," Justine screamed.

"Get the gun," Blake yelled to his accomplice.

"Noooooooo!" Justine yelled.

"You stop that fussing," the man in the boots said.

"Let me go."

"Ow. She bit me. You little—"

"Run, Justine! Run!" Rafe yelled.

She ran past him and out of the barn.

"Don't let her go," Blake sneered.

The tall man in the hiking boots ran.

Rafe only hoped his brother and Mallory were somewhere nearby so they could get to Justine before the booted man.

As Rafe and Blake continued to circle, each eyed the gun.

Rafe knew it was too far to reach without turning his back on Blake. A dangerous proposition, but he had no choice. He had to dive for it. Rafe reached it first, closing his finger over the trigger.

Blake dove on top of him and grabbed his wrist, banging his hand on the ground to release the gun. Rafe bit down on Blake's wrist until he screamed in pain, released his hand, and jumped back.

Rafe quickly turned on his back and pointed the gun at Blake. "Don't move. I won't hesitate to shoot you." Slowly, Rafe got to his feet. Never taking his aim off Blake's chest. "Now, this is how it's going to go down. You—"

"Let me go, let me go."

Rafe stiffened. He didn't take his eyes off Blake, but he knew the tall man, and not Mallory, had caught up with Justine.

"Rafe, please help me."

From the corner of his eye, he could make out Justine's tear-stained face. She was being dragged by the hand into the barn.

"Stop crying, you little brat," the tall man said.

"Bring her over here," Blake said.

"No, Daddy. I don't wanna." Justine was trying to pull away from the man, but he continued to drag her across the floor.

"If you don't stop, I'll slap you again," he snarled at Justine.

Rafe wanted to kill them both.

"Come here, Justine. And stop crying. Or I'll have to hurt your friend Rafe." Blake grabbed Justine and held her in front of him. "Cal, get over to the landing strip. Make sure the plane's ready. I'll be there shortly."

Rafe had no idea how Blake thought he would get out of this. He just sent his backup away, and Rafe was the one holding the gun.

"Justine, did you know your mommy used to be in love with this guy? Imagine a nobody like him. A criminal," Blake sneered. "I found his letters to your mommy. She loved him more than me, you see, and I couldn't have that. I knew one day she'd come running to him. So, I had no choice but to destroy him. Set him up for a crime he didn't commit." Blake laughed. "I did a good job."

"I want my mommy." Justine sobbed, tears streaming down her face.

"That's not going to happen unless your friend here gives

me the drive and the gun. Otherwise, your mommy will never see you again."

Rafe didn't move. This was the man who tried to destroy his life. Now he understood how Blake knew so much about him. Rich, powerful people could find out anything. "Put her down, and let her come to me, and then I'll put the gun down."

"You think I got as far as I did by acting stupid? Far from it. I sent the threats to Mallory. I needed her scared so she'd leave the house and I could get the laptop and the drive inside that damn teddy bear. I was the one who vandalized the house. It was easy. I had the key, and my fingerprints being everywhere wasn't unusual. Remember, it was my house. But I didn't count on her taking the laptop to a computer store. And I certainly didn't count on Justine taking that stupid bear with her," he sneered. "It doesn't matter anymore. From the beginning, I've been tracking the two of you. So, no. I'm far from stupid, and we're going to do this my way." Blake continued to hold onto Justine, inching his way toward the first stall.

"Stop moving," Rafe shouted.

"Or what? You coward. I'm holding my daughter. You wouldn't take a chance of hurting her. Would you?"

"Stop. We've all been dancing to your tune since you disappeared. You've been pulling the strings. No more."

Blake let out a laugh that sounded more like a bark. "You've watched too many bad movies. I'm holding all the cards. I'm the one who arranged for that plane to go down. Those people knew too much. Now, it's only you, me, and Mallory who know what's on that drive. Isn't that right?" His lips curved into a menacing smile. "Give me the gun, goddamn it, or someone's going to get hurt." Blake moved toward the barn door.

"Owww. Daddy, you're hurting me," Justine said.

"Am I?" Blake said.

Rafe noticed him squeezing harder.

"Daddy, stop." Justine's face turned red.

"I can keep this up for a long time. So long, in fact, there's no telling what could happen to her tiny little organs."

"You are as awful as Mallory said you were. Actually worse. What kind of man hurts his own child?"

"Happens every day. This is not a kind world," Blake said.

"No, Daddy, stop."

"Shut up." Blake turned her around and smacked her across the face.

Something in Rafe snapped. He pulled the trigger and shot Blake in the foot.

Justine screamed.

Blake fell to his knees.

The look of terror on Justine's face let Rafe know she was afraid of both of them. "Let her go."

Blake shook his head and dragged himself to the first stall, holding Justine against his chest like a human shield.

"Stay where you are."

"No. Give me the drive. Give it to me, and I'll leave."

"Not going to happen. Stay where you are. I mean it, Blake. I'll shoot you if I have to."

"Doesn't look like you have a clear shot, does it?"

"Stop right there. Do not move." The strong voice came from Agent Shore. She was standing at the entrance of the barn, Agent Byron a few steps behind. Both took a wide-leg stance with their arms straight out, aiming their guns. "Get up slowly. Now."

The next few seconds seemed to happen in a slow-motion blur. Blake let go of Justine, and Rafe ran for her while Blake rolled toward the first stall, reached in, and pulled out a small revolver. Blake stood and aimed at Rafe, who was holding Justine.

Rafe dived into the next stall—the sound of gunshots ringing throughout the barn. When the gunshots stopped, he looked around the edge of the stall to find Blake lying face down, not moving. He turned back and slumped against the stall. "Justine, are you okay?"

"Uh-huh," she sobbed. "But you're not, Rafe. You're bleeding."

Chapter 20

Rafe stared out the rain-splattered window. The dreary day made his hospital room feel depressing. He sensed his father before he heard him clearing his throat. It was that Old Spice cologne he'd never stopped wearing. A dead give-away. Rafe turned his head toward the doorway.

"Can I come in?" his father asked. The humble look on his face made his six-foot-two frame seem a little smaller. The white hair didn't seem so dashing and the expensive suit and tie weren't intimidating.

"Sure." Rafe waved him in. "Sit down."

The judge sat in the teal blue leatherette chair positioned near Rafe's hospital bed. *¿Cómo te sientes...hijo?* The words were slow, soft, and deliberate.

"They say I'm going to get out of here in two days, so I must be doing better, but I don't think my leg got the memo."

His father gave a slow smile. "I bet it hurts. It took guts to do what you did."

Rafe shook his head. "No, anyone would have gone after that little girl. I just happened to be there."

"And you happen to be in love with her mother. Aren't you?"

Rafe ignored the question and instead asked one of his

own. "What are you doing here? I hate to bring it up, since you paid for the private room and all—"

His father raised a questioning eyebrow.

"Max told me. But anyway, we're not exactly on speaking terms. What do you want?" Rafe tried to keep the anger and the hurt out of his voice. He'd been through a lot these past ten years, and this last month had made him realize he wanted to live for today. He was in love with Mallory, and while he'd been lying in this hospital bed with not much else to do but think, it was her that his mind focused on. They'd both seen their share of bad times, and now they were both free to create whatever future they wanted. He'd come to the realization that he wasn't going to chase after people for their affection anymore. That included his father. He knew now that he deserved to be loved.

"Rafe, I can't make up for what I did. For the way I treated you. I'll never get that time back. I was wrong. Dead wrong." The judge's voice cracked. He paused and looked at the ceiling.

Rafe knew he was trying to compose himself; his father's facade had never weakened until now, and he could see that this was difficult for him.

"I realize you may not want to forgive me. And if you don't, I understand. I wanted you to know that not only was I wrong, but I love you, and in my way, I never stopped loving you."

Rafe stared at his father as the tears rolled down the side of his face. He said nothing. These were the words he'd waited ten years to hear, but somehow, it wasn't enough. It wasn't nearly enough.

The judge got up, took a handkerchief from his back pocket, and blew his nose. "I'll be going." He started toward the door. "If you need anything, you know where to find me."

Max came in as the judge was heading out. "Hey, Pop." The judge nodded and hurried through the door.

"What happened?" Max asked. "Pop looks pretty upset, and so do you."

"Nothing, just nothing."

"I don't want to pry, but it can't be nothing. I know it took a lot for the old man to come here today."

"Yeah, you're probably right. He had to swallow his pride—admit he was wrong."

"Well, that for sure took something out of him," Max said.

"You don't get it."

"Enlighten me."

"I'm his son. He should have loved me no matter what. He should have believed me. He raised me, and he knew what kind of man I was. I didn't want to hear that he was wrong. I wanted to know that he was sorry he could have ever thought that of me. Mom knew the truth. I've waited years for a reconciliation. I just didn't realize until today how angry I was about the whole thing. And it's going to take a minute for me to get over being pissed off."

"Hi, Rafe." Justine bounded into the room. "We bought you a sub sandwich with lots of mayo 'cause Mom said you were getting sick and tired of hospital food."

Rafe quickly wiped his eyes, plastering on a smile. "Thank goodness, I was about to starve. Did you bring chips with that?"

"Of course, silly." Justine giggled.

Mallory walked in, huffing. "Justine, I've told you not to get too far away from me."

"Soo-rr-yy, Mom," she said in mock exaggeration.

"Hey, Max." Mallory smiled at Max and instantly recognized she'd interrupted. "Punkie, let's wait outside for a minute. Max and Rafe are in the middle of something."

"But, Mommmmmm…"

"Yeah, yeah, no buts, come on, we'll get a soda from the cafeteria."

With Justine and Mallory gone, the only sound was the ticking of the clock on the wall above the doorway.

"Max, you've always tried to be the peacemaker. And because of you and Mom, I'll tell you what. I'll give it a try. But this is going to have to take a natural progression. If we make it, we make it. Nothing forced. At this point in my life, I'm obliged to nothing and no one."

Max nodded his understanding.

Two weeks after his release from the hospital, Rafe was still on crutches. Most nights were spent with Mallory at Ellie's house. She'd wanted to stay until Rafe was fully recovered.

"Hey," Mallory said, walking into the living room. "Guess who I got a call from?"

"The lottery commission? You won a million dollars."

"Ha-ha. Very funny. No, it was Ellie."

"Is she okay?" A look of concern crossed his face.

"Oh yeah, she's fine. She said after spending so much time with her sister, she realized she didn't want to come back to this big old empty house, so she's decided to stay there indefinitely."

Rafe could sense concern in her voice. "Is that a bad thing?"

"Well…no… She asked me if I wanted to stay here and rent the house. And, well… I hadn't really thought about it. I know my dad is waiting for us, but now that Blake is really dead, I truly have my life back."

"Come here." Rafe held out his arms. "Sit." He patted the sofa cushion.

Mallory sat beside him, and he put his arms around her and pulled her in close. "Let me ask you something. Do you want to live with your dad and his new girlfriend?"

Mallory sighed. "I love my father, and I want to see him. But this place, Hollow Lake, it's become home again. And with the FBI, CIA, and Interpol making all those arrests, and Agent Shore blasting out to all the agencies that we were never able to open the drive, we don't have to run anymore. I'm safe." She looked up at Rafe. "We're safe. And Justine's so happy here. She can even start school in a week. I hate the idea of uprooting her again."

Rafe pulled her in closer. "You know what?"

"What?"

"I love your smile." He kissed her lips.

"And your beautiful green eyes." He kissed her eyelids.

"And, well, there isn't anything I don't love about you."

"I bet you say that to all the women you go through a near-death experience with." Mallory laughed.

"Well, I have to admit, I'm looking forward to taking you back to the lake house just for fun. Next time we'll leave all electronic equipment at home." He lightly kissed her lips again. "But seriously, why not stay here. This is a great house. And you just said, Justine is happy here. And it is home. And you have me, and the entire Ramirez clan."

The idea of Mallory and Justine living in Hollow Lake made him enormously happy. He'd lost her once to the big city, and he wasn't ready for that to happen again. "Listen, I'd love it if you stayed. You can visit your father. Visit him every month if you want."

Rafe kissed her temple. "Mallory, I've spent a lot of time pushing people away. Not getting involved. For the last few years, I've been polite but distant. Never wanted to get too close because I was convinced there was no future for me. But now that I've officially, officially cleared my name, there's nothing in the way."

"Rafe, I still can't believe it was Blake who framed you." Mallory looked down at her hands. "It was my fault."

Rafe leaned his head against hers. "The fact that you kept my love letters—well, I was surprised to hear that."

"I suppose I've never stopped loving you."

He turned her face toward him. "Those eyes of yours, they hypnotize me. You captured my heart a long time ago. You've broken down walls I'd spent a few years building. I love you, Mallory Kane. I want to be with you and share my life with you."

"What are you saying?"

"Marry me. Marry me."

Mallory embraced him. "I will marry you. Yes. Yes. Yes."

Rafe kissed her firmly on the mouth. When she deepened the kiss, he was lost.

Mallory pulled back. "Rafe Ramirez. I love you."

Epilogue

The clock above the mantel at the judge's home struck seven.

"Don't worry, Pop, they'll be here," Max said.

The judge grumbled under his breath. "They're late to their own engagement party."

"Pop, it's only just seven," Zack said, as the doorbell rang. "See, that's them now. I'll get it."

Rafe, Mallory, and Justine were greeted by the entire family. Ellie and Claudia rushed up to Mallory and Justine and hugged them tight.

"You look great. I'm so happy to see you," Ellie said.

"How's my little *chiquita*?" Claudia kissed Justine on the cheek.

"Come on, now. Let them take their coats off and come in," the judge said. "Welcome."

Rafe smiled at the balloons, streamers, and signs announcing their engagement that were strewn across the living room.

"Oh look, Mommy, a dog. A real pretty dog." Justine tugged on the judge's pants. "Hi, I'm Justine. Is that your dog?"

The judge laughed. "That's my dog all right. His name is Elliot, and if it's all right with your mother, you can go over and pet him. He's old and gentle."

"Can I, Mommy?"

Mallory nodded and took off her coat, handing it to the judge. "It's nice to see you after all these years."

"Mallory, the feeling is mutual. The rest of the family is dying to say hello." While Mallory knew Ellie and Claudia's children from high school, she hadn't seen them in years. She was grateful for their help and hugged each one.

When Mallory came to the end of what had become a receiving line, she was surprised to see Zack standing next to Agent Taylor Shore. "Agent Shore, what a nice surprise."

"Please, call me Taylor. I'm not on duty."

"Okay. That's going to take a little getting used to." Mallory thought she looked so different out of her FBI garb. Her red hair fell loose around her shoulders, and her emerald green sheath dress hugged her in all the right places. She thought Taylor was beautiful. "I didn't expect to see you here." Mallory turned and waved Rafe over. "Look who came."

"Wow," Rafe said. "Look at you."

Taylor blushed, and it nearly matched the color of her hair. "Um, Zack invited me."

Mallory did a double take.

"Bro?" Rafe said. "Is this a date?"

Zack grinned sheepishly and put his arm around Taylor's shoulder.

"Let's get this party started," Max said, clapping his hands together.

Rafe held up a hand. "Can you give me a few minutes?" He turned to his father. "Pop, can we talk?"

The judge nodded and tilted his head toward his study. Rafe squeezed Mallory's hand and then followed his father.

Rafe lowered himself into the leather chair opposite the desk and stared at his hands. His mouth was dry, and he didn't exactly know how to say what he was feeling. The time he'd spent recovering gave him a chance to reflect. Something he hadn't done in a long time because he was too busy being angry. Almost losing his life changed everything. It made him realize nothing's guaranteed and that making the most of the time with your family is more important than holding on to hurt feelings. While Mallory and Justine completed a big part of him, he recognized there was a hole that would be there forever unless he made peace with his father.

Rafe blew out a breath and looked up. "Pop, thanks for the party. It means a lot."

"You're welcome, son." His voice filled with emotion. "For a minute, I thought you wouldn't show. I thought maybe you couldn't forgive me. I'm just so terribly sorry—"

In one smooth motion, Rafe was on his feet, embracing his father. "Let's not rehash." He whispered in his father's ear, hugging him tightly and then patting him on the back before straightening.

The judge brushed away a tear.

"No time for crying, Pop—"

"Who's crying? What are you talking about?" He cleared his throat and put his arm around Rafe's shoulder. "Come on, we've got a party to get started."

The judge opened a couple of bottles of champagne and made a Shirley Temple for Justine. "Please, everyone—" he lifted his glass "—I want to toast my son, Rafe, and his beautiful bride-to-be. Mallory, I can see you've made my son a very happy man. And for that, I am grateful."

Mallory blushed.

"May you be happy and healthy and continue to enjoy each other's company for years to come."

"Hear, hear," was the chorus from all present.

The initial awkwardness Rafe felt when walking into his father's home for the first time in years washed away. He was with the woman he loved and surrounded by his family. He was being given a second chance, and he wasn't going to mess this up. For the first time in too long, he felt whole. The last missing piece in his life was falling into place. After all these years, his family was together. They were complete.

Rafe raised his glass. "To the woman I love, to family, to futures."

There wasn't a dry eye as the rest of the family lifted their glasses.

* * * * *